THUNDER
VOICE

THUNDER VOICE

S.W. BROUWER

V VICTOR BOOKS

A DIVISION OF SCRIPTURE PRESS PUBLICATIONS INC.
USA CANADA ENGLAND

Copyediting: Liz Duckworth, Barb Williams
Cover Design: Paul Higdon
Cover Illustration: Chris Cocozza

ISBN: 1-56476-426-5

1 2 3 4 5 6 7 8 9 10 Printing/Year 99 98 97 96 95

To D.E.H.

Thanks for enthusiasm, sound advice, and friendship.
I owe you a lot, as does Sam Keaton.

I've always loved the glories of the old Wild West, and I would like to express my gratitude to the historians whose dedication has preserved that era, allowing the rest of us to cherish its spirit of freedom.

To them, and to you who may be reading this as more than a mystery, I would like to apologize for any of my research mistakes which I may have passed on to you in my attempts to make the fiction as historically accurate as possible.

SWB

THUNDER VOICE

Wyoming Territory, Laramie, July, 1876

ONE

LEANED BACK IN MY CHAIR, heels propped on my desk, and Stetson brim down to my nose, I should have been relaxed to the point of snoozing. The marshal's office afforded shade, and with windows and door propped open, it caught a good amount of breeze, making the hot spell tolerable. I'd cleared last night's drunks from the cramped jail cell at the back of the office, and I had no pressing marshal duties until the town's annual Fourth of July celebrations began at noon, more than an hour away.

Yet much as I tried to empty my mind to find sleep, my thoughts kept returning to the latest issue of the *Laramie Sentinel*, folded and flat on my desk beside my empty coffee cup. A headline filled most of the top half of the front page, bold, black letters two inches high: **CUSTER AND TROOPS SLAUGHTERED AT THE LITTLE BIGHORN.**

Only nine days had passed since the slaughter. I could remember a time—before telegraph wire and rail tracks crisscrossed the continent—when news of the battle would have taken weeks, even months to cross and escape the frontier. Not now. Because of it, folks spoke and speculated of little else. *Was the U.S. Army powerless? Did this mean the*

Sioux were going to sweep through the settlements? Even here folks worried, where such fears were laughable in the face of simple geographical facts.

Called Greasy Grass by the Sioux, the Little Bighorn river was more than two weeks of hard travel to the north of Laramie, up into the Montana territories. Fed by the Bighorn Mountains directly south, the Little Bighorn wound through sprawling grassland hills, prime buffalo hunting grounds for the Sioux, who each summer set up encampments made of hundreds of tepees. A war party large enough to threaten Laramie would never undergo the effort and danger of traveling this far south from the Little Bighorn.

Still, nearly three hundred soldiers had been slaughtered, and suddenly to many folks, especially those recently arrived from the east, it seemed like we were again living beyond the frontier.

From conflicting newspaper stories, it was difficult to decide exactly what was truth, but I could guess. George Custer had a reputation for recklessness, and he'd often bragged a handful of troopers could destroy the entire Sioux war force. Some reports said Custer's request for reinforcements had never reached General Terry, who was coming down the Little Bighorn valley from the north. Other reports said Custer and his five companies of the seventh Cavalry—coming from the south to force an intended deadly crossfire upon the Sioux—had disregarded orders to wait for General Terry. Regardless, all reports agreed on the end result. Custer had divided his men into three columns and rode into a short, frenzied battle with no survivors against the Oglala and Hunkpapa Sioux, led by the great chiefs Crazy Horse and Sitting Bull.

I'd met Sitting Bull a year earlier, at a similar summer camp of Sioux tribes, this one in the great grassland basin between the Bighorn and Laramie mountains. My memories of the encounter were painful, not necessarily because of Sitting Bull, his fearsome demeanor, and my close escape from death at his hands, but because of the events before and after. Because of those events, I did not need imagination to understand the screams and moans and horror of shattered bodies behind the ink of the headline on my desk. And because of those events, I'd lost much of what mattered to me. Time and prayer had not eased my pain; the passage of a year of unrelenting sorrow had only served to underscore the gravity of my loss.

Not pleasant thoughts for a bright, hot, lazy, July morning.

I heard the clatter of boot heels on the wooden sidewalk directly outside. I tilted my hat back in time to see Jake Wilson, my deputy, busting through the doorway. A blessed interruption. Or so I thought.

"Grab a shotgun," he said. No excitement shook his voice. Jake doesn't upset easy.

Beauregard rose from his blanket laid beside the potbelly stove, stretched, and wandered over to give Jake's boots a neighborly sniff. As a bumbling puppy, Beau had been forced upon me by well-meaning friends shortly after last summer's events. Beau was black with a tan patch slapped like careless paint across his face, and I was beginning to wonder if he would ever grow enough to match his ungainly paws.

"Sure Jake," I said, still leaning back. "Any particular reason?"

"Just get your hind end out of that chair and follow me. There's time to flap my gums on the way."

I flopped my boots onto the floor, moved to the gun rack at the far side of the office, grabbed a double-barrel twelve-gauge and cracked the barrel open. I popped in two shells and filled my pockets with more. I rested the shotgun in the crook of my right arm and pointed my other hand at Beau, who watched me with a slowly wagging tail.

"Guard," I told him.

Beauregard returned to his blanket and dropped his head onto his paws, eyes steady on the doorway. Not much here to guard, but it didn't hurt to encourage better habits than chewing my spare boots, something Beau and I had discussed on more than one occasion.

I followed Jake into the sunshine. Jake marched purposefully toward Main Street. I was hard pressed to keep pace.

Jake was a broad-chested man of medium height with straw-filled, blond hair and a blocky face. Nothing remarkable about his appearance. Except for his arms. His left arm was massive, his right arm limp and useless, which was why he preferred a revolver to a shotgun.

Marbled scars, like ugly red worms, covered the skin on the upper half of his right arm. Careful and competent as he was, he'd once made the mistake of standing too near a mean-tempered stallion. The stallion had reached around, clamped its teeth into Jake's right biceps, and ripped the entire muscle off the bone. Most men would have fallen in shock, leaving themselves helpless to be stomped to death. Not Jake. I'd decided any man with the presence of mind to escape the stallion was a good man to have at my side. Nothing since my original impression of Jake had changed my mind, nor showed me wrong for hiring him as the town's only deputy. It was part-time work; Jake also ran a livery as well as a man with two good arms.

"Jake," I said as we rounded the corner onto Main Street, "being as we're well on the way, you mind letting me know if we're chasing wild bees, or do you have a reason for working me into a sweat?"

"I told him," he replied, "I told him good, but he wouldn't listen."

"Him?"

"Fancy pants new colonel." That'd be Colonel Ricketts, replacement for the one who'd been murdered during the events of last summer. Fort Sanders wasn't much of a posting. Just outside of Laramie, it had slowly diminished in importance as the frontier had moved on with the arrival of the rails roughly a decade ago, and I'd heard rumors it might close in the next few years. As an insignificant post, it merited the same in commanders. Since arriving last October, Ricketts had been exceptionally unexceptional in the performance of duties no more spectacular than overseeing parade ground drills.

"I was coming over to visit you anyway," Jake was saying, "and I saw them soldiers coming down the street in formation with Ricketts leading the pack. Dorsey—" John Dorsey, the reporter for the *Laramie Sentinel* "—was tagging at Ricketts' heels. Along with a mule. So I pulled Dorsey aside and asked him to explain."

Jake snorted. "Couldn't think of a worse combination. Army, newspaper, and mule. Especially with the mule packing a howitzer."

"Howitzer?"

"Sam, it's a small cannon."

"I know that, you knot-headed skunk. A person just don't often hear of a howitzer on a mule's back."

Jake grinned, showing his joy at needling me. "So Dorsey tells me the colonel has in mind a military demonstration. Wants to show the folks—and the newspaper boys—a good reason not to worry about no injun attacks. Says the colonel is tired of listening to complaints from civilians in a panic since Custer."

We both gave that respectful silence. Unimaginable, the total loss of the the finest of our soldiers with the finest of modern weaponry.

For nearly a minute we walked in that silence, passing The First National Bank, its obvious wealth marked by brick construction, where two banks farther along had false-front wooden exteriors high and wide and freshly painted. Board signs of other businesses—dangling from roofs overhanging the sidewalk—read like a town directory. HILLMAN'S EATERY. THE BROADWAY SUITATORIUM—PRESSING—BOOTS & SHOES CLEANED AND SHINED. KELLER'S PHOTO PORTRAITS. MALCOLM'S QUALITY

MILL & CABINET WORKS. THE *LARAMIE SENTINEL* —
CUSTOM STATIONARY. OVERBAY'S DRESSMAKING &
FITTING. GUTHRIE DRY GOODS & CLOTHING. ELVIN
& NELSON ATTORNEYS AT LAW. And, sprinkled among
those signs were others which well explained my existence
in Laramie: the saloons. COMIQUE THEATRE AND
DANCE HALL. RED ROSE SALOON—ICED BEER. LARA-
MIE SALOON AND SPORTING HALL.

A half dozen sidestreets intersected Main, and those qui-
eter streets were the places to find smaller hotels, black-
smiths, harness makers, and liveries. At the far end of Main
Street was what I guessed to be our destination—the Union
Pacific Hotel, the train station depot and telegraph office almost within its shadows.

It was an easy guess, for I saw soldiers, horses, and a
growing crowd of people gathered on the wide street directly
in front of the hotel.

"All right, Jake," I prompted, "what kind of demonstration?"

"Ricketts aims to show the range and hitting power of
the howitzer. Figures folks will rest at ease knowing what
the injuns will come up against if they move into this area."

"But on a mule's back?"

"It's mounted on a special saddle. A new-fangled way to
get this kind of firepower quick into the field. Mules take it
faster through worse terrain than dragging it around on
wheels. Just aim the mule's hind end and light the fuse."

Jake snorted again. "The colonel believes—and I quote—
such a novel military technique will revolutionize warfare
against the Sioux and gain him reknown and promotion."

We were within a hundred yards of the crowd. I had to
mop my face against sweat, even with stiff wind blowing in
from the Medicine Bow Mountains to the west.

"Jake, you believe different from the colonel?"

"What I believe is your shotgun will come in mighty
handy."

TWO

FOLKS STEPPED ASIDE to give us room as we moved into the crowd. More than a few nodded friendly hellos and howdy-dos. Marshaling seemed to fit me, and feeling like a part of this town was one of the few things which had made life tolerable over the last year.

When Jake and I got to the front of the crowd, I understood immediately Colonel Ricketts' intentions.

A short, compact sergeant—sweat stains spreading beneath the armpits of his blue uniform—faced the blindered mule and held its reins, one in each hand, from where he stood several steps away from the animal. The howitzer, cradled on a small wooden stand strapped to the saddle, pointed backward along the spine of the mule's back. From where Jake and I stood, I could follow the sight line of the howitzer's barrel, aimed down a wide gap between the two sides of the crowd. The target, a large water barrel, was set up a few hundred yards away, on the edge of the Laramie River.

"I don't see anything about this needing a shotgun or marshal, Jake. Miss high, the cannonball hits water. Miss low, it hits dirt."

"What I see," Jake said in a low voice, "is a colonel more

interested in impressing his lady guest than listening to the common sense I tried to pass along."

Jake pointed.

Colonel Ricketts stood at the head of a column of soldiers. He looked the way a man would look after three hours of spit and polish preparation—although I'd be willing to bet the three hours on his shoes, belt, buckles, and creased uniform had been an enlisted man's time, not the colonel's. Every strand of the colonel's dark, greased-back hair was swept back with precision. He held his hat so as not to spoil the appearance of his grooming.

Beside the colonel was a tall woman, her face lost in the shadows of a bonnet.

"According to Dorsey," Jake said, "she's a widowed heiress. Arrived with two servants and three baggage trunks. Dorsey don't know why she's here. But you should have seen Ricketts bowing and scraping to her as the procession moved through town. Dorsey says Ricketts promised her a real show."

Whatever Ricketts had promised, it was about to happen. The crowd's babble dropped to an expectant hush as Colonel Ricketts raised his right arm.

The tall, stooped soldier scratched a match into flame. He waited until the colonel dropped his arm. As the soldier raised the match to light the fuse, the wind blew it out.

The soldier cringed and tried another match. Same result. He shot a sideways glance at Colonel Ricketts who was shaking his head in disgust.

The tall soldier turned his back to the wind and sheltered his next match. He grasped the end of the long string fuse and managed to get the flame touched against it.

At first, nothing happened. Then the gunpowder caught. It hissed as it flared.

"Watch carefully," Jake said. "If I know mules. . . ."

The fuse sputtered and hissed. It might have been the noise. It might have been the phosphor and gunpowder sparks

against the mule's hide. Whatever the cause, the mule reacted the way Jake had predicted. Unable to see the source of
the unfamiliar noise, it braced against the reins and kicked
and bucked.

Its handler yanked on the reins. The mule brayed and
swung its hind end around, pointing the barrel directly into
the thick of the crowd opposite the colonel.

Men and women screamed and ducked and fell to the
ground.

"Hold that animal!" Colonel Ricketts shouted at the
handler.

Men, of course, don't win many contests against mules.
Neither did this handler.

The mule kicked and bucked and brayed, swinging its
hind end the other way, directing the hole of the barrel at the
other half of the crowd. Soldiers behind the colonel scrambled
out of formation. Civilians sprinted, arms and legs flailing.

"Shoot the mule," Jake said. He'd raised his voice above
the shouting and screaming, but nothing in his tone suggested panic.

It didn't seem I had much choice. The fuse was half gone,
the mule growing more frenzied, the handler down to clutching only one of the reins, and a five-pound cannonball ready
to blast any direction, depending on the whereabouts of the
mule's hind end when the fuse touched off the howitzer's
powder load.

I ran to the side of the sergeant who was still clutching the
mule's reins. This close, I could see the wildly rolling eyeballs
of the mule and its yellow teeth as it pulled against the bit.

I hefted the shotgun to my shoulders. I needed to shoot
down the gap toward the waterbarrel so that the lead pellets
did not harm the spectators huddled on the ground.

My shotgun was chest-level to the mule. The width of
ribs between its two front legs was an easy target, for the
handler and his grip on a single rein was effectively anchoring
the front end of the mule, no matter how wildly its back end

swung around in those dangerous, crazy, half circles.

I held off squeezing the trigger. I loathed death, and this beast was undeserving of the spray of lead which would rip bone and muscle into a geyser of gore.

Maybe a quarter of the fuse left. I had a moment of clarity which sometime arrives in the heat of battle.

Two shells in the double barrel of the shotgun. If the first shot missed, I'd still have one left for the mule. But only if I moved quickly.

As the mule's hind end swung to my left, I stepped with it, raising my shotgun slightly and taking aim on the front of the howitzer itself, where the fuse entered the molded brass.

With no hesitation—because I couldn't afford it—I squeezed. The shotgun's roar deafened me and the mule burst back in a galvanized buck of panic which tore the remaining rein from the handler's hands. The mule spun and galloped away from us, in an ungainly, side-lurching, dust-raising drumming of hooves, taking with it the saddle and the howitzer bouncing atop it.

I held my breath, keenly aware that the black hole of the howitzer faced me and the sergeant and Jake.

No explosion from the howitzer.

I'd guessed right.

From close range and with the resulting dense spray pattern of lead from the shotgun, it would have been impossible to miss the fuse. I'd simply shredded the lit fuse before it could touch off the howitzer's load of gunpowder.

Time slowed to normal, and I became aware of the weight of the shotgun in my hands, the hot sun, the dust choking my dry mouth, and the sound of one person clapping politely.

The woman in the bonnet.

I gave her a long look, trying to decide if she meant it or not. Colonel Ricketts beside her had not moved and was staring at me with the rigidity of a man in deep shock.

She kept clapping until the remainder of the crowd joined in.

I tipped my hat and moved back to Jake, glad when the spectators took their attention off me and began to babble among themselves.

"Remind me not to take you hunting," Jake told me. "That mule was close enough to spray spit in your eye, and you missed like it were a mile away."

THREE

BEFORE I COULD THINK of an appropriate reply to Jake's mocking grin, a man in a broad-brimmed straw hat waved for my attention as he stumbled a weaving path through the dispersing crowd. It was Old Charlie, drawing flinches of distaste from more respectable and less ripe townsfolk.

"Sam! Sam!"

Jake turned to follow my eyes. We both watched Charlie's progress, both frowning. Two things were wrong about this. Old Charlie usually avoided sunlight, preferring the smoky interior of the Red Rose Saloon to pass daylight hours. And Old Charlie was in a hurry.

"Sam!" he called again.

I licked my forefinger and tested the breeze. I never minded conversation with Old Charlie; I did, however, find it more enjoyable to be upwind of him. I'd move accordingly when he got closer. Jake could fend for himself if he wasn't smart enough to do the same.

"Sam," Old Charlie said, wheezing like creaky, old bellows, "you ain't in your office."

"Had business here."

He squinted at me, a web of wrinkles spreading across his coyote-thin face. "Well I got business for you too."

"Go on," I told him. "I'm listening."

Old Charlie wheezed more and coughed, hacking phlegm into bullets that rolled through the dust at his feet. Jake, opposite me, edged sideways, trying not to wrinkle his nose. Old Charlie smelled of the dried sweat of whiskey-soaked nightmares and of the accumulated stink of months without a bath. He looked exactly the way he had when I'd put him into the jail cell the first of countless times since. His pants were little more than worn canvas. His shirt had lost most of its buttons and hung wide open to reveal the faded, full-length, red longjohns he wore underneath.

"Sam, remember you told me keep my eyes and ears sharp for any talk what involved Franky Leonard?"

I did. My blood ran far colder than it should have in this July heat.

"Down at the Red Rose," he continued, "two men been asking about him. I owe you more than a couple favors and I—"

"You know these men, Charlie?"

Half drunk or not, he caught the sharpness in my voice.

"Ain't seen 'em ever before," he said. He drew himself up straight. " 'Course, once they asked about Franky, I listened real close. Sounded like Texas boys. But I didn't stay long. No sir. What with you needing to know about this. All the way to your office and then the commotion here. . . ."

"Thanks, Charlie. Next time I provide you a place to sleep, I'll buy you a coffee right off my potbelly stove."

He grinned, showing black stumps along his lower gums. "Shoot, Marshal, that ain't coffee, that's roof tar. How about a whiskey someday?"

I grinned back. This was old territory for both of us. Old Charlie spent one or two nights a week serenading me from the jail cell, the nights he drank so much he was in danger of drowning in horse troughs along the streets. He knew he'd never find whiskey in my office, for I had enough difficulty fighting the temptation without putting it in plain reach.

"Charlie, those men still in the Red Rose?"

"Could be." He scratched his belly. "Chances are they've moved on. As I was stepping out the door, I heard them asking directions to Franky's shack."

Charlie had said enough. Jake was already in full stride. With me close behind, reloading a couple of shells into the shotgun.

FOUR

FRANKY LEONARD. To the best of my knowledge, only Jake and me and Doc Harper knew how the man had died. Except, of course, for the murderer.

The story had begun with Old Charlie. Sometime in mid-November of the previous year, I'd realized nearly a week had passed since locking him up. When I went looking, I found him almost dead of pneumonia in the isolation of his miserable shack. Doc Harper pulled him through, and as November turned into the fierce winter of December, I'd begun the habit of riding to the edge of town once every second or third day, making the rounds of his shack and all the others on the wrong side of the rail tracks.

Noble as it might have sounded, my intentions held a degree of selfishness.

Surveying the desperation in the lives of the men in those lonely shacks rid me of much of my own self-pity. It also reminded me I might be only a plunge into a whiskey bottle away from those shacks myself—seeing a man shiver and wipe frozen vomit from his mouth was as good a reason as any to deny my urge for the false comfort at the bottom of a bottle.

In mid-January a blizzard had roared across the plains at the dawn, so thick with snow a man could get lost attempting to cross the street. When the wind had finally died in mid-afternoon, leaving the leather-crackling cold of minus thirty, I'd wrapped myself in a buffalo coat and walked beyond the rail tracks, fearing for the lives of the men huddled each in their own shacks as they burned dried horse manure and scraps of wood to keep warm.

I'd only found one dead. Franky Leonard. But the storm had not killed him. A bullet in the back of his skull had done it much more quickly. I wasn't all that shocked he'd died to a bullet; Franky Leonard was a mean drunk, well hated, and in this shanty area, he lived among rough company.

What shocked me was that the murderer had not been content to stop there.

I'd immediately gone for Doc and Jake and returned with them less than fifteen minutes later.

Doc, who had seen death in all its forms over more than three decades of doctoring, had paled and trembled at the sight. Jake's reaction had been like mine—he had heaved his stomach empty in the snow just outside the shack.

It was a sight which I wished I'd never seen. Someone had murdered Franky and waited—in the shack or returning later—until the body was frozen to the core. We knew that with certainty; the only blood in the shack was a small frozen dark puddle from the bullet wound, neat and small-caliber precise at the base of the skull. Without that wait, a warm body would have spilled blood by the gallon, for the murderer had taken a saw and dismembered the body into a half dozen pieces as hard and rigid as board lumber, which he'd left scattered around the inside of the shack.

Aside from the saw—which showed evidence of flesh and bits of bone—we could find nothing in the shack pointing to a murderer or a motive. Franky had been just another drunk, weaving his public appearances covered with filth and rags, often so inebriated it seemed like another drink would kill him.

What could he have owned to tempt a thief?

If the murder had been an act of rage, why the horrifying deliberation of waiting for the corpse to freeze?

With no clue to these answers in the shack, and with a good idea of how folks would react to the news of such a horrible and unnatural act, Doc and I and Jake had placed the pieces of the man in a coffin, nailing it shut from public view. We carried on as if cold had killed Franky, not a bullet.

Over the next weeks, each of us asked around casual, hoping to find any scrap of gossip to point us toward the murderer. To the best of our knowledge we had done a satisfactory job of managing those questions without betraying any hint at the brutal act of violation done to Franky's body.

Unfortunately, we'd found no answers—not even the faintest trace—and I'd prayed on each new journey to the shacks that I would not find another man in the same condition, for who could explain such depraved lunacy and guess whether it would strike again?

Winter had eased into spring with no more deaths. A couple of the drifters had moved on, but none had been brutally murdered. Blessedly, no rumors or fearmongering about a dismembered body had disturbed the town folks.

Spring had eased into summer.

While life continued in Laramie as if Franky Leonard had never existed, Jake and me and Doc always watched and listened for anyone to betray knowledge of the murder.

We'd learned nothing, all the more frustrated because of any murder, this seemed most horrifying, the most compeling to solve.

Now, nine days after Custer's futile stand at the Little Bighorn, someone had ridden into town with questions about Franky Leonard.

FIVE

AT FIRST GLANCE, it appeared a strong wind might knock over the collection of shacks at the far edge of town. Were this true, none would have lasted more than a week, for winds blew often and hard through our wide valley, formed by the Medicine Bow Mountains to the west and the Laramie Mountains to the east.

Instead, ramshackle as they looked, the shacks were ingeniously assembled from bits and pieces of scraps of lumber and tin scavenged—or more likely—stolen. I'd heard of drifters who boarded stationary freight cars as the steam locomotives took on water and coal and hid until the train was pulling away from Laramie. Just out of town, safe from the eyes of roving Union Pacific guards, these drifters would throw building materials to the side of the tracks to be retrieved later.

Some of the shacks had aged to silver gray, others were almost green with new lumber. Last I'd counted, there were twenty shacks, with ownership shifting—as drifters came and went—according to some unwritten code which the drifters followed as fiercely as they rebelled against any written laws on the other side of the tracks. Franky Leonard's shack had been taken within a day of his death; probably a half dozen men had used it as their home since.

Here and there were small garden plots, and flowers planted at the edges of crooked doorways, usually near shacks occupied by older men who clung to traces of their former lives among women and children. I often wondered at the histories which had led the older men to escape to these solitary lives. But I never asked, for escape like this also meant they had shut the door on memories of better times, with liquor the best and surest deadbolt.

We saw nobody wandering among the shacks. I wasn't surprised. Most of these were men of twilight and darkness; daylight was something to be endured on makeshift cots in the relative cool of their shacks, or, if they had found any money, in the saloons.

The wind now came into our faces as we moved, bending the tall, sun-browned grass almost sideways. Above us was the pale blue of a sky dry of moisture for hundreds of miles in all directions.

Jake and I slowed our half run to a cautious walk. I guessed Jake, too, remembered the horror which we'd found on a previous trip to Franky Leonard's shack, when hard crystals of snow had crunched beneath our feet.

We saw two horses first, reins tethered to a post near Franky's shack, hides caked where dust had blown onto sweat lather, then dried. It told me these men cared little for their horses, or their business at the shack was too urgent to walk their horses to a nearby livery for a rubdown.

"How do you want to do this, Sam?"

We were still forty steps away. No sign of the men. But the crooked door to the shack hung open. If they were inside Franky's shack, I doubted they were expecting company.

"Might be best if they don't know you're here to back me up." I pictured the small confines of the shack. "I'll go in, try to get a drop on them. If you don't hear shots, assume I've got them covered."

"And?"

"And you lead their horses away."

"To keep them from riding out on us? But if you've got them covered. . . ."

"While I'm talking, go through their saddle bags. Don't take anything, put things back the way you found 'em. Later, we'll compare their story against what you find. Soon's you're done, wander back and drop in on our little chat."

"And if I hear shots fired from the shack?"

"Well," I said, "if it ain't the shotgun you hear, you'll know they were faster than me. If that's the case, I expect the town council will hire you as Laramie's new marshal."

****

They were definitely inside Franky's shack. I stood at the side of the half open door, listening to light thuds and muttered grumblings.

As I debated the best method of entrance, the door swayed in the wind. Its hinges were only strips of leather and the bottom edge of the door dragged in the dirt floor of the shack.

That was my biggest problem, not knowing their intentions. If these men were involved in Franky's death, I was not being foolish to assume the worst. My eyes would take precious seconds to adjust to the darkness inside, while I would be framed perfectly against the light from outside. As I came in with my shotgun, those seconds were ample for them to draw and fire from close range. On the other hand, if I called them out from where I stood, I would be equally blind to their actions, and they could easily aim in the direction of my voice and slap bullets through the thin, plank walls of the shack.

Behind me, Jake was waiting alongside their horses. I decided I did not want the men stepping outside to see Jake. I wanted to discover what they were doing in the shack.

I could rush in or move slow and quiet.

I choose to move slow, slipping through the doorway with my shotgun at waist level and getting my back against the wall of the shack.

"Go easy, gentlemen," I said. "Get your hands high."

My fears had been in vain. Enough sunlight filtered through cracks in the wall to give me good vision of the interior. The two men each held a metal rod, upright as if they were holding a flagpole. The light thuds I heard were explained easily; I caught one of them in the act of thrusting the end of the rod into the dirt floor. A pattern of circles dented into the ground showed they had been poking the dirt with vigor.

They dropped the rods, slowly raising their hands. In one corner of the shack, a man was snoring, hat over his head, flies crawling across his neck.

"This ain't your business," one said, the older of the two. Old Charlie had been right to guess Texas. His words were a slow drawl.

"The badge pinned to my vest makes it my business. I'd appreciate hearing what brings you to Laramie. And to this shack."

They watched me with great calm. As if they were holding a gun on me. Small as the shack was, it suddenly felt much smaller.

"I'd also appreciate it if you boys dropped to your knees."

"What?" the younger one said. He had a square face, droopy moustache.

"You'll be doing yourselves a favor, gentlemen. Right now I'm as nervous as a chicken in a fox den. I'll be a lot less likely to twitch on this shotgun when I get a chance to relax some."

The first one dropped to his knees. Then the second.

"Good," I said. "Now lie forward. On your stomachs. Careful to keep your hands clear of your holsters."

"Stomach?" This from the younger one.

"Consider your position," I said. "I am reluctant to kick a man in the face, but I am prepared to make an exception."

They eased themselves onto their stomachs.

"Hands on your backs."

No questions from either as they obeyed.

I stepped around, leaned down, and plucked their revolvers from the holsters and tucked them into my waistband. The drifter in the corner continued to snore.

"I feel much better, gentlemen. Why don't we get back to a quiet discussion of your presence here in Laramie."

"Why don't you suck milk from a dead goat," the younger one said.

I thought of firing a shot into the dirt in front of his face, then realized the noise would carry and might throw an equal scare into Jake as he was searching the saddlebags.

"I'm not sure if I've explained myself clear enough. I marshal here in Laramie. I've found you two engaged in what appears to be theft, even if there ain't much to be stolen from a shack like this. I'm holding a gun. You're not. I won't shoot to kill, but I will shoot. And I can think of one or two places where you'd regret carrying a piece of lead for the rest of your life."

It was a bluff. I knew with certainty I could not pull the trigger against unarmed men.

"Marshal," the first one said, speaking into the dirt, "you've pushed us as far as we go, and the only reason you got us this far was we weren't particular about that twitchy trigger finger of yours. If you intend to shoot unarmed men already on the ground, you'd best shoot to kill, 'cause if we ain't dead, we'll add plenty misery before we shorten the rest of your own life."

Bluff called. I wondered what to say next.

I looked around the shack, puzzled at what these men thought they might find here. Aside from the snoring drunk, there was a wooden crate chair in the corner. A few filthy blankets crumpled in a heap against the far wall. Empty bottles beside the blankets. Nothing else, except a strong cat smell, the result of months of vagrants too lazy to push themselves outside to answer nature's call.

"You gentlemen don't scare easy," I allowed. "What would it take for us to get into a discussion about Franky Leonard and what has you asking around about him?"

"We already told you this weren't your business," the second one said.

This was getting us nowhere. The more I threatened them, the more I felt a fool. I had little cause to jail them, as few judges would see much crime in two men searching a shack which legally belonged to no one. And jailing them for any other reason would be pettiness on my part, for I doubted time behind the cells would get them to talk.

It didn't leave me much, except for maybe what Jake might have found in their saddlebags.

I turned on my heels and walked back into the bright sunshine. Leave them wondering what I was up to now, I figured. Since I didn't know myself, they could at least share my uncertainty.

SIX

I *EXPECT THEY'LL STOP BY* to get their guns in the morning, Doc." I sipped on my coffee and waited for his response. We were sitting in Chung's Eatery, letting our food digest after our usual bachelor's supper together, and I'd already recounted most of the day's activities.

Doc regarded me across his own cup of coffee. "Why's that, Sam?"

"Pride," I said. Beuregard was lying on the floor beside my chair, slowly thumping his tail at the familiar cadence of our voices. "Texas Ranger pride. They won't let a lowly town marshal get the best of them."

Doc and I had met a few years back, while I was looking into the events which had led to two men found shot dead in the bank vault of the First National. Since then, I had rarely seen Doc dressed in anything other than the same dull brown suit he wore now, in his office, at funerals, or as he set out in his horse and buggy. The suit, well short of his wrists and his ankles, gave him the appearance of an awkward school boy. Doc Cornelius Harper, of course, was at least forty years beyond school, his age obvious in the slow, grating way he walked, obvious in the thatched hair almost white, obvious in eyes deeply sunk into a worn, narrow face.

"Texas Rangers?" His voice reflected the disbelief I'd had earlier upon hearing from Jake.

"Yup," I said. "While I was in the shack, Jake found papers in their saddlebag. Written orders, giving William French and Leroy Stockton authority as Texas Rangers to lawfully arrest and confine a man named Tom McCabe."

Texas Rangers. Were it true, it greatly explained why they'd shown so little fear looking into my shotgun. Some fifty years earlier, the Texas government had formed volunteer units of "ranging companies" to guard the Mexico border, patrol the countryside, and defend against Apache raids. The need had been so great, it didn't take long for the companies to become a full-time force, paid by the government. Texas Rangers—it was said—could not survive a day of work unless they were four men rolled into one; they had to be able to "ride like a Mexican, track like an Apache, shoot like a Tennessean, and fight like the very devil." It was not an exaggeration. Those who rode for the Rangers were indeed men to be reckoned with.

"Texas Rangers," Doc repeated. "Seems unlikely they'd be this far north. After all, papers can be forged."

"I won't disagree with you there, Doc. But I'm thinking if they were *posing* as Texas Rangers, they'd have made a point of letting me know, of showing me the papers. Not only that, they acted like men who had every right to be in that shack. Still. . . ."

I glanced up as Kam Yee Chung stopped by our table to pour more coffee. His was the best eatery in town, and I had no sympathy for fools who stayed away because it was run by a man they figured should be laying tracks somewhere on the rail lines. Without fail, Kam Yee and his wife made me feel like I was at home having a peaceful supper. It had gotten to the point that I brought bags of candy every time one of their boys had a birthday. I'd even helped them name their youngest a year earlier, providing the swing vote which determined he become Michael instead of Thomas. Kam was determined his boys grow up as true-blue Americans.

"Still," I continued as I blew on my freshened coffee, "I have to wonder. No reason they couldn't have stopped by the marshal's office and asked me about Franky."

"And what does Franky Leonard have to do with the papers Jake found in their saddlebags?" Doc asked. "I thought you just said they were trying to arrest a man named Tom McCabe."

"That's going through my mind too. Behind all of this, there's the fact that Franky Leonard is dead. And, of course, how we found him. I can't believe it's coincidence these Rangers ride into town looking for him."

I studied the rim of my coffee mug, as if it held the answers. "While we're at it, I'd sure like to know what they hoped to find by poking through the dirt floor. Trouble is, I just can't see a way to get either of those two talking unless they want to."

Doc nodded. "Think the telegram you sent might help?"

"Only if I get a reply before these Rangers visit my office. *If* they visit. Otherwise I'll just have to do my best with what Jake finds by following them."

We lapsed into a stretch of silence, not unusual for us. The eatery consisted of six tables, and, as usual, the evening was late and all were empty. Doc and I made it a habit to supper here, and more often than not, prolonged it as long as possible, with discussions that ranged from theology to women to local politics. I'd never asked Doc—this was a pattern we'd established slowly—but I think he had the same reasons for this routine as I did. A late supper here killed empty evening hours at an empty house, better than filling the emptiness with whiskey or other forms of hard living.

The door to the eatery opened. My back to the wall, I could watch the visitor without making it obvious.

What I saw took my mind off the Texas Rangers in a big hurry.

This was a woman who did not belong in a dusty plains town like Laramie. While her ribbed skirt was so wide she barely swished the material through the doorway, the upper half of her dress was tight and displayed an hourglass figure much to be admired. I doubted she had need of a corset to form the hourglass; it didn't take much more than a first glance to note the firmness of youth in a flawless face, cream-white skin sprinkled with light freckles. Coiled hair fell to her shoulders, red almost faded to blonde. A plumed hat rested atop her head.

She stared straight at our table and advanced toward us. Beauregard rose, reached ahead with his front paws and stretched. Doc and I rose too, although, unlike Beau, I managed to refrain from wagging my tail.

"Samuel Keaton," she said, not as a question, extending a white glove hand toward me. "I was informed to look for you here."

Her refinement did not stop at her looks. She'd moved with the effortless grace probably learned with much effort at a finishing school. Her accent was untraceable to any region, her voice—and perfume—soft as a butterfly's touch.

"Yes, ma'am," I replied.

"You're the marshal."

"I am."

"How marvelous," she looked me up and down and did not hide the fact she was looking me up and down. "The stories about lawmen carrying guns were not wild exaggerations."

Before I could reply, she faced Doc, her smile lingering.

"Cornelius Harper," he said, accepting her handshake. "Pleased to meet your acquaintance, Miss. . . ."

"Mrs.," she corrected him. "Mrs. Leigh Tafton. I am equally pleased to make your acquaintance."

"Would you care to be seated, Mrs. Tafton?" Doc asked.

"No, but thank you. I do not mean to impose upon your conversation. I merely wish to request that Mr. Keaton join me for a late lunch at the Union Pacific Hotel tomorrow afternoon."

"Yes, ma'am," I said.

She waited for me to ask the reason for our meeting.

I smiled.

She waited longer.

I smiled, although curiosity did burn.

"I'm pleased you are able to visit," she finally said, her own gracious smile in place. "Perhaps two o'clock?"

"Yes, ma'am."

She curtseyed and departed with the same effortless grace of her arrival. Her slight shoulders remained squared, her head straight and level. I wondered if the mistresses of finishing schools forced their students to walk with books on their heads, and in watching Mrs. Leigh Tafton, I was prepared to believe it to be truth.

Rain or shine, between her and a couple of men who may or may not be Texas Rangers, I expected the next day to be of considerable interest.

SEVEN

THE PREVIOUS SUMMER, I'd been given cause to rig a leather strap beneath my desktop, one which allowed me to hang a cut-down shotgun out of sight but within easy reach of my hand as I sat at the desk. It had been months since I'd actually placed a shotgun in the strap, but when I returned to the office, first thing in the morning I hung the shotgun in the strap.

I set a couple of chairs opposite my desk, then returned to the chair behind my desk, sat, leaned back and scratched Beau's head as I turned to the first pages of a new book about a young rascal named Tom Sawyer.

Reading choice was an on-going argument Doc and I had. Fewer things got him riled faster than mocking his literary taste, something I did often simply for the pleasure of listening to him debate. Doc favored the convoluted French novelists who took five pages to describe the anguish a man felt over deciding which gloves to wear to a dinner party. When I'd told him *Les Misérables* was an aptly named reading chore, he'd snorted and said the simplistic country humor of the new fellow named Twain was just a passing fad. Folks should be reading something which took thought, Doc always said.

Maybe Doc was right, but I was always ready to argue the writer should be the one spending the thought to make things simpler for the reader, and if a man was going to lay down a dime for a book, it wouldn't hurt to be entertained instead of worked to death.

I turned pages, stopping occasionally to add coffee to my cup.

Not much later, just as Tom Sawyer was bragging on the twelve marbles, a piece of bluebottle glass, and a one-eyed kitten which he'd received for allowing his friends the privilege of whitewashing a fence, the Texans arrived, their spurs clanking as they walked into the office without knocking.

I marked my page and set the book down.

"Gentleman," I said, still leaned back and comfortable. "Take a load off your boots."

They sat in the chairs opposite, and faced me and the hidden shotgun. I sized them up in the same manner they were studying me. The tall, lean one wore a black shirt with tan vest. He shifted a high-crowned Stetson hat from his head and placed it in his lap, showing him to be almost completely bald. Some men would have tried to hide the baldness by leaving the hat in place. It told me something about him. Sun-leathered face, glittering dark eyes, hooked nose. I guessed him to be mid-forties, still strong and vigorous.

His partner had foregone a vest to show off more of his pearl-buttoned, blue-flannel shirt. He wore his hat, a southwestern style with brim curled, crown flat. He was much younger than his partner, with an uncreased square face and a drooping moustache, blond in direct contrast to long, dark hair dragging on his shoulders. A bulge of chewing tobacco filled the left side of his cheek. I guessed he'd be brash enough to spit the juice directly onto my floor.

The older man unfolded a sheet of paper. "Marshal, this here writ authorizes us as Texas Rangers to be in your jurisdiction."

He extended the paper and placed it on my desk. I shifted

forward in my chair and made a show of reading it through.

"This have something to do with Franky Leonard?" I asked.

"That's what we're here to ask you. We find it mighty peculiar that you busted in on us yesterday like you did. "

His partner leaned over and spit a stream of juice onto the rough wooden floor of my office. I reread the writ, as if searching for their names.

"You William French? Or Leroy Stockton?" I asked the younger man, looking over the paper.

"Stockton."

"Leroy Stockton, you may be a Texas Ranger, but if you spit on the floor again I'll remove you from this office. My dog is particular about where he walks."

Leroy tried to stare me down. I smiled in return.

"Do as the man says," French said in a weary voice. "Your tobacco plug ain't a hill to die for."

Leroy shrugged, stood, and walked heel-to-toe out to the street. By the time he'd returned, I had pulled a desk drawer open, removed their revolvers and set both of them on my desk, the butts of the guns toward the two men. The revolvers were loaded; a risk, but one I felt necessary to convince them I believed their story.

"Help yourselves," I said. I dropped one of my hands casual beneath the desktop, keeping it close to the shotgun. "I don't expect a pair of Texas Rangers will give me any cause for grief. 'Course, it would be nice if you gave me some answers. San Antonio to Laramie does seem a fair bit to ride."

Leroy glanced quick at his senior partner. William gave him the nod.

"I suppose we could tell you we got our reasons and leave it at that," Leroy drawled, "but being as you are the law in these parts. ..."

He left me no doubt of his disdainful opinion of local marshals. If I hadn't caught it in his tone, I could have sur-

mised it from the fact they had preferred not to visit me first
with their questions about Franky Leonard. Not that I blamed
him. Despite the cherished illusions of dime novels sold back
east, marshaling mostly consisted of strong-arming drunks or
shooting stray dogs. It didn't take much in qualifications to
wear a badge.

"Mighty kind of you to be so generous." I kept my voice
neutral. Let him guess whether I was sarcastic. I pointed at
the writ, still lying flat on my desk. "How about telling me
what the arrest of Tom McCabe has to do with Franky
Leonard?"

Leroy shot another glance at his partner.

"Show him the photo," French said.

Leroy unbuttoned his chest pocket and pulled loose a
small photo.

I took my time studying it. It showed a head-and-shoul-
ders portrait of a man who looked much younger than the
Franky Leonard I remembered. Short-clipped hair parted in
the middle, goatee. High-starched collar of a white shirt, tie,
and striped suit.

I handed him back the clipping. "That's Franky Leonard.
If you take the whiskers off the photo." Leonard's greasy face
had, at the most, shown gray stubble, but never a beard or
goatee. "But you asked around enough to know that already."

In other words, they weren't showing me anything I
hadn't already found out for myself.

"Yup. Only his name is Tom McCabe," French said. "And
we heard he died during a blizzard."

"Yup," I said.

French waited until he realized I'd said all I intended on
the subject.

He sighed. "We've been on Tom McCabe's trail for some
time now. We got wind he was hiding out here in Laramie,
calling himself Franky Leonard."

Stockton's revolver was a Smith and Wesson Army Mod-
el 1875. A single action .45 caliber gun, with a six-shot cylin-

der which broke open at the top. He'd popped the cylinder and was aimlessly spinning it as his partner spoke. I was glad I'd left cartridges in the revolver. An empty cylinder would have raised his suspicions real quick.

"Interesting," I said. "How'd you get wind Tom McCabe was hiding here in Laramie?"

French shook his head no.

"All right then, why were you on his trail?"

Again, French shook his head no. "Marshal, how about *you* tell us some about Tom McCabe and his days in Laramie as Franky Leonard?"

I obliged them, telling them no more than what they would have already learned on their own. I told them Franky Leonard was a mean, friendless drunk, who drifted into town sometime last fall, unmourned even by those who lived in the shacks around his. I did not, however, describe the state in which I'd found Franky's frozen body.

"Marshal," French said. "That ain't much for us to go on. Why don't you explain what brought you to the shack same time as us. And why you'd even care to bust in on us."

I shrugged. "Maybe I could help you more if I knew where to start looking. And I'd know where to start if you told me exactly why you'd ride up here from Texas for the man."

"It's Ranger business. And we'll take care of it our way," French said.

"Then I reckon we don't have much left to discuss."

"Reckon not." William French set his hat on his head and stood. Leroy Stockton did the same. They stepped outside without looking back.

In the silence of their departure, I wondered if I was playing this wrong. I told myself I would have learned little by arresting the two at the end of our conversation. I told myself I was going to learn more by what they might do as free men in Laramie, with Jake outside somewhere nearby, planning to remain hidden as he dogged their trail.

I thought of the telegraph wires strung along the hundreds of miles between here and San Antonio and wished for the impossibility of being able to converse through those wires instead of relying on brief telegrams. Were that the case, I'd be much better able to judge my best course of action, for what little information I'd learned through telegram had only raised more questions.

My own telegram to San Antonio's marshal had been short: PLEASE CONFIRM AUTHORIZED DUTIES OF RANGERS WILLIAM FRENCH AND LEROY STOCKTON IN WYOMING TERRITORIES. STOP.

The reply I'd received had done little to ease my mind, especially in light of how I'd found Franky Leonard: RANGERS FRENCH AND STOCKTON MISSING SINCE MAY. STOP. BELIEVED DEAD. STOP. IMMEDIATELY FORWARD REASON FOR REQUESTED CONFIRMATION. STOP.

These two Texans, then, were either French and Stockton, or men posing as Texas Rangers. If Rangers, why were they missing and allowing themselves to be counted as dead? If not Rangers, what was their game? And how did all of this tie into a man named Tom McCabe who had died under the name of Franky Leonard?

I'd have been pleased to forward my reasons for requested confirmation. Only I wanted to know more about these men before I did so. Trouble was, I had little idea where to begin. To worsen matters, depending on how long they were going to be in town, I probably had little time as well.

EIGHT

YOU MAY HAVE SAVED MY LIFE YESTERDAY," Leigh Tafton said, offering a gloved hand as greeting in the same manner she'd done the evening before. "For that, Samuel Keaton, you have my gratitude."

I'd arrived early at the Union Pacific Hotel. Seated at the dining room table, I had passed time by worrying about Jake and the two Texans, then I had risen to greet Leigh Tafton as she crossed the room not even one minute past the hour of two.

I shook her hand, keenly aware of perfume and lace. The top of her head was the height of my chin, her hair strawberry blonde in the sunlight angling in through the dining room windows. Eyes the lightest of green. Tiny smile creases at the corners of those delightful eyes.

She knew I was keenly aware of perfume and lace, and held my gaze a fraction longer than necessary. I stonewalled my stirrings of interest; this was a married woman, and besides that, I'd spent the last year growing accustomed again to the safety of solitude.

I pulled her chair away from the table, and she graciously allowed me to assist her as she sat, tucking her wide dress beneath her and setting a small hand purse on the table as I set the chair forward. She had plucked her gloves loose by the time I was in my own chair and facing her.

"As I don't recall how I might have saved your life, you have me at a disadvantage," I said.

"You're not accustomed to a lady having you in that position?"

I didn't reply to her teasing grin.

"My, oh my," she said. "A serious man."

She rested her elbows on the table, intertwined the fingers of both hands to form a steeple, and rested her chin on top. She peered upward at me, such a parody of coquettishness that I was forced to grin.

"Thank you," she said. "The last thing I wanted was a dreary lunch."

"Dreary, ma'am, is the last word which comes to mind in your presence."

"My, oh my. A serious man with a degree of gallantry."

It was difficult to judge whether she was mocking me, an effect I decided was deliberate on her part. I put a polite smile on my face and left it there. I had no idea where this lunch was headed, but my smile was armor as good as anything else.

"*Yesterday* was dreary," she said, adding false gaiety to her voice. "I was forced to pretend adoration and awe during a certain military spectacle which only become interesting when a certain marshal appeared with a shotgun, saving me from death by cannon. My, oh, my. Such bravery and elan in the face of danger. Enough to make a woman's heart flutter and tremble."

So this was the widowed heiress who had been standing beside Ricketts. Rich, beautiful, and unattached. She seemed like she was accustomed to running roughshod over men. It would make for a long lunch, and I had no desire to be bullied.

"Ma'am?"

She raised her eyebrows, giving me permission to continue.

"If you continue in such a manner, I'm guessing by the time we finish lunch, it might be just like a large herd of cattle has moved through this dining room."

"I beg your pardon?"

"You're throwing a plenty big pile, if you get my drift."

Her eyes widened briefly and she stared at me as if reappraising me.

I left the half smile in place.

"This *will* be interesting," she said. Only this time she'd dropped the false gaiety. "Perhaps you are the right man to see."

"And not an incompetent U.S. Army colonel?"

Now she grinned, almost wolfish. The woman had more moods than Wyoming had weather changes. "Am I that obvious?"

Our waiter stopped at our table. He had the same slight build as Kam Yee Chung, but not nearly the same cheerfulness. Of course, I was biased in Chung's favor. I didn't expect the Union Pacific Hotel's fine dining to come close to Chung's Eatery in quality or quantity of food.

We ordered. To my surprise, she requested steak, rare. I'd figured her for a fancier and easy-to-mispronounce dish.

"I'll repeat myself," she said. "Am I that obvious?"

I wanted to tell her she was so unpredictable, and so alluring because of it, I was enjoying myself in a way I hadn't thought possible again, especially conscious as I was of the fact she was not a married woman, especially with the freckled, cream skin of her shoulders and neck and my passing speculations on its softness and warmth.

"You're not obvious," I replied. "It was just a guess based on common sense. A widowed woman doesn't cross the country from Philadelphia to Laramie unless she's got good reason. Appears your first stop here was the colonel. If you've moved on to me. . . ."

I let it hang.

She ran a long finger down her cheek, tracing with the edge of her fingernail a curved line which matched the real one across my own cheek. "I'm intrigued by the scar, Samuel Keaton. How did you get it?"

"Youth and stupidity. What brings you to Laramie?"

"You're not easily distracted."

"Depends on what's distracting me. Flying bullets, for example, do a fine job of taking my attention away from the matter at hand."

"And women? Will they distract you?"

Amazing. Skittish one moment, direct the next.

"I've been distracted before," I finally said, not allowing this was rapidly becoming one of those occasions.

Leigh Tafton held my gaze again, daring me to look away. I didn't, hoping I had on my best poker face. After long enjoyable moments, she blinked first.

She opened her purse and pulled out a folded envelope. "Marshal, please read the letter inside."

I took the envelope. Return address *Johnstown, Pennsylvania*. Delivery address *Leigh Tafton Ellerslie, Chestnut Street, Philadelphia, Pennsylvania*.

"Go ahead." Her invitation was soft, almost sad.

I read slowly the slanted feminine handwriting on the paper in my hands.

On this day of April 15, in the year of our Lord 1876

Dearest Leigh, I can only presume this letter will be waiting you upon your return from the continent. How I envy your escape. (And you of any person alive would understand the full meaning of that statement.)

My situation has only worsened, and I am at wits end here beneath the gray, gray skys. I miss so much the balls of Philadelphia, the parties, the luncheons. (THE GOSSIP!)

I pray you might hasten to visit me, even if a steel town in the mountains sounds dull after London and Paris. I

NEED you, if only to brighten my life for a month or two.

I can promise you Frederick will be on his best behavior. He has been stranger by the day since his return, but I have been ill of late and this has softened him. (To gain his sympathy, I hardly need PRETEND my dizzy spells are real, and that is my only consolation throughout this puzzling ailment.)

Upon the very day you receive this letter, PLEASE, PLEASE, PLEASE send me a telegram promising your visit forthwith.

Your loving sister, Aurelia.

I refolded the letter and placed it across the table beside Leigh's dinner plate.

"Escape?" I asked.

"She did not mean my escape to Europe, although, of course, it was. Father married us to older men. Older wealthy men. As a way to protect the family fortune. They were not so much marriages as political alliances. Aurelia always said we were held prisoners, by our family money and by our husbands. Mine died, George Hamilton Ellerslie the Second. With no third to carry on his family name. His death was my escape. From him. And back to my family name, Tafton."

"You still have your family money," I said.

"And much of George Hamilton Ellerslie's. It lessened much of Father's hold upon me."

"Your father does not approve of a woman traveling to the territories."

She smiled. And I was distracted because of it. Jake would have a few unkind words for me if and when he found out I'd been dining with a rich, widowed, beautiful heiress as he endured the hot sun and gritty dust to stay on the heels of the Texans.

"Father's death lessened the remainder of Father's control," Leigh said. She lightened the tone of her voice. "However, I'm sure he's kicking against his coffin lid at this very moment because of my travel here."

I rubbed my face. "Mrs. Tafton—"

"Leigh."

"—I'm still not sure what all of this is. Nor why all of this brings you to Laramie."

"I happen to know Frederick visited Laramie. That's the trip mentioned in her letter."

"Frederick. Aurelia's husband."

Leigh nodded. "Frederick Blackburn. Owns a steel mill in Johnstown."

"You have a habit of raising more questions than answers. I can't figure a man like him having the need to travel to Laramie. Nor do I recall seeing or hearing of the man. And in a town this small, starved of entertainment as it is, he'd surely be noticed and gossiped upon."

Her smile, which had not entirely left her face, widened to the wolfish grin I found captivating on a face so unwolfish. "I understand, then, you indulge in gossip."

"On the listening end. Makes marshaling an easier task when you've got a sense for the town's happenings."

She opened her mouth to speak, but was interrupted by the waiter bearing silver trays of food. We both held silence as our meals were set before us.

I bowed my head for silent grace, then lifted my eyes back to hers. She was poised to cut into her steak.

"Leigh, let me see if I understand this. You're here because your sister says her husband has been acting strange since returning to Johnstown from Laramie."

She set her knife and fork back down and gave me her powerfully direct gaze. Only now I saw sadness in her eyes.

"Marshal, I'm here because my sister was dead by the time I managed to get to Johnstown. And I'm convinced she was murdered."

"Murdered?"

"Murdered. Deliberately drowned. That's why I'd like to know what you can tell me about the man Frederick Blackburn visited during his stay in Laramie."

"I'll do my best," I said. "It seems near everybody knows near everybody in this town. Who's the man Blackburn visited?"

"McCabe," she said. "Tom McCabe. Anything of interest about him?"

NINE

AS DUSK APPROACHED, I began to worry for Jake. Our rough plan had been simple. He'd watch the Texans throughout the day, taking pains to remain unseen. If it appeared they were heading out of town—leaving us no opportunity to learn more of their intentions—Jake was to leave them to find me, and we would round up a few men to form an official posse. The Texans probably would not be in a hurry, and it would be easy to trail them. I'd arrest them then, and keep them in jail until I received direction from San Antonio.

On the other hand, if the Texans stayed in town, Jake was to find a time he could leave them for a few minutes—perhaps as they ate, or if they were in a card game—and get me here at the marshal's office. He'd instruct me as to their whereabouts, and I would take a spell watching them.

I was anxious to talk to Jake in light of discovering Leigh Tafton's reason for arriving in Laramie. Until today, I could have believed Franky Leonard's death was a freak act, unsettling because of its apparent randomness. Now—because it was impossible that unrelated coincidence had both the Texans and Leigh Tafton in pursuit of the dead man—I was able to think otherwise. Jake and I could throw questions and theories back and forth as we tried to make sense of it. We could decide on a course of action; while women are much wiser in this regard, action for its own sake, useless or not, always seems to ease a man's soul.

Another hour passed. Doc was making a sick call at a ranch a half day's travel south of Laramie, which meant I'd have to sup alone. I decided instead to rely upon a good novel to help pass time. I lit the oil lamp and adjusted the wick to give me brightness to read.

Where was Jake?

I could not concentrate on the words of the pages. I set the book down, leaving Tom Sawyer rafting on the Mississippi River with his pirate friends.

Where was Jake?

I got up and paced the confines of my office. Beau followed me on my tight turns, sniffing hopefully at my palms for the dried beef I occasionally tossed him.

Pacing didn't help.

I stepped outside into calm, warm air. Most evenings in this wide valley, the wind died shortly after the sun disappeared. The sky was deepening to purple black, the moon a glow behind a bank of clouds. It was a quiet time in Laramie; family folks long since retired, saloon folks yet a couple hours from the peak of their carousing.

These were generally the most difficult hours for me. It was the time when a man should be strolling with the woman he loved, the time when whispered words would hang on still evening air, the time when the touch of a kiss spoke so much more than those whispered words.

Too briefly last summer, I had had those times. Since then, these hours were reminders of regret and sorrow for me, leading me to understand love is much more than the incredible mingled joy and peace of the moment. Love needs the promise of a shared future. Without that promise, love during the moment is merely a hollow joy, endurable only because the moment has not yet faded; without the promise of future, remembered love rings hollow that much more sadly.

As I had done many evenings before, I glanced northward into the dark night sky, imagining her among the Sioux, paining myself by wondering what she was doing at this very moment, wondering if the man she had chosen to be her husband was indeed whispering words against her soft skin.

In the society of whites, her name was Rebecca Montcalm; among the Sioux, she was Morning Star.

She had been born in London to a Sioux woman traveling in a Wild West show. Orphaned as a baby, she had been raised among English nuns as Rebecca Montcalm. At her coming of age, she had returned to America, determined to find her family. It had been my good fortune—although then I had not seen it as such—to be the guide she chose for her search. She was a contrary woman, choosing to travel filthy and unattractive for fear of unwanted advances on my part. During the first days of shared hardship I had seen her as merely an irritating impediment to travel. Naturally—since at that moment I'd been angry with her at yet another disagreement—my sudden awareness of her as a woman had been a total surprise. That first real introduction to her, along with the less than formal circumstances for it along a Nebraska creek the previous summer, was a favorite and well-visited memory of mine.

Considering our travel urgency back then, she had taken what I felt was far too long for bathing privacy, and I had returned to find her in longjohns, the red material wet, her upper body covered by her shirt, also wet. Draped over a nearby branch were her pants, dripping dry. It explained why it had taken so long for her to call me. She'd washed her clothes too. Gone was the filth.

She was standing in bare feet at the side of the creek, leaning sideways to squeeze dry her unbraided hair. She smiled at my approach, leaned the other direction, and repeated the squeezing with her hands, water streaming down her wrists and dropping from her elbows.

"Would it be a great inconvenience if we waited here for the breeze to—" She broke off.

I hadn't returned her smile. The time she'd taken to wash was time that had let me grow even more angry at our earlier disagreement.

"You, ma'am, have been a great inconvenience," I said. "Furthermore, you've played me for a fool."

"Have I?" She studied me. The muscles around her eyes tightened and her voice lost its light happiness. "My understanding of fools is that generally they only have themselves to blame for their foolishness."

I snapped my mouth shut. She certainly had a way of getting a man's attention. I found myself looking closely at her, which became, in truth, my first occasion to truly see her as she was.

Filthy before, her braids had been sloppy pieces of rope; here, her loose hair fell over her shoulders in thick, if damp, luxury. Before, the flashes of her face had shown greasy, smudged dirt; here, her skin was a light dusk stretched smooth. Before, hidden by the bulky coat, she had walked bowed and head cast downward as if in shame; here, she stood tall and proud, and her shirt, weighted with water, clung so that it was impossible to conceal the womanhood I had not suspected.

She returned my gaze with a dignity of calmness that defied the essential absurdity of a barefooted woman in saggy, wet, red longjohns. In that moment, my cloud of anger dropped to be replaced by an awareness of Rebecca Montcalm as the woman she was, and my breathing developed a hitch.

For she was beautiful. Definitely Sioux, but beautiful.

Strands of her black hair danced against her forehead and high curved cheekbones. Her face showed a haunting, untamable wildness, yet to me her half smile promised joy and long shared nights. Her features were unblemished and perfect, yet duskiness of her skin stayed any porcelain fragility.

At her rebuke, I took my hat from my head, held it humbly against my chest, and searched for any words to break our awkward silence.

"Ma'am, what say I go back to my horses, turn around, come up here just like before. Except this time when you smile and ask about inconveniences, I won't say anything that gives you the opportunity to rightfully accuse me of being selfish or foolish."

It had been enough of an apology for us to start from fresh as man and woman thrown together in travel. Fitting in with her contrariness, she would never have decided to love me had I earlier been attempting to impress her. Instead she took it into her head to love me for all the things I'd done during our first days of travel, uncaring of her watching eyes and unaware of the beauty she hid.

Although we were both stubborn—and at times it seemed against both our wills—our love had grown from that day along the Nebraska creek. I had proposed last summer, joyful at the thought of spending the rest of my life with Mrs. Rebecca Keaton.

Within a month, our dreams had been torn in the hurricane of events neither of us could withstand. I'd been fortunate to survive my encounter with Sitting Bull, but had not seen it as good fortune. Without Rebecca, I had no desire for life. Worse, our separation was, and would always be, a situation where I could take no action; there was nothing—futile or not—I could do to ease my soul of the pain of losing her.

To my shame, I had tried violence and whiskey and been saved only through faith.

Nor could any other woman fill the void. Yes, Leigh Tafton had indeed been the first to briefly lighten my heart in all this time. Yet away from Leigh's physical presence, the memory of her strong allure held no candle against the overwhelming love I carried for a woman I had not seen in a year and would never hold again.

I blinked my thoughts away from Rebecca and stared sightlessly at the towering cloudbanks on the horizon. Much better to worry about Jake than to torture myself further.
Where was he?

Beauregard had slipped through the door. He bumped his head against my leg, seeking my hand with his nose. I obliged and scratched behind his ears.

"Beau, how about you wait inside?" I led him into the marshal's office and pointed at his blanket on the floor near the potbellied stove. "If you see Jake, give him a message I went looking for him."

I had no idea where to begin looking. But at least I would be doing something. And just in case Beau neglected to pass along my message, I left a note on my desk saying the same thing, letting Jake know I would be back by ten o'clock.

****

Within a half hour, I learned Jake had not been seen recently at the Red Rose Saloon, nor at any of the other saloons. Nor at Chung's Eatery. Nor at his own livery. I told myself he was waiting for me at my office and hurried back.

Main Street was well lit by the wide windows of saloons. The side street to my office, however, was almost totally dark, the only light coming from a crescent moon, stars, and the occasional shine of an oil lamp through open curtains. Because of this, I saw too late the shadow which stepped out from a gap between two buildings.

I also heard too late the distinctive click of a gun's hammer drawn back.

"Stop right there, Marshal." A Texas drawl. Belonging to Leroy Stockton, the younger Ranger. He held his Smith and Wesson waist high, pointed at my stomach. "I see your hands even twitch, you're a dead man."

Briefly, very briefly, I thought of rolling onto the street and drawing as I tumbled, hoping for a lucky blind shot to take him where he stood. But if he wanted me dead, he would have fired already. I'd look for a better chance later.

I stopped on the wooden sidewalk.

Soft boot steps approached from behind me. I resisted the impulse to half turn. I tightened, waiting for a blow into the back of my head.

"On your knees," Stockton told me. I could hear the mocking grin in his voice. "Then on your stomach. As I best remember, ain't that the way it goes, Marshal?"

I hesitated.

"Do it," William French said, speaking from behind me. "I'm holding a blackjack in my hand, and it won't bother me none to knock you down. Except if we do it that way, you'll be a while getting up again."

Slowly, I lowered myself, pressing my face into the rough wood of the sidewalk.

French grabbed my left wrist, and manacled it in handcuffs, locking it to my right wrist behind my back. He yanked me upward by the collar of my shirt.

"On your feet," he said.

Stockton moved closer as I stood, so close I could see the gleam of his teeth beneath the shadow of his hat brim.

"Been looking for a deputy?" he asked,

Fair guess they already knew the answer to that one.

"We'll go for a little walk," Stockton continued. He spit a large splash of tobacco juice onto the toe of my boot. "Soon enough you'll find him."

TEN

IT WAS A SILENT WALK. The Rangers did not volunteer information; I did not ask. We met no people as we walked to the edge of town and onto the flat ground beyond, leaving the buildings and scant lights behind us.

Moonlight and starlight and eyes adjusted to darkness made it easier to walk through the scattered sagebrush and open ground as we began to cover the half mile gap to Laramie's stockyard, downwind on our approach. The muted lowing of hundreds of restless cattle reached us clearly, as did the pungent aroma of manure.

The railings of the stockyards were a low line against the night sky and stars. Beyond that, some stationary rail cars, and siding tracks which led to the main Union Pacific line. Come morning, many of the cattle would be shipped out, while others would remain until spoken for by eastern markets. All told, the stockyard held some thousand head, divided into a series of pens connected by cattle shutes and drop gates.

It gave me some hope. The stockyards were patrolled to guard against rustlers. If it was our destination, there was always the chance of a timely diversion.

No such hope.

We stopped a couple hundred yards short of the stock-yard, and Stockton pushed me roughly down a steep path into a narrow gully, cut through the soft soil by sporadic flash floods.

Jake was waiting at the bottom, wrists handcuffed, ankles handcuffed.

"Sit beside him," French said.

I had little choice. I sat, drew my knees up, and leaned back against the gully wall.

French manacled my ankles together. He then untied the hanky from around Jake's mouth. "Deputy, tell him we mean business."

"They mean business, Sam."

"Hey, Jake," I said. "Comfortable?"

"Shut your mouth," French said to me. "Unless it's in answer to our questions."

Both took the opposite side of the gully wall. The sharp angle of shadow covered them; Jake and I sat in a pale slice of moonlight.

"And we got plenty of questions," Stockton said. "Now, if you don't feel the urge to tell us what we want, there's plenty ways we can get you to talk. Down in Texas, we learned some good tricks. Maybe we'll drop a scorpion in your shorts. Or maybe we'll dispense with the fancy stuff and carve your eyeballs. Fact of the matter is you ain't in a position to do anything but tell us what we want."

I waited.

"For starts," French said, "what's got you so all-fired interested in Franky Leonard? Like I said this morning, it's peculiar you'd show up in his shack the way you did. According to most folks, he was just another drunk. In a normal situation, the town marshal wouldn't care none about drifters."

I was trying to make sense of this, trying to see my actions through their eyes, and wondering why my answers would be important enough to risk kidnapping a U.S. marshal. Maybe if I played along—as if I had a choice—I could learn from their questions what they did and didn't know about the situation.

"Franky Leonard died strange," I said. "Strange enough I had plenty questions of my own."

"How strange?" French asked, his voice coming soft and dangerous from the shadow of the gully wall.

"Bullet," I said. "Not exposure to cold like we told folks. We kept it quiet because—"

"Hold on," Stockton interrupted. He was playing with the cylinder of his Smith and Wesson again, the oiled clicking of the revolving cylinder barely audible above the stockyard noises of lowing cattle. "You should first know we already asked Jake the same question. Thing is, Marshal, if you give us an answer that don't match his, I'll gag him to keep him quiet and hold a lit match under one of his ears."

Stockton laughed. "It makes this whole conversation complicated, but we got all night."

That, I didn't doubt. This gully was invisible until you stepped on it. Stockyard guards would have no reason to stray this far from their patrols.

"Jake," I said. "Did you tell them the truth?"

"Well, Sam, I—"

Quickly, so quickly it gave me new respect for William French, he was across the gap with the barrel of his pistol pressed to Jake's temple.

"Another word, Deputy, and I splatter your brains."

"Think about it," I told French. "I'm just asking if he lied or not. Because if he told you the truth and I know it, then I'm forced to do the same. And when you get matching answers, then you can rest easy knowing you actually did hear the truth."

French glared at me until he finally lowered his pistol. "Deputy, nod your head if you answered us true."

Jake shook his head no.

French slammed Jake's skull with the butt end of his pistol. Jake slumped sideways.

My hands shuddered in clenched, helpless rage.

"Let's start over," French said. "We want answers. Pray you don't happen to match up a lie to one of his, or you're both dead."

I had a feeling Jake and I were both dead anyway. These men weren't in for a polite two-step and a goodnight at the end of the dance. It seemed the best I could do was drag this dance on as long as possible. "There's a real simple reason for my interest in Franky Leonard," I said. "Probably a lot more simple than yours."

"Our business ain't your concern," French said. "Get on with telling us why you appeared at the shack."

"I've been hoping to learn more about Franky Leonard since the day he died." I explained why, telling the truth. Pride and horse-trading for information—the way I'd hoped to do it earlier with them in the marshal's office—seemed of little importance now against the need to survive as long as possible.

Silence greeted me when I finished.

A coyote came trotting up the gully, caught wind of us almost as he reached us, and turned in a spurt of dust.

"All right," French finally said. "What about the money?"

"I don't know of any money." Not until now. I guessed that explained why I had found them prodding the dirt of his shack. It also told me why they were on his trail.

"Marshal," French said, "that is probably the most unfortunate answer you could have given us. If you do know about the money, we're going to find out anyway, anyhow."

Which told me it was a safe bet there was plenty money involved.

"And if you really *don't* know," French said, "it's your bad luck to have gotten in our way. Because by the time we finally believe you don't know about the money, you and your partner are going to be so close to dead you'll be begging us to put you out of your misery."

French stood and dusted off his pants by slapping his legs with his hat.

"Leroy, keep good watch on these two. I'll be back shortly."

French directed his next words at me. "Because if your misery ain't enough, it will be right handy to have Leigh Tafton here to sing out what we need."

ELEVEN

SHORTLY AFTER FRENCH DEPARTED, I tried to help Jake. Because I was cuffed from behind, I had to twist my back sharply to lift my manacled hands high enough to grasp the upper part of Jake's shirt sleeve.

Stockton slapped the cylinder back into his Smith and Wesson. "Leave him be."

I ignored Stockton. Not only was I concerned for Jake, I knew whatever slight chance we had would occur if Stockton reacted according to emotion, not thought.

I pulled at Jake's shirt. It strained my shoulders badly, but I was able to get leverage.

"I said, leave him be." Stockton cocked the hammer of his pistol.

"This man's unconscious," I told Stockton, keeping a firm grip on Jake. "His tongue falls in his throat or if he's bleeding inside his mouth, he might suffocate."

"Marshal, I'm warning you. . . ."

"Empty warning," I said. "You ain't gonna risk letting a gunshot bring folks here on the run." I gave a final heave and managed to get Jake sitting up. His head lolled against my shoulder.

I said nothing more for ten or fifteen minutes. I hoped it would bother Stockton, my minor victory.

"You do think you're smart, don't you, Marshal." Stockton's voice was sullen from the darkness of the shadow as he finally broke the silence.

I didn't reply.

Jake nudged me with his elbow, just enough to let me know he wasn't unconscious. Where we would go from here, I had no idea.

"Fact is, Marshal," Stockton taunted, "it didn't take us long at all to figure through your little game. Not long at all."

I'd guessed right. Stockton was young, needed to bolster his ego.

"How's that?" I asked. Maybe if Stockton kept talking, I'd figure a way out.

"How's that?" Stockton laughed. "First thing we did when we left your office this morning was go to the telegraph office. Told the man we was Texas Rangers. Imagine our surprise when he asked us if we was here because of the dead ones you wired about earlier."

"What business did you have at the telegraph office?" I asked. Jake left his head on my shoulder.

"None of your concern. What does matter is it shed a whole new light on our little talk. French figured real quick you was playing possum, trying to give us rope to hang ourselves. Once we started looking around, it didn't take long to spot your deputy sniffing our tracks. We let him follow most of the day. He watched us drink beer and play poker. Come dark we waylaid him as slick as we got you, Marshal. All we need now is Leigh Tafton."

"Leigh Tafton?"

"There you go again, Marshal, trying to play dumb. You had lunch with Leigh Tafton. Remember? She's the pretty one who's been asking around about Tom McCabe too. We figure it's our business to know why. 'Course, with her, it will be a downright pleasure to find ways to get her to tell us what we need to know."

Tom McCabe—who had lived and died here as Frankly Leonard. Somehow—if Leigh Tafton was right—he had been part of the reason for her sister's death. Now it looked—even dead for six months—like he'd be the cause of a few more, Leigh's included along with ours. How could a man make sense of this?

Stockton spit more tobacco juice. "Marshal, why did you wire San Antonio?"

"You're so smart," I said, "you tell me." I was stalling, even as I was forced to admit how useless it was. Jake's hands were cuffed behind his back. His ankles were manacled as tightly as mine. Jake and I would have difficulty subduing Stockton even if the man threw away his gun and fell asleep.

Stockton moved from the shadow and squatted in front of us. He set the Smith and Wesson on the ground and withdrew a Bowie knife from his belt. He touched the tip of the knife against my chest, turning the wide blade sideways. This was a man who knew how to slip a knife between ribs.

The whites of his eyes gleamed. Beery, tobacco breath washed over my face. "I don't like your attitude, Marshal. See, I push this a half inch forward and you die. No gunshot to bring folks in on the run. Just your heart pumping you dry of blood."

Jake nudged me again. The slightest of movements. *What was Jake thinking?*

"You got French's permission to act on your own?" I said, scornful. "Seems to me he leads you around like a little puppy dog."

Stockton's total focus was on me. His nostrils flared as he drew on his anger. The knife pressed harder. "I am my own man and—"

I'd been waiting for something from Jake, but even prepared, it still caught me by surprise. Jake lashed his head forward from my shoulder, clamping his teeth on Stockton's wrist.

Stockton's instinctive move was to try to shake loose. He roared with pain and yanked his hand away from my chest. Jake hung on, half falling forward into my lap.

Stockton kept roaring.

I scrambled sideways, my back still to the gully wall.

Jake kept a bulldog grip. He must have been grinding down on Stockton's wrist bones with considerable force, because Stockton's roar kept rising.

Stockton tried to stand, but Jake's weight staggered him. Stockton pulled and yanked until he realized he wouldn't free himself that way. Stockton began to flail at the back of Jake's head with his other hand. I couldn't see how Jake could take the punishment much longer.

Hands behind my back, ankles trussed together, I only had one weapon. I pushed to my feet, wobbly and uncertain of my balance. I dove forward, bringing my head down to butt Stockton in the face.

I caught him with the round of my forehead, somewhere near the tip of his nose. He fell backward, me on top. I waited for his hands to wrap around me, readying myself to bash him again with the front of my head.

Nothing.

A solitary groan, but no movement.

I rolled off Stockton.

Jake was gagging and spitting into the sand. I became conscious of warm wetness running into my eyebrows. I must have split the skin of my forehead against Stockton's teeth. I was helpless to do anything against the blood except to blink it away; with hands cuffed behind my back, I couldn't even raise a shoulder to wipe my eyes.

Jake finished his spitting. "I believe I gnawed off some of the man's wrist bone."

He looked at me and grinned at the blood flowing from my forehead.

"Always maintained you were hard-headed," Jake said. "Just never knew it had a practical purpose."

"Maybe instead of impressing me with your wit, you should figure a way to get us out of these cuffs. Hopping ain't going to get us far, and the other's gonna be back."

Several seconds of silence. Jake knew what I did. We had extremely limited movement. Given a couple hours, we might be able to hop to the stockyard, if that.

"How about his gun, Jake?" I said. "Wriggle around and get it in your hand."

"And when t'other gets back, you expect me to gun him down while facing away from him?"

"No, I'm trusting you to shoot off my handcuffs."

"Behind my back, shooting between your hands behind your back," Jake said. "This ought to be good. And if I miss and shoot you in the hind end?"

"I'll find a new deputy sheriff."

"I'm ready to quit anyway. Chewing on grown people weren't what I expected when I signed on."

Stockton groaned again.

"Probably wouldn't hurt to commence soon, Jake."

Jake commenced, shuffling to the Smith and Wesson a few feet over in the sand. He turned his back on it, grunting as he rocked to get his good hand low to the ground. He grunted again in satisfaction.

"Got it."

We maneuvered ourselves to sit side by side again. "I lift my hands," I said. We were working by feel, and I wanted to go slow. "You hold the gun so I can get the hand-cuffs in front of the barrel. When I say it, fire."

It would have worked. Jake would have been firing away from my body, and at the worst, I would have suffered powder burns. With free hands, I could have then shot his hand-cuffs loose, then taken care of our manacled ankles.

Only one thing kept us from our freedom.

We ran out of time before William French returned. Along with Leigh Tafton.

TWELVE

AFTER MY ENCOUNTER with Sitting Bull last summer, there had been a spell in which I'd done my best to kill time in a way which allowed it to return the favor as quickly as possible—taking to drink as a way to escape my misery. Those weeks were a blurred memory, the clearest event a single sharp moment in which Doc Harper had forced me to choose a different path. Since then I had not tasted even a single drop, although the temptation to look upward into the bottom of a bottle had never entirely left, with some days more difficult than others.

Because of that, a portion of my body welcomed with relief the whiskey William French began to pour down my throat.

Stockton was sitting to the side of our small group, holding a handkerchief to his face and mumbling curses. Leigh Tafton, hands and feet bound by coarse rope, sat nearby. Jake, still as manacled as I was, sat on the other side of her.

"It's like this," French said. "Your lady friend has done saved me and Leroy plenty of time. And you oughta be thanking her for saving you both plenty of anguish, being as we learned enough from her to forgo the unpleasantries."

With one hand, he had the neck of the bottle jammed hard against the roof of my mouth; with his other hand, a firm grip on my nose, plugging it as he tilted my head almost straight back.

It was drink or choke.

The whiskey burned its familiar burn. Uncomfortable as it was to drink in such a manner, it felt like my body was a parched cactus, soaking water after a long drought.

"Keep going, boy. Still plenty left."

The burning eased, my shocked throat now numb. Still he poured. Still I gulped to keep from drowning.

Halfway through, he withdrew the bottle.

"Get some air."

My eyes watered fiercely, mixing tears with the sticky blood on my cheekbones.

What had happened to change French's mind about questioning me about the money? Why was he pouring whiskey down my throat?

I managed a quick glance at Leigh. Most of her face was in shadow. The set of her shoulders and angle of her head showed her to be angry. Not afraid. I wondered how I appeared to her, helpless in my handcuffs and my own face plastered with blood.

"Led me get some licks in," Stockton said to French from behind his handkerchief. "I owe dem. My node beels like its done busted."

"Shut up," French said. "You got what you deserve. Two men in handcuffs and they almost beat you."

French plugged my nose again and poured more whiskey. Another rest to give me breath.

Even on my worst days, I hadn't drained whiskey this fast. Its warmth snaked through my veins. My head began to wobble. And half the contents of the bottle still remained.

Abruptly, French set the bottle down and stood. He grapped Stockton by the collar and yanked him to his feet, dragging him down the gully out of earshot.

I have no idea how long they conversed. By then, time was beginning to become sludge in the old familiar way.

"Leigh," I said. "Did he hurch—" I shook my head and willed my tongue to work around the words. "Did he hurt you?"

"Knocked on my hotel door bold as anything and put a gun to me. With my servants just down the hall in another room! Marched me down the stairs and through the lobby with the gun hidden in his vest. Promised to shoot me and anyone whom I called for assistance. Threw me on a horse and rode me off into the middle of the night."

Her voice softened from anger to concern. "You Samuel? You look hurt very badly."

I shook my head to say no. The stars and moon spun in circles of blurry white lines. "Can't feel much."

Which was true. The whiskey was slamming me with the suddenness of a hurricane. My tongue had become wood and it was all I could do to remain balanced.

"Sam," Jake was saying. "I don't like this, not being able to figure their intentions."

All I could do was smile tightly at Jake.

"Intentions?" William French had returned, alone, dark above me in the pale moonlight. He picked up the bottle again and poured more whiskey down my throat.

"Intentions?" French repeated. "Deputy, when we're finished, folks will think you and the marshal here took the lady on an ungentlemanly midnight picnic. Too bad you won't be alive to defend your reputations."

****

Although I never lost consciousness, it is difficult to piece together exactly how the rest unfolded. At some point, French removed the handcuffs from my wrists and from my ankles, and the handcuffs from Jake's ankles. He did not, however, loosen any of the rope which bound Leigh Tafton.

I have a vision of Leigh thrown over French's shoulder, her hair cascading down French's back as he gripped her feet somewhere around his waist. I remember stumbling along in front of French as he pushed me up the narrow path onto the flat ground. Then the four of us in a procession toward the stockyard, me dimly conscious that Stockton had not joined us.

I remember shadows which swayed, and roaring in my ears and drunk giggles and fighting for balance.

I don't remember too much after except in fragments: The horizontal line of the stockyard railing at the edge of my tunneled sight. The muted bellows of cattle in those pens. A downward slash of French's fist and a belated realization as Jake lay crumpled that he had just knocked Jake's skull with a gun butt again. Leigh laying on the ground beside Jake, her pale face turned moonward. Me suddenly alone, lurching and weaving overtop of them both. And helplessness as my fingers refused to listen to my brain's disjointed instructions to loosen the knots.

A shouting in my ears. Someone shouting for help. Until I understood the shouts came from Leigh Tafton. Vigorous shouts. Words unslurred as she cried for help from the men who patrolled the stockyard.

I tried to shout along with her, but the whiskey had incapacitated me so badly it felt like I was mewling.

Dim figures in the distance waved and shouted in return.

Then the sun rose.

At first, that was the only way my brain could comprehend the blooming of light at the rim of the horizon just beyond the stock pens. Then the light flared and danced and became flames along the wooden rails on the other side of the stockyard.

Cattle bellowed and bawled.

Gunfire erupted somewhere near the sudden flames.

More bellowing. The mass of cattle shifted, pushing its weight against the fence closest to us. The front line of cattle stopped against the fence, bulging it toward us. The cattle behind were so filled with panic they attempted to climb over the cattle in front of them.

More gunfire. Rising flames.

The wooden railing fence burst open and the cattle stampeded toward Jake and me and Leigh.

I wobbled, as afraid as I'd ever been, paralyzed by the alcohol poisoning.

Leigh screamed, a shriek of terror lost in the thunder.

Something bumped into my palm. I looked down. Beau licked at my palm.

A man stood beside me. Dropped to his knees. Raised a rifle.

Beau braced himself and started to bark, a deep roar of frantic rage.

The cattle were so close, the ground shook beneath my feet.

The man with the rifle shot into the front of the cattle. Levered another bullet, shot again. And again. A repeated booming that rolled and crashed above the roar of stampeding cattle.

Cattle dropped at one side of the wave, the bodies tumbling ahead and blocking the cattle behind, turning the wave of cattle slightly.

Then the wave was upon us, the cattle so close I could reach out with my hat and brush them.

We formed a wedge just past the island of fallen cattle, Beau at the front and barking rage. The man beside me firing the last of his bullets. And Jake and Leigh at our feet, lost to sight in the billowing dust as the cattle pushed by, rising and falling in the rhythm of galloping panic.

Then the cattle were by, and the thunder faded as the thousands of hooves drummed into the distance.

Someone was shaking me.

"Sam! Sam!"

I tried to respond but the words could not form in my

head, let alone leave my mouth.

"Sam! Sam!"

The man shaking my shoulder and yelling into my face was Doc Harper. I understood no more as the ground swallowed me into blackness.

THIRTEEN

DISTANT SHOTS PENETRATED MY NIGHTMARES. Without opening my eyes, I woke to the same ache of bones and discontented, stretched nerves which had been close companions during my whiskey time the year before.

I tried half opening one eye and decided sunlight hurt as badly as any knife. I groaned.

"Water's in a glass beside your bed."

The familiar voice of Doc Harper.

"I'll work up to it." I tried the other eye and managed to keep it open a couple of seconds, so I followed with the other.

I was in my own bed in the small, wood-frame house I'd purchased last fall on the strength of a loan from Mayor Crawford at the First National Bank. It hadn't been my idea, but Crawford's, who insisted I make the investment. Things were booming in Laramie, and it had been good advice. The house was worth nearly double what I'd paid. But it was still a house. Not home. Not without a woman who lived somewhere north of me among the Sioux.

I forced myself into a half-sitting position and managed to get a shaky hand around the glass of water, only because the rage of thirst was greater than my reluctance to move.

"Jake told me the most of it," Doc said, lifting his head from a well-worn Bible in his hands.

"Then you know more than I do."

I refilled the glass from a jug and drank deeply again, wondering if I'd be able to hold it down. I vowed never to allow solid food into my stomach again.

Doc marked his page, and shut the Bible.

"What were you studying, Doc?"

"Ecclesiastes. The more I doctor and the more I learn about folks because of it, the more I'm struck by the wisdom in that short book. King Solomon had it right. Times change, but people don't."

He paused, and cocked his head to a sad smile I'd seen often on his face. "Mostly though, it seems there's only one way to acquire wisdom. Through the tests of pain."

"Amen to that, Doc." I grimaced. "And from what I'm learning from my body at this particular moment, that ol' king ought to be asking *me* for advice."

Doc removed his spectacles and held them up to the light, inspecting the lenses for dust. The angle of sun darkened the lines of his face. I realized with sudden sadness he was indeed old, probably exhausted from his vigil here.

"Craving whiskey, Sam?"

"In the worst way."

"Figured," he said. "That's why I'm here."

"Gonna hold my hand all day, Doc?" I stretched my face into a grin. That hurt too.

"If that's what it takes."

I found comfort in his presence. Doc had had his own fight with the bottle. He hadn't spent much time in discussion of the details, and I hadn't pressed him, for by then I'd already heard the rumors of a successful practice abandoned back East.

Doc was a practical man, and an enquiring man impatient with fools who moved through life oblivious to the questions life raised. As a practical man, he wasn't content with spoonfed, church religion. He tried to fit what he saw in this world—especially what he learned through every new year in doctoring—with what he understood through faith. In his contemplations of how God had designed us, he'd told me our souls have a powerful homeward calling to God and His love, an instinct of remembered Eden as our souls cross the long, hard desert from birth to death. Without love, we try to fill our terrible yearning for God. With anything. Money. Women. Booze. Or we try to deny the God-hunger. With hatred. Evil. Revenge.

Telling me that, Doc had removed his wire-rim spectacles and polished them—as he was doing at this moment—and he'd informed me a man drinks for the warm peace that fools him into thinking the hunger has ended, like he's on the far side of the desert.

Those thoughts had served me well, keeping me from whiskey during times my own yearning had been as terrible as winter without light.

Except now, after months of temperance, my body was a sponge, desperate for another drop of whiskey.

"Why'd he do it, Doc?" I asked. "The whiskey, I mean. Aside from you and Jake, folks around here don't know about my drinking days on the other side of the Territory."

"I doubt he knew either, Sam. Near as I can tell, it was a handy way to get you all killed and give them time to clear Laramie."

The images of the previous night started to come back. Stumbling through the sagebrush. The brightness of the flaring night sky. The thundering of the cattle. The man with the rifle.

"Doc," I said, almost surprised, as bits and pieces of recollection ran through my mind. "It was you with the rifle. How...."

"Thank that ugly dog of yours. I stopped by your office last night—"

"He been looked after, Doc?" Normally, if I slept past dawn, Beau scratched at my bedroom door and whined until I shuffled out of bed and muttered complaints while I fixed the both of us breakfast.

"He's got food, water, and company, Sam. Don't fret."

"Fret? I ain't fretting. Not over a hound dog. Just go on with your story."

"Last night I was looking to unwind some, to see maybe if you had some coffee on the stove. There was your note, telling Jake you'd be back at ten. Only it was past eleven. No sign of Jake either, and I knew he was supposed to be trailing those Rangers. Naturally it raised concerns. I grabbed a rifle, and took Beau out looking for you. He kept running ahead and coming back, leading me on like he knew exactly what I wanted. Nose to the ground, he took me out toward the stockyards."

"You couldn't have showed up a minute later, Doc. Almost unbelievable, you showing up like cavalry cresting the hill."

"Sam, I'd been there at least ten minutes, waiting, watching, trying to figure what was happening. I saw the Texan run and couldn't make sense of it. Not until the cattle broke loose."

Doc shook his head. "They figured it real slick, Sam. The woman started screaming for help and you were standing over top of her. Stockyard guard said he saw it plain enough to think you were attempting something ungentlemanly. If those cattle had run the three of you over. . . ."

I reached for more water, wishing it would have the whiskey burn on the way down. "You said it was a way for them Rangers to clear Laramie?"

Again, distant shots.

Doc caught the puzzlement on my face and answered both questions with the same explanation.

"Jake's heading up a couple dozen men trying to clear the streets of Laramie. I expect some of those longhorns are so grizzly-mean the only thing to stop 'em is lead poisoning."

"Longhorns?"

"Two thousand head of cattle busted out of the stockyard last night, Sam. It's past noon now and there's probably still a hundred longhorns in Laramie itself. Probably still another thousand head upriver, downriver, and scattered to all points north, east, west, and south. By the time things settle down here, those two Texans are going to be a hundred miles clear, and nobody will have noticed them in all the confusion."

I swung out of bed, groaning again. "Jake needs help," I said. All I was wearing was a pair of cut down longjohns. I stepped barefoot onto the floor. For a moment, I teetered, half certain my head was about to explode. I forced cheerfulness into my voice. "Where's my boots, Doc? Where's my clothes? Where's my hat?"

"Out in the parlor, Sam, but I wouldn't—"

I patted Doc on the shoulder as I passed him in his chair. "Don't worry about me, Doc," I lied. "I'm fitter than a new fiddle."

"Sam, you don't want to—"

I pushed the bedroom door open and made it maybe a half step beyond. Beau ambled over to greet me. Doc had mentioned Beau in company with someone else, and I saw her on the stuffed chair in the parlor.

I froze in my tracks, smiled and nodded, then backed into the bedroom and let the door shut behind me and my longjohns.

"Let me guess," I said to Doc. "You were trying to tell me Leigh Tafton was waiting outside."

FOURTEEN

DOC CONVINCED ME THAT JAKE could handle the longhorn roundup just fine without me. I, in turn, convinced Leigh whatever she wanted to talk about could wait another hour until she met me at Chung's Eatery. After I shooed Doc out along with her, I went about trying to convince my body it had some living left to do.

First thing I did after getting dressed was to make a dozen trips from the water pump out back of the house to my bathtub inside, filling the tub with bucket after bucket of cold water.

Then I stripped off my shirt, took a jug of water, stepped into the sunshine again and commenced to chopping wood. July or not, it never hurt to get cords stacked and ready for the winter. Beau, lazy as he was, stayed in the shadow of the house, lying on the dirt, watching me with one eye until he began to doze.

Within two minutes of chopping wood, my body began to shake. The sun blazed at its highest and hottest, and the house blocked any cooling breeze. My mouth and throat were so parched, it felt like my skull was packed with sand. I was forced to rest, trembling like a whipped dog. I commenced again and within minutes stopped again, this time to bend over and retch dry heaves that rolled through me like booming echoes of cannon fire. After the spell passed, I returned to splitting logs. Sweat began to slide off me like grease, and I paused frequently to gulp water from the nearby jug. It wasn't a cure Doc might have prescribed, but I was determined to filter out all the whiskey poisons, no matter how high the cost.

I continued long past the point of reasonable endurance, hoping my body would learn the lesson that punishment would follow whiskey. After drinking the entire jug of water, I finally quit my wood chopping to return into the shaded interior of my house, where I eased myself into the cool bath water.

It was probably my first smile of the day.

It was also the first time I was able to think clearly. As I closed my eyes and let my body absorb welcome relief from heat and sweating, I ran through the events of the previous night. I still had no way of knowing whether Stockton and French were renegade Rangers, or were men who had killed Stockton and French and stolen their papers. I did know they were after money, enough money they were willing to murder lawmen. I also knew that they had not found the money here. Had it once been in Franky Leonard's possession? If so, how and why? Could I perhaps believe that whoever murdered Franky had also known of the money? Had Franky's murderer found the money? And how had the Rangers known Tom McCabe was here living as Franky Leonard?

A snippet of French's cold conversation came back to me. *Your lady friend has done saved me and Leroy plenty of time. And you oughta be thanking her for saving you both plenty of anguish, being as we learned enough from her to forgo the unpleasantries.* The unpleasantries of finding a way for Jake and I to tell them about money of which we knew nothing.

What then, had they learned from Leigh Tafton?

If I could figure that, maybe I could figure the direction French and Stockton had taken. If so, I would definitely follow. This matter had become a personal one, and I wanted them to answer for it.

****

Leigh Tafton again proved the only thing I could predict about her was her unpredictability. She arrived at Chung's Eatery dressed in jeans and a flannel shirt. She'd pinned her hair into a compact bun, showing more of the elegant lines of her soft throat. She gripped a riding quirt in her left hand, a man's cowboy hat in her right hand.

I allowed myself the luxury of a raised eyebrow as she reached the table where I was standing and waiting.

"Good afternoon, Marshal Keaton. Do you approve of my attire?"

"I will admit Jake don't put the same kind of curves into his jeans."

"I did not mean in terms of fashion." She was grinning as she said it. "I meant in terms of practicality. This is suitable for riding horseback, is it not?"

"Depends which horse and how far you intend to ride."

"I believe you're being deliberately difficult. I shall forgive you, however, for I wish for you to escort me on a ride through the countryside."

"You know enough about horses not to fall off?"

"Take your chances."

"Any reason for the invitation? Chung here makes food as good as anyone, and the chairs don't bounce a person around."

"Take your chances."

I liked her spunk. I liked her uninhibited wide grin. I liked my chances.

"It might take a few minutes to get some horses ready."

"Both are waiting outside. Jake saddled them up for us."

And Jake, the old woman, would be waiting in my office to pester me for every detail upon my return.

"That was very kind of Jake," I said.

"He's a very forthright man," she told me, still grinning. "Unlike you. I spent a very profitable half hour with him at the livery."

"Wonderful."

"*I* thought so. What was that other widow's name?"

"Ma'am?"

"Helen Nichols, I believe. The one to whom you returned a gold mine after her husband was murdered."

"Silver mine."

"Jake said she was beautiful. Jake said she practically threw herself into your arms."

Helen Nichols was beautiful. In the way a person should be. Kind. Honest. Loyal and loving to her husband and his memory after he had been found dead in suspicious circumstances in the First National Bank vault. Helen Nichols was determined to raise her sons right. God-fearing. But Helen Nichols was not beautiful in the way Leigh's smirk implied, for if Helen had thrown herself into my arms, her bulk would have crushed me. I had simply helped clear her husband's name and had returned the legal documents which rightly gave her a producing silver vein in Colorado, where she had promptly moved with her sons.

"Jake tends to exaggerate," I told Leigh, trying to hide my own smile. Jake also liked to stir the pot.

"Did he exaggerate about the dance hall girl? The one who gave up the saloon life and broke the hearts of all the cowboys in the territory because she mooned over you?"

"Jake should have told you the rest. Suzanne married a preacher. They moved down to Kansas. Last I heard, she's got twin boys, and expecting again."

"Next you'll tell me that a respected physician like Cornelius exaggerates."

Cornelius? It took me a moment. Doc Harper. If he was

letting her call him Cornelius, it must have meant she'd exerted considerable charm. . . .

"Cornelius told me how you first got the marshal job in Laramie. Gunned down one of the biggest outlaws in the territory."

I'd had help, but in my embarrassment of discovering the source of that help, had neglected to pass it on to Doc.

"And Cornelius told me about the snake preacher, and how you shot two snakes out of the air. Cornelius told me—"

"Mrs. Tafton."

"What will it take for you to call me Leigh?"

"As we speak, two men are getting farther and farther away from Laramie. These are two men who tried to kill you last night. These are two men I'd like to see behind the bars of the marshal's office. I figure if you get around to telling me the sorts of questions William French asked you, I can get a handle on the direction they're headed. It'd be real nice if we got around to discussing that matter instead of wasting time on tall tales or horseback riding."

"You may rest your fears, Samuel. I believe I know exactly where they are headed. And you need not hurry to catch them."

I raised a quizzical eyebrow again.

She reached up and pushed my eyebrow down with the tips of her elegant fingers.

"In fact, if you prove to be a considerate escort, I may even tell you by the end of this afternoon."

WE FOLLOWED A TRAIL into the hills on the eastern edge of the wide valley, our view dominated by the backdrop of mountains dark with the hazy purple-blue of distant conifers. When I turned my head away from the mountains to look north or south, the horizon was a shimmering edge in the summer heat. Those not accustomed to the vast distances of the territories often feel a fear to be so alone and so small; for me, the view brought welcome peace.

Leigh's horse followed mine. As we moved upward, I remained silent, and took in the smell of sage, its fragrance released as the horse hooves crushed the foliage. Our silence brought to us the rustling of tall grasses, and the shivering pain of the morning's hangover seemed like fragments of an unsettling dream.

I enjoy being on a horse beneath the wide-open sky.

Our souls are always yearning for God, but it's not until I'm away from the flimsy wooden or brick structures which we use to protect ourselves from the frightening immensity of the universe that it feels like my soul begins to reach upward for Him.

I tilted my hat and glanced with envy at a soaring hawk,

lost as it was in the quiet, limitless solitude of the sky. To me, hawks are as free as any creature alive, able to soar for hours until the earth's demand for penance brings them to the ground or branches of a tree.

The hawk reminded me of a line of thought I'd occasionally pursued with Doc during our evening conversations. In the next life, how will we pass our time? After all, here on earth, it seems the closest we come to time in its eternal form is during pain, boredom, sorrow, fear, and worry. Happy moments always seem fleeting, as difficult to grasp as oiled beads. I cannot believe God expects us to do nothing, even if basking in His glory would suffice for an eternity. I argue with Doc that God's glory—once we are released from the confines of our body—will be visible wherever we are in the universe, that we need not be held still and unmoving in a massed group to sing His praises. To me, part of the joy is in the promised freedom of our souls, to be unfettered as the soaring hawks, yet having no fear of any force able to claim us prisoner again. In our next life, will God then permit us to eternally roam His universe in a way we could never dream, exploring the vastness between the stars, skimming overtop the waves of oceans on faraway worlds? In our next life, will God give us the gift of escaping the greatest and most unyielding prison—time itself—by allowing us to reach into the massive unstoppable river at our leisure, dipping into the water to sample one eon, then the next, tasting a thousand years in a moment or holding one moment a thousand years?

God has a reason for everything, and I believe it was with unfathomable wisdom He designed vessels of flesh and blood to carry and confine the soul through its earthly first journey. As Doc said, we learn truths from pain. There is nothing noble in our bodies, doomed to age and decay even while carrying the soul, destined to become rotting shells when the soul has vacated. Yet there is shining grace in our daily struggle against the body's efforts to hamper our soul in its pursuit of an eternity of love—while only grace through faith delivers us to our Lord, it is the struggle against our burden of flesh and blood for a fleeting four score years which will allow us to fully understand and appreciate our freedom in the next life.

"Sam?"

Leigh had urged her horse forward to walk directly along-side mine, so close that my knee almost touched hers.

I took my thoughts away from the hawk.

"Either you ignored me or didn't hear me," she said. "I was inquiring if you knew our destination."

I almost told her I had been pondering the same issue.

"For this afternoon, yes, I do know where we are head-ed," I replied instead. "After that, I figure it depends on what you tell me about those two Texas Rangers."

She reached over and grabbed my reins.

Her poise and balance did not surprise me. Early after our departure from Laramie, I had moved our horses into a trot, the surest way to determine a rider's ability. Instead of inex-pertly bouncing helplessly in the saddle, however, she had eased into the horse's rhythm with her shoulders, belly, and hips riding so smoothly she could have carried a full glass of water without spilling.

My horse stopped as she tugged on the reins.

"We've traveled an hour with little chance to speak," she said when she was assured she had my full attention. "Then your first conversation turns us back to those Rangers. I hardly call you an enjoyable escort."

"What do you suggest, Mrs. Tafton?"

"I am deeply tired of your aloofness. And I hope it is pretended." Her lips tightened. Mock anger or real, her next words were definitely a command. "Down from your horse."

I crossed my arms in defiance of her command.

She pushed me, a move so unexpected it succeeded where her command had failed. My only hope of keeping my balance was to follow the momentum of my upper body and try to land on my feet.

My hat fell, and I almost speared it with my left boot heel

as I hit the ground, keeping my feet beneath me and stagger-ing upright. I was dusting the hat as she came around the front of my horse.

She stepped closer, grabbed my shirt with clenched hands, and pulled my head down toward hers. She kissed me long and hard. Whatever breath remaining after that surprise soon disap-peared in the following prolonged stretch without air.

Just as abruptly as she had kissed me, she released my shirt and pushed me away.

"I have never before been so bold," she said. "I only do it because I assume you have no idea of my interest in you. I assure you, however, I will not make an advance again, for I do have my pride."

I massaged my lower lip and tasted blood. She'd been that fierce.

She stared me full in the eyes. I thought of any number of responses and chose silence.

"I will say it more plainly." Her voice husky. "There is only a single step between us. The obligation to step forward has now fallen upon you. And we are very, very alone out here."

Whiskey would not have hit me harder than the fire I felt looking at the half smile and thinking about the passion of her kiss.

Why *not* step forward as invited?

Fear probably. Remembered love, remembered pain. The knowledge I was no longer a boy and this would not merely be a casual kiss stolen during a flirting moment.

I continued searching for a reason to stop me, which in itself told me I was rapidly losing the fight. Had she stared at me another five seconds, I would have moved into her arms.

Leigh, however, removed the need for decision.

She crossed the distance between us, reached up again, and slapped me full across the face, spun on her heels, and marched upward along the trail, away from me and the hors-es. By the time I collected my wits, she had disappeared around a bend, leaving me with the rustling of long grass, the creaking of insects, and the swishing of horse tails as they cleared themselves of flies. In my life, a handful of times I've been shot at and missed, twice shot at and hit. Leigh's actions had about the same suddenness and unexpectedness. The bullets, however, had not resulted in the grin of admiration now across my face.

If I could have figured out what to say, I would have followed her up the trail to attempt to apologize. I also took into consideration the fact that last summer somehow I'd managed to survive Sitting Bull, and there was no sense now in pressing my luck further. I decided she would need a horse to return to Laramie, and as these were the only ones available for miles, it was more prudent to remain where I was.

It took Leigh a half hour to return, her chin high with pride as she stepped down the trail.

I was sitting in the shade of my horse. I stood at her approach.

"I won't apologize," she said. "Not for the kiss. Not for the slap. Not for walking away."

Even with a half hour, I had not found anything I could say. Stupidly, I tried anyway.

"Leigh, I. . . ."

"Finally. You've stopped calling me Mrs. Tafton. And don't try to explain yourself. I did what I wanted. And failed. You owe me no apology."

Her frown slowly became a tentative smile. "Actually, do explain. Much as Cornelius divulged about you, he remained stubbornly silent about the reason you have no wife." She shook her head. "For that matter, Jake was equally protective despite everything else he told me. I envy you for your friends."

"You have no friends?"

"My sister is dead."

I saw, or rather understood, much in that statement. She was protected by money, servants, the customs of the rich, whimsical indulgence of her fancies, and a knowledge of her desirability. All I had—and worth much, much more—were two friends. And memories of another, the woman I loved, Rebecca.

Leigh's lapse into quiet vulnerability touched me, and I found myself talking, explaining the events of the previous summer. The massacre of Sioux. Then of soldiers. The show-down with Sitting Bull. How, despite love we shared, those events had forced Rebecca away from me.

Some time later, when Leigh interrupted me with a question, I found us sitting on a large flat rock, with her holding my right hand between both of hers.

"It must be difficult," Leigh said. "Have you heard from her since?"

"Rebecca lives among the Sioux. To them, and to her husband, she is Morning Star. I'm a marshal in Laramie. She doesn't get supplies at the general store. I don't stampede buffalo over cliffs."

I shrugged. "It's better this way. I'm not sure I could bear to see her. Or hear from her. It would only be a painful reminder of what could have been."

We shared a long silence. Shadows came and went as clouds passed. I watched an ant struggle up the side of my boot, then tumble into the dust.

Leigh toyed with the tips of my fingers. "Do you enjoy this role?"

"Role?"

"The tragic figure. Holding out for your one true love."

I blinked away anger. Tried to pull my hand away.

She tightened her grip. Smiled.

"Don't pout, Samuel. I'm not trying to make light of what happened. I just think it would be a shame if you felt sorry for yourself for the rest of your life."

Now the anger was too great to blink away. I jumped to my feet, yanking my hand away from her. If my voice blazed with the heat I felt, she did a remarkable job of not flinching.

"You have no right—"

"If you were the only person in the history of the world to have lost love, perhaps not." Her calmness contrasted with my anger.

"You presumptuous, selfish, spoiled—"

"Are you angry at me, Samuel? Or angry at the truth?"

"Don't push this any farther or I'll—"

"Her memory is too sacred?"

I had three choices. Strike her. Cuss at her. Or walk. I walked.

SIXTEEN

LET ME GET THIS STRAIGHT," Jake said. He stood beside a black gelding. On a small bench at his feet were iron nails, a hammer, tongs, and four horseshoes. The livery door was open, giving us the last of the evening's sunshine. "You're taking a train to Pennsylvania. Tomorrow."

"I am asking a lot."

From a loose fist, finger by raised finger, Jake ticked off my requests. "Step in as marshal. Feed Beau. Tend your garden. Water Beau. Keep Doc company." He ran out of fingers, formed a fist again, and started over with his fingers. "Keep Beau company. And run your horses every second day. Leave a note at the marshal office letting folks know they can call on me here at the livery. And be sure to feed and water Beau. Did I miss anything?"

"It's not that I'm particularly worried about Beauregard. Shoot, a man can get another dog most anytime. Most days I figure he's more trouble than he's worth."

He gave me the look which said we both knew otherwise.

"I'll make sure he don't run under the wheels of no carriage." Jake grinned. "This sudden departure. It got anything to do with a certain fair redhead who took you up into the hills today?"

"Jake, I imagine you want to shoe this horse before it gets dark."

"It can wait. 'Till morning, if need be. I'd rather hear about Leigh Tafton."

"There's plenty, Jake." I frowned at his widening grin. "Plenty in regards to Franky Leonard, you old woman."

"And plenty more, I'll hazard a guess. You stepped in here mighty perky."

I wasn't about to tell Jake that after stomping away from Leigh, I'd walked close to a mile before she rode up behind me, with my horse trailing hers. By then, I'd cooled down some, enough to realize Leigh had been closer to the mark than I wanted. We had both pretended my angry half-yelling had not taken place and had finally gotten around to discussing William French, Leroy Stockton, and Tom McCabe.

"Jake, yesterday at this time, those Texas Rangers had you hog-tied. Since then, we've been beat up, stuck square in the path of a cattle stampede. You spent the day rounding up longhorns, and I—"

"Spent the day mooning over a rich widow."

"And I haven't had the chance to sit down and tell you what I learned from Mrs. Tafton about Franky Leonard."

Jake pointed at a hay bale.

"So sit."

Jake led the gelding back to its stall.

I moved to the hay bale, with no need to watch where I stepped. Jake kept a clean livery, raking out the horse manure twice daily. He raked in the same one-armed manner he pitched hay and straw, with a narrow sling nailed to the top of the handle. He'd slide his left hand through the sling and grasp the handle halfway down—the sling around his upper forearm gave him the leverage he needed to rake or lift without the help of his useless right arm.

I took a deep breath, inhaling the sweet mixture of hay and horse sweat. Jake pulled out another hay bale and sat opposite.

"Jake, Leigh Tafton traveled here to learn more about a man named Tom McCabe. The Texas Rangers—if they are Texas Rangers—rode in to find Tom McCabe."

"Franky Leonard."

"One and the same. Both parties were surprised to find him dead."

"Do you think they were both looking for him for the same reason?"

I shook my head. "No, and I'll get to that in a minute. Bear with me as I try to get my thoughts straight."

I recalled my conversations with Leigh. "It's like this, Jake. Leigh's here because her sister died back in Johnstown."

"Johnstown?"

"Pennsylvania."

"Where you're headed tomorrow."

"Remember, bear with me. I'll try to make sense. Leigh believes her sister's husband killed her sister."

"Sam. . . ."

"I know, I'm getting a headache too. The husband's name is Frederick Blackburn. He traveled here—"

"Here as in Laramie?"

"Yes, Jake. Here as in Laramie. To meet with a man named Tom McCabe."

"Tom McCabe. You mean Franky Leonard."

"One and the same, Jake. After they met, Frederick Blackburn returned to Johnstown. Leigh is convinced something happened during that meeting which led Blackburn to kill Aurelia once he returned."

"Sam, my head is spinning. Aurelia?"

"Leigh's sister. Who left behind an estate worth ten million."

Jake whistled.

I was in agreement. Ten million dollars *was* an incomprehensible amount. A good cowboy made $30 a month.

"Ten million," I repeated. "It does seem to make murder

a real possibility."

Jake rubbed his face with his good hand and sighed. "Blackburn comes to Laramie. Meets Franky Leonard. Returns to Johnstown. Murders Leigh's sister. Leigh shows up here to find out more about Franky Leonard." Jake dropped his hand. "That's the drift?"

"Yup."

"How did Aurelia die?" Jake asked.

"She was found drowned. Leigh tells me her sister was terrified of water. Yet she went for a midnight rowing excursion by herself. They found the rowboat the next morning, and her body drifted to shore. Leigh insists it was murder."

Jake groaned. "Lawmen aren't fools out East. If it was murder, they'd know. They'd be on the trail. Especially since it involved a wealthy woman."

"Not if Frederick Blackburn is a steel mine owner, former town mayor. A candidate for governor. And so far above suspicion no one would even consider it."

"And Leigh has considered it?" Jake asked.

"Leigh's got her sister's diary. She says there is enough in there to make it worth considering. She's hired me on to investigate the murder. I've accepted. To keep this fair, you'll be collecting my wages for marshaling in my absence, something I cleared with Mayor Crawford."

"Sam. . . ."

"Jake, Leigh traveled all the way out here to inquire about Tom McCabe. That should tell you there's something to all of this."

Jake snorted. "I'll say. She's a rich, bored widow." He grinned. "With a new interest in a western lawman."

"Before you put both feet in your mouth Jake, realize a couple things."

He waited.

"One. Two men ride in as Texas Rangers with questions about the same man: Franky. That in itself should tell there's more to this than meets the eye—aside from the fact that this same man was found dead in a way we had to hide from the townfolk."

"The second thing?"

"Ask me when Frederick Blackburn arrived from Johnstown to visit the man we knew as Franky Leonard."

"Sam?"

"January. The middle of January. Right around the time we found Franky Leonard frozen dead and scattered around his shack."

Jake understood, and his eyes narrowed. "That makes Frederick Blackburn a prime consideration for the man who murdered Franky Leonard."

"Especially because it seems he came into town as quiet and invisible as he left. Like he was hiding. If he's not the murderer, he should at least be able to answer a few questions to point us toward the murderer. And those answers might tell us more about the reason these Texas Rangers showed up here in July. Once we understand who Franky Leonard was, we should understand most of the rest of this."

Jake was nodding now, more serious and less skeptical. "You hope to sit down with this Blackburn fella in Pennsylvania and ask him those questions."

"There's a little more to it than that, Jake."

He snorted again. "Right. The rich widow. I presume she'll be on the train with you?"

Jake had the dogged persistence of a badger.

"You asked me if Leigh Tafton and the Rangers were both looking for Franky Leonard for the same reason."

Jake nodded.

"Now you know the answer," I said. "Which is no. Leigh wants to prove Frederick murdered her sister. Stockton and French? They were checking the dirt floor in Franky's shack. Looking for money is my guess. When they had us hogtied, they asked about money. Enough money they were going to try a few ugly tricks on us, thinking we were hiding what we knew about the money. Enough money to risk murdering the both of us."

Jake nodded again.

"Jake, you might recall what William French said when he returned to us out near the stockyards. He had Leigh Tafton with him and told us she'd saved us both plenty of anguish, as he'd learned enough from her."

"I do recall. Instead of aggravating us, he kindly stampeded cattle in our direction."

"I asked Leigh what they'd talked about. The short of it is that she told French everything she told me."

"And?"

"And she has informed me those two Texas Rangers are headed straight for Johnstown, Pennsylvania, where I intend to make them answer a lot of our questions. And where I intend to make them answer for last night. Which are the real reasons I let Leigh Tafton hire me on."

SEVENTEEN

TIME AND AGAIN, flashed memories took me unaware as the steam locomotive hauled us eastward, memories I hardly knew existed until the slowly changing landscape brought back to me impressions of myself as a boy who now seemed a distant stranger.

It had been '50 when my ma and pa made the decision to follow the Oregon trail to their dreams. I was boy, barely ten years old, my brother Jed only a little older. We'd left our home town of Lancaster and its heavily wooded hills, thinking the mountains in western Pennsylvania truly were mountains, amazed at the distance it took us to reach Independence, then overwhelmed at the naked horizons and limitless sky across the great plains.

Ma and Pa had died badly at the hands of Crow braves while attempting a cutoff from the main trail through the Bighorn mountains, with only Jed and me as witnesses in a hidden compartment of the wagon. Jed had died later, to a bounty hunter taking prisoners from us, leaving me alone as the keeper of our family's memories, leaving me alone without even gravestones to remind me of their passing.

Now the Union Pacific was retracing for me the path I

had taken nearly three decades earlier from my birthplace, moving effortlessly over land which I'd walked, day by day, behind a covered wagon and oxen, across stretches of prairie where instead of iron tracks, the trail had been marked by bleaching bones of perished livestock.

Sand flats along the Platte River took me to the Fourth of July celebration, a day when I'd spiked myself by falling into a thorn bush. Seeing the muddy waters brought back the vivid perfume of my mother's bonnet and the gentle humor in her eyes as she removed each thorn.

Leigh and I crossed the Missouri and the eastbound train kept moving me inexorably farther and farther back into my memories. As the landscape changed from flat, brown, and endless to the first rolling hills of Iowa, I found myself becoming sadder and sadder for all that time had changed in my life, and sadder for the enforced realization that time would continue as irresistibly as the heavy tonnage of the steam locomotive. Someday—too soon—Doc would die. Jake would. Leigh Tafton would become wrinkled and gray as time wore her down to her final breaths. On this earth a hundred years from now we would all be forgotten dust. What a curse to live—alone in this manner among all animals—with the knowledge of our own mortality. And what a blessing to know faith gave our lives meaning despite the certainty of death.

Iowa's rolling hills became the rich, dark soil of Illinois, Indiana, Ohio, until the clumps of trees became clustered closer and closer and the land became rocky hills of green foliage on the western edges of Pennsylvania. I found myself chuckling to remember how I had once allowed the hills to impress me as mountains.

Not all of the journey was a melancholic recollection of an almost forgotten boyhood.

I took advantage of the enforced leisure and finished *Tom Sawyer,* occasionally reached down absent-mindedly to scratch Beau's head, only to be pulled from the adventure when I realized I was on a train and Beauregard was hundreds of miles behind in Laramie.

If the train was a prison of sorts, it was a guilded prison.

Leigh Tafton secured luxury berths each time we trans-ferred from one rail line to another. Her servants fretted over the transfer of baggage, including mine, so I had none of the worries most travelers must endure. My only constraints were meal schedules, and Leigh and I spent long hours in the dining car, where breakfast, lunch, and dinner became events attended by waiters in dark suits and white gloves.

While the air grew more humid as we left the arid plains, the rushing wind through open windows helped considerably, and each night I slept well to the swaying and clacking of rail wheels, managing because of the sleep to resist without great difficulty the temptations of wine or whiskey as a way to soothe all the emotions evoked by this journey away from the frontier.

Leigh Tafton and I held to an unspoken truce. She did not mention Rebecca again. Nor did I. With high humor and lively banter, we discussed politics, religion, fashion, and writers. I often found myself gazing at her lips and speculating on more of the bruising passion she had so briefly shown, yet we were almost formal in our manner and treatment of each other, as if a chaperone hovered over our meals and conversations.

All told, it was a pleasant week. I could understand why the rich choose to travel for amusement. My payment, of course, was due to be rendered among the streets and steel mills of Johnstown, for Leigh Tafton had purchased the rail fare in exchange for my promised help.

We passed through Pittsburgh and continued deeper into the Allegheny Mountains of western Pennsylvania. Johns-town was ahead of us, a town the conductor informed me which was founded in the steep, narrow, Y-shaped valley which had been gouged as the result of the three rivers flowing into it — the Little Conemaugh, the Stoney Creek, and the Conemaugh. It was important because of the coal and iron ore native to the area, and well connected through two railways and a shipping canal.

We finally reached Johnstown, where I stepped off the train and out of the station to ominous gray, beneath mid-day clouds and steel mill smoke. I surveyed the crowded streets and the hills which rose steeply into the haze, waiting for Leigh to step beside me.

Instead, a constable in a derby hat appeared and smashed me across the side of my head with a wooden baton.

EIGHTEEN

MISTER, STAY ON YOUR KNEES," the constable said. He whacked me across my shoulder, numbing my left arm.

I was down on all fours, like a dog. Through blood-smeared vision, I was dimly aware of a gathering crowd. Of my hat on the cobblestone beside me. Of sharp pebbles biting into my knees and palms.

He slammed my ribs.

I groaned and hung my head—a weakness not difficult to feign. I groaned again and before the groan ended, leaned my weight to one side, and lashed out with my boot, catching the front of the constable's kneecap square with my heel.

He tumbled with a curse.

I sprang upon him, punching him once in the face and knocking him on his back. I jumped onto his chest.

He rapped me with the baton again, an ineffectual blow because my knees had him pinned. I yanked the baton from his hand, lined it across his throat, and with a hand on each side, pressed down on his Adam's apple.

Small rivulets of blood were trickling from his nose into a blunt moustache. His face was fat, his eyes a washed-out gray. I stared down on him, and splatters of my own blood from the gash across my head dripped onto his nose.

I pressed the baton until his eyes, white like fish bellies, rolled back in their sockets, and only then did my rage fade and sanity return.

I rolled off him and wobbled to my feet.

The crowd had become quiet. Rumbling of nearby steel mill furnaces sounded like distant thunder.

Leigh was at the front of the crowd, her gloved hand pressed to her mouth in shock. Her servants stood behind her, holding her travel trunk between them. I wondered if she had seen the constable hit me, or if she believed I was a wild man who attacked local police for no apparent reason.

I had no chance to explain.

Two men, also in uniforms and derbies, stepped between us. I assumed they, too, were local police.

"You're not finished already?" one asked quietly. He had droopy bags beneath his eyes. A middle-aged man with a small gut. "We're in no hurry."

I wiped my face, soaking my sleeve with blood.

"Finished?" I asked.

The other leaned forward and spoke even more quietly. He was young enough to still be pimpled. "We're doing our best to restrain you, can't you see? Yet somehow you've managed to pull loose and get in a couple good kicks."

"Aye," his partner said when I refused the invitation. He stooped over and picked up my Stetson hat from where it had fallen after the baton blow to my head. "No one's knocked him down before. It would be a shame to let the chance go by. He's a real pig, that one. You'll be doing something we often wished we could do. And once you're in jail, he'll get to punish you just as bad for one kick as twenty. You'll be well off making it worth your while."

I ignored the fallen constable. Blood interfered with my vision. "In jail?"

"Only when you're ready to stop resisting our valiant

attempts to hold you back. . . ." The first constable nodded wistful hope toward the fallen man.

Then Leigh was beside me, offering a perfumed handkerchief.

"Gentleman," she said, chin set, eyebrows furrowed, voice grim. "Perhaps you'll explain why a member of Johnstown's constabulary attacked my traveling companion."

"Ma'am!" The middle-aged constable handed me my hat, then removed his derby. His partner missed the hint, and the older constable nudged him into hasty compliance.

"Why was this man attacked?"

"We received word of theft aboard the train," the older constable said.

She arched her eyebrows.

"A telegram from Pittsburgh," he explained quickly. "We've no choice but to investigate."

"What does this have to do with us?" She demanded. She had the authority of a queen. Money is a great mantle of power.

"One of the pursers witnessed the crime." The air was steamy humid, but I doubted that was the reason perspiration sprang from the man's forehead.

I continued to press Leigh's handkerchief, now sodden, against my aching head. I held my hat with my other hand. No sense in placing it on now and filling it with stains.

"What does the theft have to do with this man?" Another imperious demand.

"We were told to look for a man in western attire. He was the only one to fit the description. The purser followed him to his berth, managed to get his name."

"Then this should be a simple misunderstanding, easily cleared," I said. "My name's Samuel Keaton."

They both stared at me. Their expressions were not encouraging.

"Maybe get another kick in," the younger one suggested. "Before he comes to."

"This is ridiculous," Leigh said.

I would swear in court the older constable flinched at her tone. I'm also nearly certain he jumped.

The fallen constable groaned.

"Search me," I said. I waved my hat in the direction of my suitcase. "Search my luggage. I didn't steal anything."

"Certainly then," the older constable said. "Best if we do it before he awakes."

They shooed away the crowd and popped open my cardboard suitcase, lent to me by Doc Harper.

It took the younger one less than thirty seconds to straighten. His voice held a mixture of regret and triumph. His hand held an earring which twinkled despite the gray sky.

"Looks like a diamond," he said. "A gift for a lady friend?"

The groans behind us grew louder.

I shook my head no.

The older constable was studying Leigh's face, now ashen.

"Ma'am?" he asked.

"It's *my* earring," she said. Slowly she lifted her eyes to mine. Gone was the queen of everything she surveyed. Instead, Leigh was a quiet little girl in her sudden disbelief. "Samuel, if you needed money, you should have asked."

NINETEEN

I AM NO STRANGER to the interior of prison cells. In fact, I had awakened behind cell bars upon my first acquaintance with the marshal's office in Laramie. On that occasion, a bullet wound had drained me of enough blood to leave me laid out unconscious for the previous two days, and waking on the wrong side of the bars had been a surprise.

On this occasion, it was not a surprise, nor was I unconscious entering the jail cell. But I wished I was.

I'd been arrested and handcuffed by the constables, abandoned by Leigh Tafton. I endured stares from every new passenger to step from the train station. The younger constable had found water to throw on the senior constable until he sputtered back to life. The middle-aged one had held my Stetson and spun it nervously in his hands.

As I waited, I did my best to orient myself. Friendless and alone in unfamiliar territory, it was all I could do to relieve some of my helplessness. The sky, however, was no guide, for the gray haze gave no clue to the sun's position. Grimy brick buildings—three, four, and five stories tall—seemed haphazard—giving me no sense of pattern. The hills on both sides of this narrow, steep valley were featureless in the haze. I had no idea of north, something which bothered me more than it should have. I was not on the open plains—my life didn't depend on a sense of direction. But old habits die hard, and the frustration added to my sense of helplessness.

I contented myself by trying to memorize street names as the three constables escorted me through Johnstown. We began our walk at Iron and Station Streets, the site of the Pennsylvania Rail Station. We headed away from one set of hills toward the other, down Washington. Along Washington, a rail yard dozens of tracks wide and filled with freight cars testified to the prosperity of Johnstown's steel mills.

We continued down Washington. The two junior constables kept exchanging nervous glances, as if they were waiting for the water-soaked constable to erupt in violence again.

The air was filled with noise, smoke, coal dust, sour gas of sewers. The streets were cobblestone, smeared with fetid mud.

At Market Street, we bore left, crossing Locust, continuing until a block later we reached the public square at Main. Throngs of people. A small park with wilted trees guarding trampled grass. Benches and statures whitewashed by pigeons. County Courthouse. Firehouse. City Hall. Jailhouse. All the buildings were turreted and had gabled windows and were still gray and grimy and depressing despite these best efforts of architectural optimism.

The constables nudged me up the steps of the jailhouse. As the doors banged behind us, the senior constable moved to the rear of my left shoulder and spoke his first words to me since staggering to his feet at the train station.

"The name's Ben Currie. Behind my back, folks call me Blackjack Ben." He paused, as if savoring his words. "They've got good reason for it."

There was a whistling sound, the only warning before a sharp pain against the meat of my collar bone, so sharp and brutal I first thought he'd thrust a knife. Then the whistling of his blackjack again and another white-hot dagger of pain.

I fell into a wall, leaning against it to stay on my feet.

A man just down the hallway looked up from papers at his desk, surveyed the situation with blank eyes, then resolutely cast his attention back on the papers.

"I've got a special touch," Currie said, whispering garlic breath into my face. My eyes were sparkling with black dots, so I heard, rather than saw the leer on his face. "I don't break bones. A man rarely passes out. I can get fifty, sixty blows in. I'm told it feels like falling into a rock crusher."

The sharp whistle of warning. A blow against my thigh. Another against the side of my ribs.

Time ceased to have meaning as the whistle of blackjack continued. I could not block tears of pain, grunts of agony. I slouched lower and lower to the floor.

"This is a foretaste," Currie said when he stopped. "In the morning, you'll get more. So think about it tonight. All night. Because I promise you won't be able to sleep."

Currie pushed me roughly. I fell sideways to my knees.

The other two constables lifted me under my arms and dragged me down the dim hallway.

"Should have got your licks in when you could," the older one whispered. "You'll have no more chances at satisfaction."

TWENTY

I *WAS A RAG DOLL* propped into the corner of the jail cell. While I was aware of a couple of other men in the cramped quarters, I gave total attention to breathing as shallowly as possible, trying to reduce any lift and fall of my battered ribs.

Currie had beaten me so thoroughly I could not even crawl. The only movement possible without pain was blinking my eyes. Once I tried to lift my arm to wipe blood from my nose, but I gave up and let the blood run unheeded until it slowed and dried. Thirst overwhelmed me, but I could not move to search for water.

I had no energy for thoughts. Or worries. Or hopes. I was just enduring time.

"Now, Murphy?" I heard one of the men ask. His voice was like one from a dream. It seemed as if dark shadows loomed above, between me and the dim lights of the lantern in the hallway outside the cell bars.

"Too easy," came the reply. "Wait 'til we can make sport of it."

The shadows moved away and I lapsed back into my trance of pain. When I thought it could get no worse, my body began to shake and shiver, taking me away from whatever comfort I had found in the refuge of my trance.

I began to count. For no other reason than to take my mind as far away from my body as possible. I tried to divide the numbers into minutes, then hours, for the effort of my calculations provided further distraction.

Well over two hours later, shouting broke through my determination to remove myself from the cell.

"George! George! How they treating you?" Loud, drunk. "No surprise seeing you in there among the sinners!"

"Hey! Hey!" Sounds of struggle. "Let me in the other cell with George! No need to throw me in with strangers!"

The scuffling continued, grew closer. I opened my eyes. In the hallway, a giant man was wrestling two constables. Handcuffs or not, he might have won had he been sober. Drunk, however, he could not throw them off his shoulders.

"You'll get these mates instead," one constable snarled. He jumped away from the giant man and opened the lock to my jail cell. "Come morning, you'll see the magistrate."

They pushed him toward me and quickly slammed the cell door shut.

"What about me handcuffs?" the giant man bawled at their retreating backs. He lifted his hands helplessly behind his back. "Surely to goodness you'll let a man have free arms."

Both constables ignored him. Their footsteps echoed as the giant man stared down the dim hallway until they had disappeared.

I lost interest. Closed my eyes. Tried to count myself into fitful sleep.

"You don't look like no cowboy," the giant slurred.

I opened my eyes. He was not speaking to me however.

There were two other men in the cell. One was short, thick in the chest, bearded. The other, nearly as tall as the giant man, nearly as heavy, but fat heavy, with a double chin. The short one was wearing my Stetson. I had no recollection of the constable throwing it in the cell with me. I had no recollection of the short man picking it up.

"I said, you don't look like no cowboy."

"And you look like a dead man if you don't shut your mouth."

"Hey. . . ." The giant man dropped his voice ridiculously low, as if trying to shush a baby. "Just making conversation."

"Shut your gob," the other said. "Or I'll shut it for you."

For a moment, I thought the giant might rush them. He teetered, as if considering it. Then he must have remembered his handcuffs, because he shrugged and stepped back to the cell wall. He lowered himself down the wall to sit beside me.

"How about you?" he said to me. Whiskey smell filled my nostrils. "You a cowboy?"

I swallowed a few times, trying to get moisture into my mouth. "Sure partner. Soon's you find me a horse."

The cell was too dark for me to see much of the features of his face. I heard him chuckle. "I just might do that."

As it hurt to talk, I just nodded.

Minutes later, the giant was snoring, chin on his chest. He relaxed and slowly slumped more and more of his weight against me. I was in the corner of the cell, and was unable to move away from him. He leaned his head against my shoulder in his sleep, pinning me harder, and I winced with pain.

He began to slump farther. In any other situation I would have found this comical. The man was so big it felt like a buffalo was squeezing me, yet he was childlike in his sleep, snoring, wiggling into me for warmth as if I were his mother. He slid to a position on his side, curling up into a ball, using my thigh as a pillow.

Just the weight of his head hurt. I could not imagine how much agony I would have to endure to be struck there with a blackjack again, and fear of the morning overwhelmed me. I forced my mind back to the present.

He slept through my own movement as I pulled off my

vest and jacket. I wadded the clothing into a pillow and set it on the hard floor, making sure the man's head landed softly as I pulled away from him.

He snuffled, clearing his throat, but did not wake. Oddly, I heard a light tink, as if a coin had dropped from his mouth. I was too weary to give it much more thought.

And the two others in the jail cell had moved toward me.

"Showing signs of life, he is," the short one said, silk soft with pleasure.

The big one leaned down, grabbed my collar and hauled me to my feet. "Right you were," he said to his partner. "More fun to make sport of this."

The short one punched me in the stomach. "This hurt?"

Blood gagged the back of my throat.

"Not too hard," the bigger one cautioned. He'd shifted his grip and was holding me from behind. "We don't want him slipping away on us. Currie worked him over good."

"Right, right." The short one spoke to me next. Conversational tones. Could have been commenting on rain. "We've been waiting in here to kill you. And that's what we'll be doing over the next couple of hours."

He studied my face. "Show some fear, friend. We like that."

"And other things," the fat one said. "Prison things. We can do whatever we want. No one will hear you scream. You'll sound like a pig. We like that."

Cold dread from the certainty of their manner filled my stomach.

Life is far too large to control. It's an arrogance—which I struggle against—to assume a man can twist the world around him into doing his will. You can't control how other people chose to respond to your actions; you can't control whatever actions people might attempt against you. All you can do is make choices for your own actions. Doc Harper had spoken of Ecclesiastes, and would have said the race is not to the swift nor the battle to the strong nor favor to men of skill but time and chance happen to them all. Once I'd understood this, it made life a whole lot easier. Whereas before I'd have fretted about making the weather right, I now choose the much simpler course of dressing according to the weather. And of adjusting my attitude to the weather, because attitude is the only thing a man can force into consistency throughout all the events around him.

These two men were going to kill me. I couldn't change that. Even healthy I'd have been up against heavy odds. But I could make a decision about the way I'd die. No matter what they did, they wouldn't be able to take away attitude.

I looked the short one in the face and spit.

"Give him another wallop," the fat one wheezed. "Then we'll make him scream."

The short one moved in close to hit me again. I lifted my knee, a lucky desperation effort which caught him solidly in the groin.

"Abe," he gasped as he held himself, "this man will pay."

Abe threw his arm around my throat and squeezed my windpipe in the crook.

The short man took a deep breath and grinned. A horrible, greedy grin, made uglier by the waxy white of his face in the dim light.

Abe squeezed harder, then relaxed as I began to slump, giving me just enough air to remain conscious. "Remember, Murphy," Abe said. "I get him first."

Murphy straightened himself with great effort, pulled a knife loose from inside his shirt. "He'll be losing blood, so you best be quick."

He weaved from side to side, summoned energy, swiped air in front of my face, taunting me. The fat one held me motionless.

Another swipe, nicking my cheek.

"Cowboy, want some help?"

Murphy froze at the sound of a new voice. Abe pushed me away to face the drunk giant.

"This ain't your game," Murphy said. "Get yourself back down on the floor."

The giant shook his head. His hands were still behind his back.

"Hit him good," Murphy told Abe. "Couple times high. Couple times low. Then kill him."

Abe laughed. "Be like hitting a baby, Murphy. Them handcuffs. . . ."

"Watch his feet, then" Murphy said. "Watch 'em good."

Abe should have watched for the giant's hands. As Abe moved in with a slow, lazy hook, the giant ducked, coming up with a fist he drove squarely into Abe's jaws. The giant followed with a few short jabs, snapping Abe's head back with tiny pops of bone against bone.

Abe crumpled to his knees, mewling in surprise.

"Your friend's right," the giant said, no trace of drunken slur. "Watch my feet."

His right foot was a blur, catching Abe in the pit of his stomach. Abe crashed onto his side and curled himself into a little ball.

The giant turned his attention to Murphy. "Hard or easy, lad. The hard way, you keep the knife. Easy way, you set it down."

Murphy choose hard, charging forward, knife extended. The giant sidestepped Murphy, brought a fist down on the back of Murphy's neck, sending him headfirst into the wall. Murphy sighed twice, then collapsed.

"Well, my cowboy friend," the giant said. "It seems a fair lady had good reason to send me here after all."

TWENTY-ONE

TWELVE HOURS LATER, I was soaking in water as hot as my skin could bear. Outside the bathroom door, I could hear low voices. One belonged to Leigh Tafton, the other to the lawyer who had successfully pleaded my case to a local magistrate as soon as the courthouse had opened for the day.

I was in no hurry to leave the bathtub and join their conversation. By remaining motionless in the heat of the water, I could pretend my body was free of pain. Currie had been true to his promise—no broken bones—but much of my body was yellowing with bruises, and the walk from the jail to the courthouse to this hotel had seemed like a thousand miles. The thought of toweling myself dry promised enough agony that I intended to spend three days exactly where I was.

It would be a pleasant three days too. The bathroom was larger than the sitting room of my own house back in Laramie. While the ornate fixtures and thick towels alone were special luxury, I marveled most at something unthinkable in the territories. Indoor plumbing.

All I had to do was reach up with my toe, turn an elaborately enameled faucet, and hot water would flow again into the tub. When I stepped out, I could use a flush toilet—no chamber pot or long walk to an outdoor privy in the darkness of the night.

Outside the door was a three-room suite equally ostentatious, with tile floors, stuccoed walls, and hardwood furnishing. In the room just outside the bathroom, Leigh and the lawyer sat on a plush sofa long enough to sleep two. The sofa faced a natural gas fireplace—Jake would swear I was making up tall tales when I told him all I needed to do was turn a switch and light a match.

There was a bar along one wall—I'd already asked Leigh to empty it of all spirits, and asked her not to ask me the whyfors of my request. Plush carpet, oil paintings, and a balcony.

The second room was much smaller, a well-lighted alcove for reading and writing, fully equipped with a roll-top desk, stacks of paper, and fountain pens with bottled ink.

The bed in the third room was so large I could stretch across it sideways and not touch either side. It had a down feather quilt to match down feather pillows, which I knew I would enjoy as much as the pleasures of the bath tub.

Four stories beneath me were a billiards room, a barber shop, a branch of the Western Union telegraph office, and a restaurant. All I need do was pull a cord hanging near the wardrobe, and a servant would appear shortly to take any order I might care to send to the restaurant—the food would appear within twenty minutes.

As for the wardrobe in the corner of the suite, it was full of suits and shirts of the latest fashion—similar to the pants, shirt, and vest laid out beside the bathtub—all fitted perfectly for me, ordered and delivered on short notice because of Leigh's insistence and bank notes.

I guessed the room to be a week's worth of cowboy wages for a single night's stay. I knew for certainty that the dandified city clothes had cost six months of a cowboy's wages.

I do not like owing debts. Including train passage, Leigh Tafton had spent more money on my behalf than I could earn in a year. To repay her, I needed to learn why her brother-in-law Frederick Blackburn had visited Franky Leonard, and—if it were true—show he had murdered her sister. And to do that, I first needed to leave the sanctuary of pleasure provided by the hot water in the bathtub.

I sighed, pushed myself out of the water. And toweled myself dry very, very gingerly.

TWENTY-TWO

ONLY PRIDE KEPT ME from hobbling as I walked out of the bathroom, dressed the way Leigh wanted me dressed, right down to a bow-tie with my vested suit.

She bestowed a smile upon me, a fitting reward for the queen's diligent subject.

"As we did not have time following your court appearance, Samuel, allow me to make a proper introduction," Leigh said. She was sitting perched on the edge of the sofa. The sight of her exquisite face and shapely body in an elegant dress stirred my blood and encouraged me to believe my body had not been damaged totally beyond repair.

"Bailey Pense, meet Samuel Keaton. Samuel Keaton, Bailey Pense."

He rose from the sofa, a tiny man with a well-oiled, handlebar mustache falling below his chin. His hair was long, slicked back and so dark I suspected it had been dyed, for his thin face was cracked with deep frown wrinkles, a fifty-year-old dandy trying to pass for one thirty years younger.

Everything about Bailey Pense was delicate—spidery fingers, thread-like gold chain to his pocket watch, silk handkerchief in suit pocket, narrow lips. Yet, in court before the magistrate's bench, his voice had proven to be anything but delicate.

To his credit, and despite his affected appearance, Bailey Pense was a true orator. I had closed my eyes several times during his articulate arguments, and had heard not a dandy, but the voice of a charming, robust man who perhaps favored port and thick cigars.

Pense had argued before the judge that the diamond earrings in my luggage were there to be held for Leigh's safekeeping. Leigh had testified the same. Pense had then argued my attack on Ben Currie, while unlawful, could be justified as self-defense, for several witnesses agreed I had been making no effort to escape as Currie slammed me with the baton.

The magistrate had made a quick decision in my favor, winked at Pense, and decreed me a free man. I wondered how much a lawyer of this influence had cost Leigh Tafton and realized my debt was growing rapidly.

"Fascinating," Bailey Pense murmured as he shook my hand. Delicately, of course. "A frontier lawman. Yet Leigh assures me you are anything but brutish."

Patronizing or not, he had taken me from the jail cell. And this was their party. I bit back a suitably brutish reply.

"Pleased to make your aquaintance," I said, "and more pleased to be making it here in the Washington Hotel."

"As compared to meeting at the jailhouse?" Pense arched his eyebrows. "My good man, I haven't stepped within its doors in years."

"Glad you could send someone instead."

Pense gave me the benefit of a well-acted, puzzled frown, easily formed by his deep wrinkles. "Oh," he said after a pause, "you must mean Louis."

"Yes, Louis. A remarkable man." And one I liked by instinct considerably more than this slick lawyer. Louis had hidden a lock pick under his tongue—the sound which I'd thought was a falling coin—and used the pretence of falling asleep as a way to gently spit it on the floor, allowing him to roll over and work it on the handcuffs behind his back.

Later, to pass the long hours of the night, Louis had shown me how to pick the handcuff lock, and insisted I practice. He'd demanded payment for the lesson—wild west stories, which I'd hardly embellished at all.

"Samuel," Leigh said, "Mr. Pense deserves full credit for the idea of sending Louis to assist you."

"Out of the blue, he called upon you with the offer?" I said, adding a grin to show I wasn't taking this too seriously. Although I was. I felt like an insect floating on a current, with no idea of what was roiling beneath. *What had transpired to get the two of them together? How could she have known I would be in danger in jail?*

Leigh gave me a sharp glance. "After the shock of your arrest, I regained my wits and came to the conclusion you would never steal from me. I immediately enquired around for a lawyer, and was ensured Mr. Pense had no compare. When I explained the situation to him, he came up with the logical conclusion. You had been set up. Someone wanted you in jail."

"Yes." Pense interrupted smoothly. "And if someone wanted you in jail, it promised danger. Ben Currie has a less than savory reputation. I find it occasionally convenient to have contacts with the seamier side of Johnstown. Louis is one of my favorites. Large, but intelligent despite his size." Pense pursed his lips, reconsidering a hasty judgement. "I mean, of course, a primitive instinctive sort of intelligence. In his way, a reliable man. It seemed prudent to send you assistance until we could take your case before a magistrate."

"He's a good friend of yours?"

"Hardly. Louis is simply a hired—"

"I meant the magistrate."

Pense grinned. Wolf-like. "We fish together. I have membership at the South Fork Fishing and Hunting Club. Very exclusive, you understand. He appreciates the chance to get away from the riffraff."

Riffraff like Louis. And like brutish frontier lawmen.

"Could you hire Louis for another job?" I asked.

"*Retain* him for another *task?*" A not-so-subtle correction. "This hotel's reputation is impeccable. I can't see why you would need further protection."

I let that remark pass. A Colt .44-40 has a considerably longer and faster reach than any man, and I'd make sure to keep my revolver close by. No, I didn't need Louis here. But I could use his help elsewhere.

"Send Louis after two men," I said. "The two in the jail cell. A short one named Murphy and a tall one named Abe."

Pense tapped his teeth with a manicured fingernail.

"As you guessed," I said, "someone wanted me in the jail cell. And that same someone wanted me dead." I explained Murphy's remark about waiting for me to arrive so they could kill me.

"Surely you asked them who sent you," Pense said. "After all, with Louis there and the both of them incapacitated, you would have taken advantage of the opportunity."

"I didn't get the chance. When Murphy came to, he shouted for a guard. Both of them were taken away."

"Hmmm." Pense furrowed his eyebrows in theatrical thought. I wondered how much extra he was able to bill because of apparent mental effort. "The idea has merit. Louis will find them, have no doubt of that. And Louis, I'm certain, has methods to convince them to give us the information we desire. Once we know who sent them to kill you. . . ."

I had given it plenty thought. Even if they were in Johnstown already, I didn't think it could be the Texas Rangers. Upon leaving Laramie, they'd have assumed I was dead to the stampeding cattle. Nor were they on the train, able to plant the earrings in my luggage.

Who then could have known I was arriving with Leigh Tafton? And who then could possibly be threatened by my arrival?

It seemed I faced a host of questions, questions I couldn't

even be sure were related. First, there was the matter of Franky Leonard, his previous life as Tom McCabe, and his horrible death. Second, and part of it somehow, were the Texas Rangers, who quite possibly weren't Texas Rangers, and who quite certainly were after money, the source and amount of which I had no idea. Third, there was Frederick Blackburn, who may or may not have murdered Leigh's sister. Fourth, there was this immediate attempt on my life in a town thousands of miles away from Laramie.

"Do me a favor," I said to Pense. "Have Louis stop by the hotel room. I wouldn't mind going with him."

Pense hesitated.

"Mr. Pense will arrange that," Leigh said. Her self-assurance was striking. She was in her twenties, probably three decades younger than he, but confident because of breeding and money. "Any reason you feel the need to accompany Louis?"

"Does Mr. Pense know the reason you have invited me to Johnstown?"

Now she hesitated. "I felt it necessary to inform him. He promised me the strictest confidentiality."

"Then you both should remember our Texan friends," I told her. "If they're in Johnstown, Louis should be able to help me find them."

"Of course," she said.

"Should we warn your brother-in-law of their presence?" I asked. "I presume they are as interested in him as we are."

Bailey Pense coughed to get my attention. "Frederick Blackburn is extremely reclusive. And has the wherewithal to remain unreachable. I doubt you should fear for him."

"Leigh?" In three days of travel together, she'd neglected to tell me this.

"It shan't be a problem, Samuel. I've already arranged for us to visit upon his return from Philadelphia. I am, after all, related to him by marriage."

I hoped my face gave away nothing of my thoughts. Because it bothered me that Pense was a part of this now, instead of much earlier when she first had suspicions about her sister's death. Why drag me in all the way from the territories when Pense was more familiar with Johnstown, and much better connected? Why hadn't she gone to him first? What could I offer Leigh Tafton that Pense could not provide?

I felt enough unease that I decided now was the moment to press Leigh for something she had delayed giving to me, despite my frequent reminders. If she refused now, I could gracefully walk away and search for the Texans with no obligation to her.

"Looks like I'll be laid up for a bit," I told Leigh. "I'd sure appreciate seeing your sister's diary. Seems like it might be a good place for me to start, and I won't be completely wasting time."

Leigh smiled. "Excellent idea, Samuel. I'll have it delivered to your room immediately. Mr. Pense has invited me to lunch. You'll be fine on your own?"

She left no doubt she was dismissing me, the hired hand. It was an abrupt change from her earlier charm as travel companion and hot-blooded woman so recently widowed. Again, I was reminded of a insect floating above deep dark currents.

She rose without waiting for my answer.

Bailey Pense allowed me another limp handshake and followed her out the door.

Which left me fine on my own, despite two attempts on my life in the previous week. Fine on my own, wondering when a trout was going to rise from the deep dark currents for another attempt.

TWENTY-THREE

SOMETIME IN THE MIDDLE of the afternoon, I yanked the cord which would bring a bellboy to my hotel room. He arrived at my door within minutes, a bland-faced young man with carefully kept hair and a pressed uniform.

"I understand you'll run errands for hotel guests," I said.

He nodded. "Yes, sir. Whatever you need, sir."

"I would like to have some telegrams sent."

"Yes, sir. Western Union will apply the charges to your room, sir."

"No." I handed him some bank notes.

Leigh was paying for the room. Last thing I wanted was for Leigh to know about the telegrams, especially if Western Union itemized the destination and recipient of each telegram.

I gave the boy the folded sheets of paper with handwriting that had occupied me during the early afternoon; at a nickel a word, it paid to be as efficient as possible.

As he hesitated before walking away, I understood how easily ignorance becomes fear. He was waiting for me to advance him a sum of money for his efforts, yet this was not the Territories, and I had no idea of the amount. I am not a miserly person and did not want to give too little; nor did I wish to appear foolish by giving too much. Minor as this was, I felt a fear of unfamiliar territory.

"Help me out," I said to him. If ignorance led to fear, then knowledge was the best defense. "Please explain to a frontier man the customary amount expected for this service."

Why was I trying to be so formal? Fear of appearing who I truly was, a small-town marshal?

"Yes, sir," he said. He told me the amount. It seemed reasonable.

"Thank you, sir." He palmed the money, gave a half salute, and walked away to deliver the telegrams.

The first was headed to San Antonio: APOLOGIES FOR DELAYED REPLY. STOP. PREVIOUS REQUEST FOR CONFIRMATION OF RANGERS FRENCH AND STOCKTON BECAUSE OF THEIR ARRIVAL IN LARAMIE. STOP. AM TRACKING THEM TO JOHNSTOWN PENNSYLVANIA. STOP. WILL KEEP YOU INFORMED. STOP. PLEASE SEND COLLECT TELEGRAM AS MANY WORDS AS NECESSARY WITH FULL BACKGROUND C/O WASHINGTON HOTEL JOHNSTOWN. STOP. SAMUEL KEATON.

The second telegram was headed to Boston. During the summer of my troubles a year ago, a fine young man had died—much too young, much too fine for death under any circumstances—and I'd played a small part in helping his parents through the situation. Although I'd only met them through correspondence, I knew the Hawkthornes to be a family of wealth and influence. By return mail, they had expressed gratitude and an offer to help in any way should I ever be near Boston. I was hoping they would be able to make discreet inquiries for me. While Boston was a distance from Philadelphia, perhaps someone in the Hawkthorne circles knew someone who knew someone who might know the Tafton family. Or industrialist Frederick Blackburn. This telegram too had taken time and care to compose: AM INTER-

ESTED IN BACKGROUND ON LEIGH ELLERSLIE NEE
TAFTON OF PHILADELPHIA. STOP. ALSO INTERESTED
IN FREDERICK BLACKBURN OF JOHNSTOWN. STOP. IN
YOUR DEBT IF YOU CAN MAKE DISCREET INQUIRIES.
STOP. IF POSSIBLE FORWARD COLLECT TELEGRAM
AS MANY WORDS AS NECESSARY WITH DETAILS C/O
WASHINGTON HOTEL JOHNSTOWN PENNSYLVANIA.
STOP. SAMUEL KEATON.

If ignorance led to fear, I wanted knowledge to arm me as
well as possible over the next few days.

****

I wore a robe and propped myself on the bed against
three down pillows as I read Aurelia Blackburn's diary. Occasionally I would stop reading and wonder at a vague guilt
which seemed as pervasive as the bruises on my body. How
could I not be enjoying life in the lap of luxury?

I shook myself from thoughts which led nowhere and
gave my attentions to the diary.

I liked Aurelia. Her words spoke to me as plainly as if she
were across the room in the overstuffed chair near the
window.

Dec. 24, 1875. What do I care if the Britains have pur-
chased most of the Suez Canal? It is the eve of Christmas,
a time for dreams and warmth in front of the fire and
roasting chestnuts, yet Frederick paces back and forth mut-
tering oaths against the Egyptian blackguards who are en-
dangering his investment. If I want to frolic in the snow,
he draws upon huge cigars and complains of rebellion in
Cuba. How can a man care so much about a world he
cannot touch, and know so little about the events in his
own life? I am tired of hearing about Turkish sultans and
possible uprisings by Serbians and Bosnians. I want to
hear about sons and daughters and enjoy the gossiping of

servants. I wonder if Leigh feels the same in her marriage.
Tonight I shall read aloud my favorite fairy tales and pre-
tend a prince has arrived to take me away from the cold-
ness of my lonely bed.

She was a faithful diary writer—not missing a single
day—and I believed I understood why. It gave her a chance to
talk, to explore, to give of herself, for it was obvious from her
writing she had no one else to share the feelings she needed
to share. Where a man tends to bury any thoughts beyond
practical ones or ones of measurement, a woman takes feelings into the light to affirm their existence; where a man lives
by seeking to forget sentiment or its cause, a woman will live
by memories, and in so doing, live more than the man.

It touched me that Aurelia had such passion, and that it
seemed so ignored by her husband.

January 1, 1876. The new year begins. Will this be the year
my womb gives life? Will this be the year I will be permit-
ted to give a baby unrestrained love and have it returned? I
hardly dare hope, yet without hope it seems I have nothing.
I feel alone always. Frederick continues to pace and mut-
ter, but his mutterings are vague. A letter arrived for him
today and it excited him badly. I cannot expect, of course, to
hear from him the cause of this excitement. I am but a
decoration, suitable for the endless rounds of dreary events
to elevate his profile in political circles. I do wish I could sit
with Leigh, like we were girls again, giggling over boys and
dresses. Adult life is not what I thought it would be.

January 3, 1876. Frederick left by train today. He refused
to tell me his destination, saying a woman has no right to
the business of her husband. I found from a servant, how-
ever, he purchased fare to take him to Laramie, a dusty
cow town on the frontier. I have never heard the name Tom
McCabe during any of his conversations. How does this

strange man have the power to pull Frederick from Johns-town and important upcoming political events? I have heard of men who upon approaching their middle years cast aside logic and pursue their lost youth. I would fear this has happened to Frederick, except I know it has not. He is too coldly rational. Indeed, a madness of this sort would give me hope for a renewal of passion. No, it must be the letter he received. Yet what could cause him to leave for the great wilderness in the dead of winter? I console myself by realizing in his absence I do not need to endure his dark moods. Nor could my bed be any lonelier or colder during his absence than it is during his residence here. I shall have to ask Leigh if her husband has the same disin-clinations. Perhaps she will find it a sour joke upon us after all our speculations in whispered conversations late at night as young women.

Had I not been resting in the Washington Hotel, had I not seen the great cities of Chicago and Pittsburgh during the travel here, I would have been angered at the suggestion Laramie was a dusty cow town. No sir, Laramie was a major stop on the Union Pacific, with upwards of four hundred peo-ple—and a military outpost. I knew now, however, equipped with more than my boyhood memories of the east, that Lara-mie truly was a dusty cow town. One that I missed badly. I thought of Doc and Jake and Beauregard and wished I were joining them for an evening meal at Chung's Eatery.

I gave sentiment no more than a minute and banished it by returning to the matter at hand: Aurelia's diary, page by page, marking passages I found of particular interest.

January 25, 1876. Frederick has returned. He is limping and refuses to tell me why. Despite his sullenness, perhaps the frontier was a tonic. Or perhaps his trip relieved him of a troublesome burden, for he regards me with a new glint in his eyes, although he did not visit me in my bedroom chamber. If only I had someone to ask questions on these matters. I do hope time flies until Leigh returns.

I was beginning to see the world through Aurelia's eyes, and she was becoming a friend. Her confusion at a new ailment disturbed me, as it would have hearing it straight from her lips.

February 15, 1876. I cannot explain what comes over me. There are times I feel perfectly fine, yet other moments I keel over with dizziness. The physicians have assured me it is nothing more than gastric fever and should pass soon. I do hope so. I have not shown to the physicians, nor would I for fear of dire mortification, the rashes which occur on more delicate areas of my body. I take comfort, however, in the silver lining of this cloud. I can be credited for his growing dislike of social events. It must be his fear of my unpredictable behavior. We are becoming almost reclusive. Nor does he bother me with his formerly incessant talk of politics. The changes in me, it seems, have brought changes in him. I can't discuss it with him, of course, even if he were so inclined. During yet another one of his business trips to Philadelphia, I am alone again in this empty house. Truly alone, for the servants will always be strangers to me. Money is a barrier, I have decided, for it makes them nervous when I try to befriend them. It is back to a lonely, cold bed then, a loneliness which I prefer to his company, for although he waited nearly three weeks after his return from the frontier to exercise his conjugal rights, he has been cruel in a way he never was before. What is happening in my life? Are all marriages like this? Am I doomed never to be happy as long as I live in this marriage?

I hope I will have the energy to dream pleasant thoughts as sleep falls upon me. Thoughts of soft babies. Thoughts of a

*sister I long to see again. Dear God, I pray you will be with
me in my life of solitude.*

Aurelia told me more—day by day—of her strange sufferings
and of her hopes and dreams. I searched for and found the
entry she had made just before the last letter she had written
to her sister, the one Leigh had shown me in Laramie.

*April 14, 1876. My decision is made. Despite Frederick's
wish that we receive no visitors, I am sending an invitation to Leigh. She has escaped her own miserable
marriage—I hardly dare hope the evil of death upon Frederick to give me an equal escape—and I hope her joy might
brighten my life. I would write her the letter now, except it
seems I am always fatigued and dreamless sleep beckons
like a dark angel. Tomorrow then, I shall defy Frederick
and send a note of invitation. I do hope she will arrive as
quickly as possible.*

Aurelia recorded her joy in her defiance and more fond
wishes about the possibility of Leigh's visit. Day by day I
grew to care for her more, until with a shock, I came to the
last entry and realized they were the final words she had
written in her young life.

*April 25, 1876 Frederick has escaped to Philadelphia on
business. Were he here, I am sure he would merely glance
at my face and know what I have discovered. Who can I
tell? Who would believe? And what, I pray to my dear Lord,
can I do with what I have learned? Sleep will not come
tonight, I am sure.*

April 25. I knew from Leigh that was the night
Aurelia—reported to be terrified of water—had apparently
left the house to row a boat by herself in the moonlight.
Whatever Aurelia had learned, had it been enough to drive

her to suicide? Or had she learned something which had killed her?

I wondered why Leigh had not brought this diary to the attention of those looking into the death at the time. I wondered why she hadn't brought this diary to Bailey Pense much earlier. I wondered why it was me she had chosen to expose this as murder.

I wondered too about three missing pages in her diary. Missing pages neatly and almost invisibly cut from the diary by a razor, so that I'd had to bend the book open almost to the point of breaking to see the edge shorn near the binding. Missing pages which had held Aurelia's diary entries for the four days prior to her death.

I stayed on the bed against the pillows and wondered through all the questions again and again until Louis the giant knocked on my hotel room door.

TWENTY-FOUR

LOUIS DUCKED to get through the doorway. With my haze of pain reduced to a grinding ache, and helped by late-afternoon daylight, I was able to see him much more clearly than during the previous night in the jail cell.

In direct line with my eyes, his Adam's apple loomed in a neck as thick and sturdy as a wooden beam. He was in a vest—no shirt—and his skin gleamed with sweat, his arms heavy with bulked muscle.

Louis had close-cropped brown hair, a clean-shaven, massive face, and jug-handle ears. Altogether, he was a large, ungainly, friendly puppy. Maybe older than Leigh, maybe younger. Definitely alert, definitely bouncing with vigor I could not even pretend.

He grabbed my shoulder in greeting, and his grin widened in apology as I winced.

"Stove in pretty bad, cowboy?"

"Would have been worse without you."

"Don't thank me, cowboy. Remember, I was retained."

He worked his lips around "retained," saying it with the prudish delicacy Bailey Pense would have used.

I laughed. And my stomach muscles paid for it.

"Pense says to take you around, help you look for last night's friends, help you look for a couple of other cowboys."

"How about instead we sit for a couple minutes. I can call down for a beer, a whiskey."

"I don't like what whiskey does to me," he said. "Gets me fighting mean and I don't like either. Fighting. Or mean."

"You'll sit?"

"Lazy is what I do best." He moved to the sofa in front of the fireplace. I took an armchair.

"Didn't know you was a rich cowboy," he said, nodding in admiration at the comforts of the suite.

"More like a kept one," I said. "And to tell truth, it's beginning to itch considerable."

A maid had stopped by while I was reading Aurelia's diary. She'd straightened the room and left a tray of fresh fruit. Louis closed his giant hand on three apples, tossed them in the air one at a time and began to juggle, using both hands, adding a fourth apple once the first three were in the air.

"I wouldn't sneeze at being kept," he said, hardly paying attention to the intricacies of juggling. "Not by someone as pretty as the lady that swept you from jail this morning. 'Specially if she can pay for this spread."

Still juggling, he grinned. His teeth were the size of small dinner plates. "What you got that makes you so special?"

"I'm wondering the same thing myself. I'm wondering a lot of things. If I could get to the point where I feel as good as a fish out of water it would be a sizeable improvement over my present state."

He grunted. One of the apples escaped the tight circle of his tossing motion. He snapped his head forward, caught it in his teeth, let the other three plop one after the other onto the palm of his right hand, and crunched down on the apple in his mouth. Two bites, two swallows, the apple had disappeared, core and all.

"See," he said, "thing is when Pense retains me, I don't

ask questions. Not why. Not what happens next. Not right or wrong. Pense pays too good. And I don't complicate what I do by thinking about it. This here chat smells like you're waiting to ask questions. Which is too much like complications."

He squinted at me. "Chances are, you didn't want to be chasing around town. That was just an excuse to get me here."

"Too beat up to move," I admitted. "I could use an extra pair of eyes and ears in this town, but I'll settle for answers to some questions."

"Give me a reason to answer."

"How about listen to the questions first."

He shrugged.

"You remember a woman who drowned last April? Aurelia Blackburn?"

Louis didn't reply. Didn't flicker a single muscle on his huge face.

"Ben Currie," I tried. "Was it him who looked into Aurelia Blackburn's drowning?"

No reply.

"Bailey Pense and Frederick Blackburn. They run in the same pack?"

I could have been talking to my own thumb.

"Where's the best place in town to ask questions about Blackburn?"

At least I could have got my own thumb to wriggle. Shake. Twist. Louis was a cemetery stone. I was tempted to wave my hand in front of his face to see if he might blink.

"Is Pense a man you would trust?"

At that, he grinned. "Cowboy, I was raised in a traveling circus. My pa got paid a dollar a day to be a sideshow freak, he was so big. Soon's he could, he made money betting on me in wrestling matches against menfolk from town to town. I was twelve then—almost as big as Pa. Didn't take long to learn every dirty move a man could make. You tell me. Do I trust Pense? Do I trust anybody?"

He got up. Stretched. Moved to the fireplace. Took the iron poker, a hand at each end.

"Watch this, cowboy."

Louis breathed deep. He held the poker horizontally at chest level, his elbows extended away from his body. He began to apply pressure to the iron bar. The massive bulk of his arms sprang into defined muscle. Slowly, the bar began to form an upside down "u." Not once did his breathing quicken in pace. The only sign of exertion was a slight reddening of his face.

He continued until he had bent the bar so sharply the knuckles of each hand touched the other.

"Good thing the Lord built you to dislike fighting and meanness," I said.

"I'm going to help you cowboy, and I'll tell you why. Last night, you made a pillow for my head. I heard you moaning with pain at how much it hurt to take off your jacket. Still you made that pillow, thinking I was a drunk too stewed to take notice. And you laid that pillow gentle for me. It's been so long I can't remember the last time someone did something for me not expecting anything back."

He handed me the poker. Curled in on itself. I set it in front of the fireplace. Maybe later I'd tell Leigh I had been testing my arms to see if they'd healed proper to their old strength.

"Another thing, cowboy. Last night, them two—Abe and Murphy—they had you cornered like a crippled rat. You didn't holler for help. You didn't get on your knees and cry for mercy. Difficult not to like a man that stubborn. And there's another reason."

"I presume one less sentimental."

He grinned. "Exactly, cowboy. Money."

"I doubt I can outbid Pense."

"Don't need to. See, something big is happening. Pense is paying me fifty dollars a day, just to stay in town to be at his beck and call. Pense hates spending money. All I can figure is he's gambling for a real honey pot."

"Sounds logical."

"I want part of it," Louis said, still grinning. "I think you can help me find it."

"If I can't?"

He pointed at the poker I'd set aside. "But cowboy, remember I can twist bones plenty more easy than I can twist iron. Pense pays me good. You let on anything to him that happens to show I was a fool to trust you, I'll hunt you down and break you across my knee like you was dry kindling."

"Conditional trust," I said.

"I'll lend you my eyes and ears, but there's a couple more conditions."

"I'm waiting," I said.

"One, any money involved, I get half. A penny less and I'll hunt—"

"—me down and break me across your knee like I was dry kindling."

"You learn fast."

"Second?" I asked.

"Make me a present of your Stetson hat."

I didn't hesitate. "Wear it in good faith, partner."

His eyes lit. Here was a giant, boy enough at heart to enjoy the romance of the west he heard about through dime novels.

I gave him my best drawl. "Remember, son, out west we need a hat with a brim wide enough to shed sun and rain, fan a campfire, dip water, and whip fightin' cows in the face."

He stuck out his hand to shake on the deal. I'm big enough to wrestle any steer, big enough to stare down most anybody. Still, his hand dwarfed mine so bad I figured once he let loose, it would take a map for it to find its way out.

Louis grinned again. "Listen up, cowboy. Aurelia Blackburn drowned April 25. A Monday night. Husband out of town, she went out alone in a rowboat. In the rain. Some folks wondered maybe she jumped out. Suicide's an ugly word, but it was whispered more than a few times. You guessed right. Ben Currie was the one going up there among the rich folks, asking questions, finally called it a tragic accident. Best place in town to ask questions about Blackburn is the *Daily Democrat.* Editor there, Mort Shaw, about the only man in town not afraid of Blackburn. Course, down the street at the *Tribune,* Blackburn's a man who walks on water, but coming from a Republican paper that shouldn't surprise you. Do I trust Bailey Pense? Not a lick."

He paused for breath. "That about cover all your questions?"

He knew it hadn't.

"Except for the most important one," I said.

"Pense and Blackburn."

"Yup."

"They used to be thick as thieves. And a lot of truth in that statement."

"Until. . . . "

"January, maybe February. Then they had a falling out. Pense lost his richest client."

Louis grinned those shiny, dinner-plate teeth at me. "Pense, though, is a man who lands on his feet."

"Yes?"

"Soon's Leigh Tafton showed up in May, he pulled her in as slick as a carnival barker. Whatever he lost from Blackburn, he made up with her."

I kept my face frozen. Earlier in the day, both Leigh and Bailey Pense had made a point of letting me understand their acquaintance was barely a day old.

"Interesting."

"You play good poker, cowboy. Because that was my ace card. Maybe you can tell me why that was the first and only thing Pense instructed me to keep secret from you during our excursions about town."

TWENTY-FIVE

Mortimer Shaw's face was mostly forehead. The *Daily Democrat* editor was balding in such a way that the back half of his head was thick with long, graying, straight hair. The front half, bare as sculptured marble, was round and wide. Tiny eyes. Tiny spectacles. Tiny nose. A wisp of a moustache. He was comfortably middle-aged, with a round ball for a potbelly, skinny arms and skinny shoulders.

Behind Shaw, were the presses of the *Daily Democrat*, idle now that the morning edition was on the streets. I'd purchased a copy to read over breakfast—eggs and bacon at the Washington, costing a half day's wage back in the territories—and read it through twice.

I guessed the *Democrat* to be a profitable paper, clustered as it was with advertisements throughout. But then, Johnstown was prosperous. Shortly after dawn, unable to sleep with the pains that lanced through me at every turn, I had opened a window to be greeted at that early hour by the rumble of steel mills and a breeze pocked with coal dust and smoke.

Had the town been less prosperous, the *Democrat* might not have been able to afford Shaw's use of it as a soapbox.

His editorial in the morning's issue had covered the women's suffrage movement and was calculated to be as stridently irritating as any single piece of writing I'd seen, enough to make me turn to the *Tribune,* where I'd been able to complete my education on the subject. Two tomcats in a burlap sack wouldn't have had a more violent disagreement. Where Shaw had applauded suffrage supporters, his Republican counterpart had foamed virulent rage. All told, I'd been entertained.

"Boy at the front said I might find you back here," I replied to Shaw's questioning eyebrows. "Name's Sam Keaton."

"Call me Morty," he said. "Most folks do, unless they're in here to call me otherwise. That wouldn't be you would it? Already had an even dozen stomp in. If I had a nickel for every time someone cussed at me. . . . "

"I'll be happy to call you Morty."

"Read the editorial this morning?"

"Yup."

"That's encouraging then," he said. "You agree? Let them vote?"

"Question's not whether they're capable," I said. "Most times I've seen a woman's guess to be more accurate than a man's certainty. Question is whether the system could take the strain of allowing intelligent voters into the race."

"Hey!" He wiped his hands free of printers ink on an already well-smudged apron. "I like the ring of those words. Mind if I steal them?"

He was reaching for a scrap of paper as he asked.

"Not if you mind me asking about a man named Frederick Blackburn."

It was like I'd jerked a puppet string attached to the top of his head. His chin popped up, and his hand froze halfway through the scribbling he'd begun with his pencil.

"Frederick Blackburn?"

"Friend of yours?"

"No." His voice grew louder. "No, no, and no."

He glanced around before speaking again. "Can't quite place your accent, but from that and your question, I can tell you're a stranger to this town."

"Wyoming Territories." Only since arriving here, had I begun to notice what was before an unconscious act. I'd been born in the east, raised and educated here well into boyhood. It meant I did have a grasp of formal grammar, and in the company of educated folks, I spoke as they did. But I'd been in the Territories since boyhood, growing up among trappers, ranch hands, and soldiers, the bulk of whom could not read or write. Among them, I slipped into less-polished speech patterns, as if I were shucking a pressed suit for jeans and a cotton shirt. "Laramie, more exact-like," I said, wishing at the moment I *was* wearing jeans and a cotton shirt. "Done some wranglin', some marshaling. Ain't been back East fer a spell. Shore is pretty here, but I do miss my hoss. Ain't but one like him, prettiest calico a man ever did see."

He grinned at my exaggerated drawl. "Laramie!"

"Yup."

"I was there in '70!"

I hadn't been. Late '60s I'd worked as scout and hunter for Union Pacific as they laid track. Hadn't returned to Laramie until '74, never expecting the events which would lead to a marshal's badge pinned inside my vest. Still, I could guess why Shaw had visited.

"The Howie murder trial, right?"

He nodded enthusiastically. "What a trial! We came in from all over the country. Reporters, photographers, cartoonists."

In 1869, Wyoming had become the first territory in the world to give political equality to women, granting them the privilege of voting. I believe something so revolutionary occurred simply because of the Territory's isolation. A widowed woman might be left with a ranch or business and no male relatives to help. On the trail, men and women did equal work. Women didn't become homemakers, but partners. Formal barriers between men and women never really existed, and I guess folks figured it natural that women should have a say in running the territory. We followed up with the equally astounding political act of granting women the right to acquire and hold any property in their own names. A year later came the event which drew Shaw to Laramie—women jurors.

A local bad man and drunk had gambled and whiskeyed himself into a violent rage, waking up a hotel resident, Andrew Howie, who promptly shot the drunk man dead. The Chief Justice appointed six women to the grand jury. They in turn sat on the trial, wearing heavy veils to protect themselves from photographers and cartooned caricatures, eventually returning a murder indictment, which in itself was a surprise, as men in those days were hanging for horse theft, while able to shoot a man and call it self-defense if the other so much as had a hand on a pistol.

"Baby, baby, don't get in a hurry," Shaw sang, smiling. "Your mama's gone to sit on the jury."

I smiled with him. Men had stood in packs, singing the song to taunt the jurors—Wyoming wasn't entirely free of suffrage opponents.

"What a hullabaloo that was," he said. "I do remember it fondly."

He suddenly squinted. "Did you say marshaling?"

I remembered I was speaking to a newspaper man. "Some."

"Have anything to do with Blackburn?"

"Some," I finally admitted, none too pleased with myself at my carelessness.

"Why don't we find a place to sit were we can talk," he said. "Horse trading here can't be much different than it is out west."

****

I was sweating badly by the time he got me to a tavern, only a couple of buildings down from the *Daily Democrat.*

Some was from the teeth-gritting manner in which I had to walk, most was from the humid heat, worsened by the haze which seemed to hang in the narrow valley. It was a cloudless day, yet the sun appeared like a white ball seen through smoked glass. I could only imagine how hellish it would be to work in the steel mills which caused the haze.

The tavern was dim and no less relenting in damp heat. I waved away Shaw's offer of a beer and hoped he could not see how much effort it took to avoid the temptation. He ordered instead pink lemonade over cracked ice for both of us, and I sipped gratefully.

"What do *you* know about Blackburn?" he asked me.

"Runs a steel mill. Thinking of running for governor."

"Give me more," he said.

"Wife drowned in April."

"I meant give me more of what brings you in from Laramie asking questions about him."

I sipped the lemonade. Crunched on some ice, a loud sound in the nearly empty tavern.

"Come on," Shaw said. "I can't print anything unless I confirm it somewhere else anyway. Not with the hold he has on this town."

I shrugged. "You might learn more from my questions."

Shaw grinned, showing a couple of blackened teeth along his lower jaw. "Fair enough. Try me."

"I heard you're the only man not afraid of him in this town." Although I wondered at how the mention of Blackburn had jerked Shaw's head up from his notepad. "What kind of hold *does* he have on this town?"

Shaw closed his eyes, as if literally trying to search his mind. "Let me tell you about his competition first. The Cambria Iron Company. Began here hardly more than 20 years ago, when Johnstown was a village. Maybe a thousand people. Thing is, I remember it that way. Grew up here. The streams had fish, the hills had deer. A man didn't need to rub his eyes when he walked down the street. Hang a pair of bloomers out to dry, the cotton stayed white."

He sighed. "On the other hand, the steel mills support a lot of folks. Cambria Iron alone employs 4,000."

I whistled, feeling like a country rube.

"Yup. Blast furnace, covers probably a dozen acres. Steel department, 400,000 gross tons a year. Rolling department —half the rail track in this country came from Johnstown. A forge plant, got some hammers that weigh more than five tons. All told, all departments, probably over a hundred furnaces."

He grinned at my appreciation of the immensity. "Think of it like this. Out to Connellsville, the company operates near to 700 beehive coke ovens. Seven hundred! And another hundred at Bennington. Eight hundred coke ovens just to supply it with the coal it needs. Getting an idea of its size?"

I nodded.

"Blackburn owns the Washington Iron Works. Probably employs 2,000 people. Half the size of Cambria, sure, but that in itself is more than big. Difference is, Cambria's run by a board of directors. Blackburn's the sole director of his company."

"Which means?"

"He's a dictator. He can make decisions on a whim. And does. Few things more frightening than an unpredicatable man with power."

"Two thousand employed," I said. "That's two thousand families. Man, wife, say six children. Blackburn sneezes and 16,000 people wipe his nose."

"Exactly. Sixteen thousand people who'd much rather tie their lives to Cambria than the Washington Iron Works. Cambria's founder, a fellow by the name of George King, he's everything Blackburn isn't. King set up the Cambria Hospital. Maintains it for all employees who become sick or suffer injury at the mills. King funds a library for the public. Gives away more money than he keeps for himself—and that's plenty on both sides."

Shaw snorted. "Blackburn? He's got the first nickel he ever made, notwithstanding the rumor he contributes to an orphanage in Harrisburg. I'm not sure I believe it. Throw him in his own blast furnace for a week and his heart would still be ice."

It fit with the impression I'd had of the man as I'd seen him through Aurelia's eyes.

"Has he done anything strange, unusual in the last while? Anything peculiar stick out?"

Shaw shook his head no. "He keeps to himself. Always did, but more so since his wife drowned."

"What can you tell me about that?"

Shaw tightened his lips. "Not much. Blackburn has enough pull, he stone-walled it. Ben Currie called it an accident. No one else would speak to me. Maids, servants, neighbors. All too afraid of Blackburn."

"Currie." Just saying his name felt like someone had poured broken glass into my stomach. "He's a lawman?"

Shaw studied my face for close to a minute. I kept a half smile in place, sipped more on my lemonade.

"Impressive," he said. "If I didn't know better, there'd be no way to tell he worked you over night before last."

In return, I studied Shaw. Homely as his egg-shaped face was, a person stopped noticing after a bit. His eyes, the fire of his words, made him a handsome man.

"Impressive too," I said. "Back at the *Democrat,* you probably knew who I was before I opened my mouth. You played me like a half-dead fish."

"I put it together as soon as you asked me about Blackburn," Shaw said.

"Care to share?"

"Depends on what I get in return."

"Before I leave town, I'll tell you everything I know. But not before."

Shaw lifted his tiny spectacles from his tiny nose and inspected them against what light he could find in the tavern.

"I got a friend who does that," I said, stabbed with a twinge of homesickness to be reminded of Doc. "Same way as you. And for the same reason. Whenever he needs to stall some."

Shaw took a deep breath. "Friend, you got yourself a deal. I usually don't give information before I get, but I'll make an exception on this one. Because it's Blackburn."

He let the breath out, an asthmatic wheeze. "Had two reasons for playing you once you asked about Blackburn. Wasn't more than four months back, someone broke into the *Democrat* and went through my files. Stole every single article or mention of Blackburn. I couldn't even lay my hands on a tintype of that man if I needed it now."

Shaw was leaning forward on the table now, staring at me with strange intensity. "Within a week, same thing happened over to the *Tribune*. Does that make any sense to you?"

"No," I said. "It does not."

Shaw continued to stare at me. "I told you two reasons. Put yourself in my shoes, a newspaper man, remembering Blackburn's files are stolen. Then a few months later, three folks from the frontier happen to show up in the same week and ask about him. Wouldn't that tell you something was happening?"

"Three folks." I was able to work out my sums without a pencil and tablet. "Me. Two others." I put up a hand to stop Shaw's next words. "Texans, right?"

"Texans," he replied. "What do you suppose they were after?"

"Don't know. That's part of why I'm here asking questions."

Another long stare. I knew if I protested that I was telling him the truth, he wouldn't believe me. So I absorbed his stare until he was satisfied I was not lying.

"Where do you go from here?" he asked.

"I hardly know enough to know. Any idea where I might find those Texans?"

"Your guess is as good as mine. This is a real easy town to hide in."

I thought of the teeming streets, the tall brick buildings all pressed in on each other. The dozens of taverns and hotels. I had as much chance of tracking them as Shaw did of tracking bear through the mountains. I told myself that Louis was on their trail anyway.

"All right then," I said, "where would you go if you were me?"

"You haven't told me exactly what you are looking for."

Trouble was, I couldn't answer. Franky Leonard had been murdered in the dead of winter. Two Texans had come looking for him. So had a rich widow, with her own story about a sister's murder. And somehow it was all tied together.

"Mr. Shaw," I said. "I'm looking at a big ball of yarn. I'm just pulling at loose ends, hoping to unravel something."

The tavern door slammed open, outlining a the small figure of a boy against the light.

"Mr. Shaw!" the boy called. His voice told me it was the same boy who had directed me to the back of the *Daily Democrat* in my search for Shaw.

"Yes, David?"

"Come running!"

"What have you got?"

"Two men found drowned. Wedged up against the weir. They're dragging the bodies out now."

Shaw stood, tumbling his chair onto the floor behind him.

"Any idea who?"

"No sir. Someone just came running down to the office with the news. Said it was a short man and a tall man."

"You'll excuse me," Shaw said.

"Certainly."

Shaw was halfway to the door. And I remembered.

"I might be able to help," I said, catching him just before he stepped into the soupy heat outside.

I was true to my word. The weir was ten minutes of carriage riding down cobblestown streets, with Shaw pointing out local features.

When we arrived, the bodies had already been pulled loose and surrounded by a mob of curious men, women, and children. Shaw pushed through the crowd for both of us until we had our first clear view of the dead men. Wet brown leaves clung to the men, their clothes sodden, faces already an unnatural, waxy white.

I was able to identify them, for I'd seen them up close two nights before in a jail cell.

Murphy and Abe. Louis could find them now, but they were long beyond the reach of him or anyone else here on earth.

TWENTY-SIX

A COUPLE HOURS LATER, I was on another carriage ride, me at the reins, Leigh at my side. It was much longer and much more leisurely than my ride earlier with Shaw, to a high hill east of Johnstown, just beyond a village, for reasons readily obvious by the steep road it took to get there, named Summitville.

I stepped from the carriage first, and from the ground accepted the picnic basket Leigh handed down to me. I set the basket aside and reached up to help her from the carriage. She lost her balance halfway down, falling into my arms, clinging to my neck. Even through the layers of clothing, I could sense the firmness of her young body, and with her hair against my face and her perfume in my nostrils and her unwillingness to let go, I became aware of her in the primal sense which she had intended.

"How clumsy of me," she said when she finally pulled her face away from my neck. "And how gentlemanly of you. I hope it didn't hurt your poor, bruised body."

She said it in a pouty, little-girl voice, a teasing tone, which, deliberate or not, had its affect. I reminded myself this was a woman who had lied to me about her relationship with

Bailey Pense. I reminded myself this was a woman who had
given me a diary with three crucial missing pages.

"This is a wonderful view for a picnic, ma'am."

"Your resistance stirs me, Samuel." Pout gone. "I like
the challenge." She faced away from me, backed into me until
the top of her head nestled just beneath my chin, and draped
my arms over her shoulders so that we were half embraced.
"And you are right. It is a wonderful view."

We were looking west. From right to left, the unbroken
ridge of the Alleghenies ran in crumpled lines, indistinguish-
able in the distance from the blue of the sky. It was land
pleated with abruptly steep hills and equally deep and narrow
valleys. Closer, seemingly at our feet, lay the gold of grain
fields among patches of woodland. A half dozen towns—the
churches and spires were scissored dark outlines—and
countless farm houses and barns were spread in panoramic
splendor. The turnpikes formed dark webs reaching into the
woods and past the fields. Far, far below, the river was a
glinting ribbon, spanned by a train trestle. As we watched, a
locomotive turned through a bend; it puffed steam, and seconds later we heard the whistle.

The wish entered my mind so quickly I had no chance to
stop its invasion. *I want to be here with Rebecca.* I wanted to
hold her hand, rejoicing together in the life which surged
through me to feel the freedom of such a view.

"Penny for your thoughts, Samuel."

Women have an innate capacity to sense the movement
even as a man's heart shifts. That thought, however—as with
the one before it—was not for sale.

"Why was the diary missing three pages?"

"Hmmm?" She said it as if in a dreamy trance, rubbing
her face across my forearm on her shoulder. It was then I
knew with certainty I would not trust her. She fascinated
me—and it would have been dangerous to deny it to
myself—but I would not trust her. Had she stiffened, pushed
herself away, been outraged, gasped, demanded explanation, I

still could have trusted her. But to pretend a romantic moment held more of her attention than the diary pointing to her sister's murder....

"It's peculiar," I said. "She was faithful to her diary. Didn't miss a day. Yet most of the week before her death was not recorded. I looked closely. The pages had been razored from the binding."

"Yes, Samuel, there were missing pages." She continued to brush her face against my arm. "I did that."

I remained where I was. Neither pulling away nor pulling closer. She would not get a reaction from me.

"Oh?"

"Aurelia was reminiscing. There were several embarrassing stories about me as a teen-aged girl. When I had crushes on older men. I did not want you to read them."

I was tired of her game. "Leigh, I want the truth."

"That is the truth, Samuel."

"I want the truth about all of this. I want it now."

"Let's unpack the picnic basket. Such a splendid day. We can pretend we love each other. And who knows, it just might happen."

"Take the carriage back yourself, Leigh. I'm no longer part of your game."

The ground was rocky and uneven. It forced me to limp as I walked away. My actions were not bluff. While I did not intend to leave Johnstown until I knew more about why Franky Leonard died, I did intend to leave the Washington Hotel. And I intended to put and keep Leigh out of sight. Desire fades where love endures. I'd learned to live without the woman I loved; forgetting Leigh, while difficult, would be infinitely easier.

"One quarter million dollars," she called. "You find me the truth, and I will give you one quarter million dollars."

Stubborn pride is stupid. I kept walking, trying not to think on how much money each step was costing.

"Aurelia planned to kill him," Leigh said. "Those are the

missing three pages. Does that satisfy you?"

Four painful steps later, I decided it did. I turned. "Tell me about Bailey Pense. You've known him for months, not days."

"Will you return to me and share this picnic as I intended?"

"Will you answer my questions?"

Slowly, she nodded.

By the time I climbed back up to her, sweat began to soak my forehead, and she'd pulled out a blanket, spreading it on grass. I watched, saying nothing, as she readied the meal on delicate plates of fine china: grapes, cold chicken, cold buttermilk in a large jar, chunks of marbled cheese, apple pie.

"Sit," she said, patting the blanket beside her.

Awkwardly, I lowered myself. In a few days, maybe less, I would be able to move without tensing against the bruised muscles of my thighs; at the moment, however, it was beyond mere inconvenience.

She shook the buttermilk jar several times. She kept her eyes on the jar, speaking as she pried the lid's rubber ring seal loose. "Currie beat you severely, didn't he? I can see it in the way your face tightens."

"Bailey Pense," I said.

She set the lid on the blanket, taking care to keep the bottom of the lid facing up so that the buttermilk residue did not blot upon the blanket.

"Bailey Pense," I said, "tell me about him."

She poured the buttermilk into glasses. She offered one to me. I ignored it.

"Bailey Pense."

She sighed, placed both glasses back on the blanket. "You are a tiresome man."

"Why lie to me about Bailey Pense?"

The jar had been so full that buttermilk had seeped onto her fingers. She wiped them on a napkin. "I lied because of the reason I first hired him. Aurelia."

At this height, the humidity seemed much less oppressive. A breeze lifted and dropped the corners of the blanket. With my legs stretched in front of me, I was as comfortable as I had been in days.

"Aurelia wrote me other letters, you know," Leigh continued. "I couldn't show them to you. These were letters in which she openly dreamed about Blackburn's death. As time went on, she began to wonder if there was a way to encourage his death. I think..." Leigh faltered. If acted, it was timed perfectly. "I think my own husband's death prompted her thoughts. I'm afraid I may have rejoiced too openly in my own letters to her."

She reached across the distance between us to place her palm on my forearm. Hot as the sun had been on my skin, her palm burned more.

"Samuel, I believe Aurelia wished to enlist my assistance in murdering her husband. That was part of the reason she was so anxious for me to visit."

"Assist? How?"

She shrugged, although her hand remained where she'd placed it.

"I think you're lying again. You do know."

"There you are. Tiresome again."

I moved my arm from beneath her hand.

Leigh sighed again. "She was going to shoot him as he walked his property. But she was going to have me as witness to the fact she was in the mansion the entire while."

"And Bailey Pense?"

"The day I arrived, he approached me. Told me I needed to listen to a story about my sister. I listened. Bailey gave me her diary."

"No missing pages."

She smiled at my sour tone.

"No missing pages, Samuel. He wanted me to know he knew Aurelia had planned to murder Blackburn."

"Why?"

Leigh raised her face to the sun and closed her eyes. Her skin was seamless, the flesh taut. This was an incredibly beautiful woman. One who knew it.

"Why?" Her eyes were still closed. "Money, of course. Isn't that what the world is about?"

"No, but I doubt I'd be able to convince you otherwise."

She lowered her face, opened her eyes, and cast a long, studied stare into my own face. She drew a breath to say something, changed her mind, returned to safer ground.

"Pense had drawn up wills for both Blackburn and my sister. As it stands now, Blackburn is entitled to all of my sister's inheritance. If I can prove Blackburn murdered my sister, the money returns to me. Pense and I are business partners."

"A quarter million for him?"

She hesitated too long. Then she knew I knew agreement would be a lie. "A half million."

"I won't settle for less."

A flicker of surprise in her eyes. Delighted laughter. "Glad to see there are *some* temptations you can't resist."

"I'd like the agreement in a letter," I said.

"You don't trust me."

"I like business to be done in a business-like manner."

Delighted laughter again. "My, I do enjoy a man who doesn't fall at my feet. You shall have your letter."

Which told me the sums involved were staggering. If she could treat the half million each to Pense and me so casually, it must be money skimmed from the top of a deep well.

Or she'd find a way to withhold the money. Nor would I care much if she did. I couldn't comprehend that kind of money—greed for it would have been like greed for the moon. If she believed, however, my motivation was the same as hers, I'd have much better chance at getting more of the truth from her. And if the half million ever fell into my lap, I knew plenty of people back in Laramie who could use a share of it after Louis collected his half.

She turned her attention to the the chicken, wrapping a leg in a napkin and handing it across to me. I accepted.

With a mouth full of cold meat, I thought of the buttermilk and reached for a glass. In reaching, my gaze fell upon the upturned lid.

A dozen or so dead flies lay in the thin layer of buttermilk on the lid.

I chewed thoughtfully, leaving the glass on the blanket.

I watched another fly land. Not squarely in the buttermilk, but to the side. It dipped its front legs into the liquid.

I swallowed my chicken. Took another bite. Kept watching the fly. Before I had chewed and swallowed again, the fly had fallen onto its side, flailing its legs in rapidly weakening circles.

Leigh reached for her glass of buttermilk.

I grabbed her wrist.

"Don't," I said. "I think that milk is more than sour."

TWENTY-SEVEN

SHORTLY AFTER MIDNIGHT, a knock on the door took me from sleep. I pulled on my pants, tucked my Colt in the back of my waistband, and moved from the bedroom to the main suite.

The knocking on the door was repeated as I fumbled with a match to light an oil lamp. I set the lamp on the fireplace mantle where its light would first draw the eyes of my visitor.

The heavy carpet absorbed my footsteps as I approached the door. I stood to the side as I quietly tried to slide the bolt open. I knew of men who would shoot through the door at the sound of the bolt, hoping to kill from the hallway. Once in Laramie, a jealous husband had used this technique. Only he had knocked on the door of the wrong room, and was hung for shooting a tonic salesman.

Bullets did not splinter through my door. I didn't feel foolish, however, for the precaution.

I stepped well back and waited among shadows away from the lamp on the mantle and trained my gun on the doorway.

"Come in," I said. "It's open."

Louis pushed the door open. He was alone. Unarmed.

I tucked my Colt in my waistband and stepped out from

the shadow.

"I believe that was a gun I saw in your hand," he said.

"Your eyesight is good. It was."

"Always this jumpy?"

"People keep trying to kill me, I'll be even jumpier."

Louis shut the door behind him. "Pense told me some about it, but not much."

"Doctors figure it was strychnine," I said. I described the jar of buttermilk and how I seen the dead flies.

"Flies is one thing," Louis said. "But you got to weigh close to two hundred. Was there enough to kill you?"

"More than enough. Leigh was almost hysterical at the thought of someone trying to murder her. She insisted there was no room to simply guess. It cost her some, but the doctors arranged for the purchase of a hog down at the local slaughterhouse. They went down, fed the hog all of the buttermilk. Hog must have weighed five hundred pounds. It didn't live more than fifteen minutes. And it died terrible too."

Terrible was understating the case. Doc Harper had once explained to me why he didn't approve of ranchers using it to kill wolves. He said it was too indiscriminate, had seen badgers, hawks, dogs all die because they got to the poisoned meat before the wolves did. Strychnine hit the nerves, Doc had said, causing all the muscles to contract at the same time. The animals died from asphyxiation or sheer exhaustion from the convulsions.

The hog had first spasmed its legs, then its entire body in convulsions which threw it against the side of the pen. In the end, its body had arched so badly it had snapped its back.

Leigh hadn't watched long; the doctors had given her sedatives and sent her to the hotel to rest. For my part, I'd returned to the hotel to question the cooks on their preparation of the picnic basket. I'd learned nothing of use.

"You barely been here a couple days, cowboy. Twice already someone tried to kill you dead. They must want you real bad if they didn't care the pretty lady died with you."

I nodded. For all I wanted to mistrust Leigh, she was no party to who or why someone wanted me dead. She'd been about to drink the buttermilk, and that, along with her reaction to discovering it had been laced with strychnine, told me there was plenty to this situation she didn't understand either.

"Seems to me there's been a lot of dying," I said. "You probably heard they fished two men out of the river today."

"I heard."

Keeping my voice even toned, I sprung the question on him. "Did you kill them?"

Louis sat himself down on the sofa, leaned his head back, and supported it with his hands. "Not a chance, cowboy. It's not my style."

When I didn't reply, he continued. "Fact is, three years ago Pense hinted once about removing some difficulties by arranging for a witness to meet an accident. Cowboy, I nearly killed Pense myself for suggesting it. I'm no saint, but I'm no murderer either."

The story told me a lot about Louis. And a lot about Bailey Pense.

"You'll pardon me for asking?" I asked.

"Barely."

"There's a million dollars at stake here," I said. "People have killed for a lot less."

Louis sat upright. "A million?"

"Half to me and half to Pense if we can prove Blackburn murdered Leigh's sister. That's a quarter million to you." I smiled and pointed at the bent fire poker. "I haven't forgotten your deal."

Louis clapped his giant hands together. "Then let's get started. I found out where your two Texan friends have been holing out."

"This is between me and them, partner. If you like, just tell me where to find them. You don't have to make yourself part of the play."

Louis gave me the wide grin. "Appears that you are rapidly becoming an investment I need to protect."

"Only two of them."

He shook his head. "Cowboy, where we're headed you don't find lace and room service champagne served by bellboys in pressed suits. They're staying in a boarding house in a slum where men hide during the day and roam like rats at night. Stranger like you, this time of night, that part of town, you'll be up against every cutthroat who needs a drink or a dollar."

"Then I won't mind if you lead the way." And I wouldn't. I'd seen him bend an iron poker. Juggle apples. Pick locks. He was some kind of big, and some kind of quick with his hands. Although a few days after the beating my body was finally able to move without betraying me with pain at every mood, I had no problem admitting it'd be good to have this good-humored giant watching my back.

Louis stood from the sofa, an easy shifting of his weight a man half his size would be hard pressed to do with equal grace.

"Let's go, cowboy. I'd like to catch up with them before they move on to another place. From what I heard, they've been real careful about staying out of sight."

We needn't have worried.

A carriage was waiting outside the Washington Hotel for us. The driver took us beyond the steel mills, through streets growing more narrow and more crooked until he refused to go any farther.

It was another ten minute walk. We were jeered by drunks and hissed at by prostitutes. Shadows of men flitted and disappeared at our approach. Buildings were crooked, leaning against the other. No gas lamps lit the doorways.

And when we pushed open the door on the second floor of a boarding house that smelled of sweat, urine, and mildew, we found our Texans. We need not have rushed; William French and Leroy Stockton would have waited for us for a long time.

The oil lamp that Louis lit showed both were dead, lying in blood on strawtick beds.

TWENTY-EIGHT

I *TOOK SEVERAL DEEP BREATHS* and I did my best not to react. It wasn't the shock of seeing William French and Leroy Stockton dead when I'd expected the need to draw a gun on them. No, it was the blood.

Long ago, although in my dreams it seemed so fresh I often woke believing it had just occurred, I'd held my brother as he coughed blood onto my sleeve, dying in my arms after saving me in a gun fight which I had caused. My only brother. The one who'd raised me and protected me in the sad, lonely years of orphanage. Part of my payment for that mistake had been a knowledge of how much damage and pain a bullet brings, knowledge seared into my soul, a visceral knowledge which runs far deeper than knowledge of the mind. Because of it, the sight of a man's blood hits me hard. Puts my dying brother back in my arms, the churning horror and disbelief back in my stomach.

"Would you stand in the hallway and watch the door, Louis?" I wanted to run. Anything but stand inside the death stench of this filthy, cramped room. "Make sure nobody walks in on me."

"Sure, but what are—"

"No questions." I swallowed, vainly trying to settle my stomach. "Later, maybe, but not now."

He slipped back into the hallway.

I lifted the oil lamp and moved closer to the beds. A rat darted from beneath one bed to the other. Squeamishness about a rat was the least of my problems. Although I was breathing shallowly through my mouth, it still seemed as if I could smell the copper of pooled blood.

I bent over, holding the lamp close to Leroy Stockton. A bullet had taken him center of the chest, leaving much of his shirt's cloth hidden by blood. On his face, an oozing brown trailed from the side of his mouth. My stomach lurched, then I realized it was his chewing tobacco. His eyes were open, glassy. I closed the eyelids, but they would not remain shut.

I did not want to, but I put my hand against the side of his face. It confirmed what I'd learned from his eyelids.

In my efforts to be a good lawman, I'd forced myself to endure time with Doc Harper as he examined those who had died by accident or foul play. Body by body, he'd shared over thirty years of experience with me, gentle in his respect and treatment of those bodies, as if they were his patients. I knew from Doc that changes to a body were fairly consistent following the onset of death.

In a half hour, the skin becomes purplish and waxy. Within four hours, the small muscles become stiff, noticeable at the eyelids, face, lower jaw, and neck. Another couple of hours and the entire body is stiff, the rigor mortis lasting nearly a day until the body softens again.

Leroy's face was cool to the touch, and his head resisted movement. His arms and legs lifted easily, however. Dead more than four hours, less than six.

William French's body was in the same state, something I could have guessed, although I didn't, forcing myself to test the resistance of his head and jaws to any movement. It fit with what their body positions told me — they had been shot, one immediately after the other. And they'd been shot where they fell, onto their backs onto the bed behind them, as if they'd been perched sitting on the ends of their beds as they faced their killer. There was no blood elsewhere in the room to tell me they'd been shot and dragged into position.

I put myself in the murderer's shoes, wondering how I would have managed to shoot two savvy men, each one accustomed to gun play and treachery.

If I burst in on them, they'd react—diving, pulling their own revolvers, anything but passively remaining in seated positions on the end of the bed, waiting to be plugged.

So I was expected then. I'd knock on the door and wait for them to invite me in.

And they trusted me to a degree. It was not to be a confrontational meeting, or they would have been prepared for the possibility of gunplay, perhaps having their own guns drawn as I stepped inside.

No, I would have walked in, smiled, and started speaking, letting them relax further. Then I would have pulled my revolver, continued smiling and speaking, and motioned for them to sit on the ends of the beds, just far enough away to give me time to shoot if they made a move for my gun.

Even then, they wouldn't have expected to die. Otherwise they would have both rushed me, knowing at least one would survive.

So William French and Leroy Stockton would sit as commanded while the conversation continued. I could see them too being as cool facing the murderer and his gun as they had been while I held a shotgun on them in Franky Leonard's shack. They would be expecting all the while it was one more touchy situation they would undoubtedly survive.

Only this time the gun barrel would bloom with fire, because as the murderer I would have casually pulled the trigger on one of them halfway through a spoken sentence, aiming for the chest, knowing at this range it would be impossible to miss. I would have shot William French first. He was craftier, more likely to react.

So maybe it left Leroy Stockton, mouth gaping in shocked realization that the gun barrel was now turned on him. And as murderer, I would have coldly executed him before the echoes of the first shot had stopped ringing, for I would want to leave before anyone—as unlikely as it might be in this squalor—appeared to investigate the source of a gunshot.

These thoughts left me with two questions. With whom would they have made acquaintance so soon after their arrival in Johnstown? And who would they have trusted so soon? Although I still didn't know what stakes they had died for, I knew the stakes to be high enough they'd tried killing me and Jake. It didn't seem they would trust anyone easily over those stakes, let alone someone they had known less than a week. My second question was equally puzzling. What reason would this person have to kill them?

I turned to leave the room, desperate for fresh, night air. Then it struck me to wonder what the murderer might have taken as he too spun on his heels to depart.

I spent another five minutes in the room, breathing so shallowly I verged on dizziness. All that I found of interest was a single saddle bag, in the darkness of a corner, as if it had been tossed there. The saddle bag held bank notes and the usual personal effects of a traveling cowboy, but did not hold the writ I had seen in Laramie, nor the tintype of Tom McCabe which the Rangers had shown me during our discussion in the marshal's office.

I knew that this oddity should tell me something. Money untouched but picture gone. But I still could not guess what it should tell me.

The bleak loneliness of the way they had died began to overwhelm me and I could not remain in the room any longer. A man should die in his own bed, with songs of angels growing as the darkness closed in, with the tears of his loved ones falling gently upon his face.

I left them, on their beds, staring sightlessly at the broken plaster of the ceiling above.

TWENTY-NINE

WE STOOD ON AN ABUTMENT of an old, earthen
dam—Bailey Pense, Leigh Tafton, and I, looking upstream at the Little Conemaugh River. The abutment
itself was green with overgrown grass, cut in the middle
where the river waters flowed through at an unhurried pace.
The earthen dam did hold enough water for a shallow lake;
had the gap in the middle of the abutment been filled again,
the lake would have been much higher, the river itself much
less of a wide, silver ribbon glinting in the sunlight. It was
idyllic here; rounded, valley hills green with pasture and corn
fields rose on both sides, and the sky was blue, not tainted
with industrial smoke.

To get up here into the mountain hills east of Johnstown
had taken over two hours of steady travel, two hours of
strained small talk among the three of us on the open buckboard of the carriage. For my part, much was on my mind.
Four dead men in two days—Abe and Murphy from the jail
cell, William French and Leroy Stockton—all four somehow
bound to the reasons we were on our way to the appointment
Leigh had arranged with Frederick Blackburn at his country
estate. Aurelia's drowning made it five deaths. Franky Leon-

ard, if he was tied to this, six. Had Leigh and I died to the strychnine, it would have been eight deaths.

What could have driven a murderer or murderers to kill so many times? Money, to be certain, for Leigh had offered a half million for the answers. *But how much money? And how could it be taken, or have been taken?* Millions of dollars are not stolen as easily or with the comforting degree of secrecy that, say, a pickpocket lifts a wallet, or even the way a gang stops and robs a train. No, millions of dollars gouge a path as deep and obvious as any river flood. A thief who manages to take such an amount must be prepared to fight desperately to keep it.

And desperation of that magnitude leads to death.

I had not told either of my companions what Louis and I had found the night before. Louis and I had slipped out unseen, deciding it would be better for both of us to avoid the questions which would come with the discovery of two men soaked in their own blood. The boarding house had such an air of decay that for all I knew, Stockton and French had yet to be discovered. It was not a thought I wanted to contemplate long. The stench of death brings blowflies by the hundreds; Stockton and French would be paying the price for their greed by providing a hatching ground for maggots.

I took a deep breath, trying to cleanse myself of that stench of death, enjoying the air much more here in the country than in the sweltering soup of Johnstown's industrial gray valley.

The hazy afternoon heat had driven me to roll my sleeves and toss my jacket in the rear boot of the carriage, which was parked on the south bank of the dam. Pense, formal to a fault, had not even loosened his collar.

Leigh stood several dozen steps away, facing away from us, her head bowed in contemplation. Her hair was braided and coiled into a bun. She wore a wide-brimmed hat to protect her face from the sun, and her cream-colored shawl matched her long dress. I guessed her attention was on the shallow lake far below our feet, the lake in which her sister had drowned on an April night. Leigh had changed since our picnic; her eyes had quieted, her shoulders were not so square, chin not so high. To the young, death is not an enemy, they have no fear of the dragon outside the door, for to them, of course, dragons do not exist. Watching the agonized death throes of an animal fed poison meant for her, however, had brought to Leigh the whiff of brimstone that comes with the dragon's fiery breath. I could understand why her sister's death had new meaning to her.

I wondered if my thoughts were also Leigh's — in the sunshine, with the unruffled water promising coolness and relief, with the trilling of birds and the treetop buzzing of cicadas, it was that much more cold to imagine the fear and darkness which must have swallowed Aurelia as she flailed for life in her last, solitary moments.

"I may have told you about my hunting club," Pense said. "The South Fork Fishing and Hunting Club."

"You did." I was not interested in hearing more.

Pense ignored my bluntness and pointed upstream. "This valley used to hold a substantial lake. It continued up and around the bend, probably a couple of miles long. The reservoir had been built originally to supply water for the canal system used before the railway. It's been abandoned for more than a decade. And you can see—" he kicked at the ground beneath our feet "—this broken dam barely holds anything now."

"Enough to drown a young woman in the prime of her life." Her diary had brought her to life for me, and I was angry at Aurelia's death.

"Imagine it now with a dam twenty, thirty feet higher...." He swept his arm to take in the view of the entire valley, as if the death of a young woman was fine print in a document he had long ago discarded. "Build the dam high enough, you'd have a lake seventy feet deep, not ten feet. A half mile wide, not a hundred yards."

"Didn't you tell me it was about fifteen miles downstream to Johnstown?"

"Yes. What of it?"

"Say your half-mile-wide lake busts through the dam. Ripping down through the valleys, it'd be like an earthquake hit the town."

"Doomsayer. We've heard the same feeble worries from townsfolk. What they don't understand is what the rich want, the rich get. And what they'll get is a lake large enough for sailboats. Imagine that, sailing in the mountains!"

Pense nudged me. "Blackburn is one of the few to have an estate up here. What do you think the land will be worth once you bring in a lake? The rich want privacy. The South Fork Fishing and Hunting Club will not only deliver privacy, but stocked fish, protected hunting grounds. Once we buy this dam and the land—"

"Why was she out that night? Does anyone know?"

"Eh?"

"Aurelia. She was in a rowboat. At night. Why?"

With a shake of his head, he tore himself away from the utopia of wealth and leisure. "They found the rowboat. Loose. It had drifted up against the north part of these damworks. She was found in some branches." He pointed several hundred yards upstream. "There, where that tree has fallen into the water. Nobody knows for certain she was in the boat. It's just the conclusion drawn."

"Somebody could have struck her unconscious," I said. "Or held her under. Then cut the boat loose."

Pense blinked several times. "Certainly, I suppose."

I stared at him hard. He looked at me, glanced at Leigh, looked back at me, lowered his voice.

"Leigh prefers to think it was murder." He glanced again to see if Leigh had heard her name. Leigh remained still, shoulders bowed. "I agree it was no accident. Aurelia would not have gone rowing. But I believe it was suicide."

He hesitated. I realized this was really the first time

Pense and I had been alone and able to discuss this. "Aurelia was a peculiar woman. Dreamy, if you know what I mean. She believed in romantic love. I think she finally gave up hope. In love. In life."

"It is convenient for you to appear to believe otherwise."

He frowned. Then smiled. "Have I underestimated you?"

"Only you can answer that."

"Perhaps I have. Leigh has engaged me to pursue the matter. I am compensated for my pursuit."

"Or for the appearance of pursuit?" I asked.

Before Pense could reply, Leigh turned and stepped toward us. A single tear tracked down her face.

Wordlessly, we followed her back to the carriage. We all remained silent in the carriage, comforted by the steady *clip clop* of the horses hooves. Five minutes later, we passed through the gates onto the narrow driveway which led up to the impressive stone-walled mansion of the Blackburn estate.

****

"Not here?" Leigh said to the butler. "But that's impossible. We had an appointment."

We had not been invited inside. The three of us crowded an alcove in front of the main entrance. I was grateful for the shade of the mansion which towered above us.

"I shall repeat myself, madame," the butler said. "Mr. Blackburn extends his regrets."

He was a tiny man with a bulbous nose and eyes huge behind thick spectacles. He wore a black suit and spoke in a stiff, formal manner, as if he were as important as the position he had assumed.

"Mr. Blackburn is also my brother-in-law. You shall invite us in, and we shall wait for him."

"I'm afraid that is not possible, madame. Mr. Blackburn is in Philadelphia."

"No!" She stamped her foot. While I had been curious to

finally meet Blackburn, I was not outraged to have missed him. There would be another time. It surprised me, her heated reaction and disappointment. "He has been expecting our arrival at this hour for several days. We must see him."

"I assure you he is not in residence at the moment. Perhaps upon his return...."

Leigh trembled with frustration. "Where is he in Philadelphia?"

"He did not leave instructions to divulge such information."

Leigh was on her tiptoes, leaning her face into his. Her voice was restrained fury. "I...am...the...sister...of ...the...woman...who...was...his...wife."

"And I, madame, am a man in the employ of Frederick Blackburn. Until you employ me, and I doubt that day will arrive, I answer to him and for him. Histrionics will not sway me. I bid you good-day."

With that, he swung the heavy door in our faces, leaving me with only a remembered glimpse of the opulence I had been able to see past his shoulders.

Leigh kicked the closed door and shouted for him to open it.

Bailey Pense took her by the arm before she could hurt herself.

"The wealthy do not behave in this manner," he said in a low voice.

She jerked her arm away from him. "The wealthy behave in any manner they wish. And remember you are in *my* employ."

She marched ahead of us, back toward the carriage.

I remembered the horse ride which Leigh and I had taken into the hills outside Laramie, and how she had marched away in a similar manner.

"Probably best you let her cool down," I suggested.

"Of course." Pense showed no worry at her outburst. He dug a cigar from his pocket, snipped the end, and lit it, slowly rolling the thick tobacco through the match's flame.

Several puffs later, he began to amble in the direction Leigh had taken.

I shrugged and began to follow the cloud of cigar smoke. I felt part of a play in which I did not belong. Leigh's outburst seemed far stronger than the situation had deserved. What had I missed?

Halfway toward the carriage, a new thought struck me.

"Mr. Pense," I called. He stopped, but did not acknowledge me by turning. When I reached him, I made sure to stand close enough for him to feel how much I outsized him. Petty, but the only civilized satisfaction I could take.

"Why did she have to tell the butler she was Aurelia's sister? Shouldn't he have recognized her?"

Pense drew on the cigar several more times before answering. "My dear man," he said. The patronizing tone put my teeth on edge. "Blackburn has replaced his staff since Aurelia's death. It's as if he is starting a new life."

"Oh," I said.

Pense blew cigar smoke in my face, smiled in a way which brought the blood of anger to my face, and strolled forward again.

With three of us on the buckboard, not a single word was spoken the entire carriage journey back to Johnstown.

THIRTY

THAT EVENING, alone in my hotel suite, I fought restlessness and melancholy. It was a lesson in the value of money, which could only bring me the luxury of high living, but could not ease my soul.

I missed Laramie. I missed the sigh of wind through tall grass. I missed Jake's broken chuckle, the sight of Doc cleaning his spectacles. And, as always, I missed Rebecca. I have faced pain in many forms—as have most of us—and have concluded the worst pain is to face an insurmountable barrier—guilt perhaps, anger, death, betrayal—between you and someone who loves you in return. I would almost have preferred death to be the barrier, not her marriage to another man; then, at least, I could look forward to meeting her when called home beyond this life.

Brooding is not healthy for me. It tempts me to search for the false peace of alcohol. My body was stiffening as I sat, and it seemed a brisk walk might be the best remedy for both my bruised heart and bruised muscles.

I set aside the newspaper which had failed to distract me, walked past suits hanging neatly pressed in a wardrobe, stripped myself of starched pants and starched shirt, and stepped into my jeans and cotton shirt. My old leather boots fit like slippers. I wore my vest too, since I needed a way to hide the Colt .44-.40 tucked into my belt.

I forced a smile on my face and, although I certainly did not feel like it, I whistled. I've found those simple actions will dispel some gloom, and I hoped a walk would do the rest.

The evening air had cooled enough to make my exertion comfortable. Hissing street lamps gave ample light. More than a few others walked through the cobblestone streets, and carriage traffic was brisk.

It did hurt to walk; most pedestrians passed me, including an old lady who turned her bonneted head and smirked triumphantly in my direction. I reached to tip her my Stetson, a habit so ingrained I clutched twice for the brim before remembering I had given it to Louis.

I looked around frequently to keep my bearings. The jumble of buildings seemed as confusing to me as unmarked prairie might to an easterner. Because I moved so slowly, as I glanced around every few minutes, I was able to notice the oddity of another man at the same pace.

I thought nothing of it until I noticed him for the third time, still the same distance behind me, usually in shadow.

I believed I had ample reason to be suspicious. The Texans were dead, Abe and Murphy dead, and twice attempts had been made on my own life.

I walked another half hour, trying to give the air of a man with no cause for fear, glancing back less frequently. When I decided I had waited long enough to let him believe I had no idea of his presence, I wandered toward a quiet section of town, toward the steel mills along the river.

It was simple, actually. I rounded a corner and stepped into a doorway. I could have waited until he moved past, but any man who had been able to kill Leroy Stockton and William French was a man to reckon with. If he turned the corner and saw no sign of me, he'd probably expect me in any doorway ahead.

I listened carefully. When his boot heels clacked notice that he too had rounded the corner, I stepped from the doorway with my Colt pointed at the center of his belly.

"Hands clasped behind your neck," I said. "Now."

I cocked the hammer. Even with the various background noises of the town, it was a sound which carried clearly.

"This most surely is a sorry day," he said, lifting his hands high and clear. "I'd just as soon get caught with my britches down as let a northern lawman get the drop on me."

I could make a reasonable guess this was no local thug. Not when every word was drawled in Texas tones of understated irony.

"Well, partner," I said, "it's going to get worse for a bit. I'll need you down on your belly."

"I'd druther not. This town's got a stench to it. Pig manure's cleaner than these bricks."

"I've learned a man on his belly has a poor time drawing his gun. Once I'm satisfied you're clear of iron, you can get back on your feet."

"If I say no?"

"I'll plug your feet with lead. Nothing as damaging as hitting a kneecap, but it'll get your attention."

"You'd do that to a fellow lawman?"

He was grinning. I was watching his hands carefully.

"Yup," I said. "It's been that kind of week."

****

I marched him at gunpoint to the center of an old stone bridge over the Conemaugh River. His own Colt—a .45—was tucked in my waistband. I'd looked closely at his Texas Ranger badge, and was prepared to take him for a southern lawman. I was not prepared, however, to give up my advantage.

"This is as good a place as any," I said. "This time of night, folks seem few and far between. Lean on the edging, casual like, as if you're staring down on the water. I'll stay here, far enough way you won't try anything stupid. And if I need to put a bullet in your skull, it won't take much to heave you into the river."

"You this touchy on a habitual basis?"

"Nope. Just tired of avoiding the undertaker."

He whistled. "Sounds like an interesting story."

"It is. But I'll listen to yours first."

He turned his head toward me. This was a rangy man. Clean shaven, his face bulldog square. Matched my height, probably twenty pounds lighter.

"Name's Moses Muldoon," he drawled, extending his hand toward me. "Moses on account of folks in Texas figure I've been around since about his time."

I ignored his hand, maintaining the distance between us. "Sam Keaton," I said, "but I'm guessing you already knew that."

"Sure did. Asked around at the hotel. One of the boys was kind enough to point you out. Also kind enough to expect a dollar for it."

"Why not introduce yourself proper, instead of following a man around town?"

"Wanted to know where you might be going. I lose two good men, hardly knowing how or why. Then I hear two others have taken their names. Then I hear those same moved on to this steel mill town. Then I step off the train and hear they've been kilt. What I know about the situation can fit into a thimble. Seemed smart to try to get to know more before I introduced myself."

"You might recall I was the one who passed on the telegrams."

He shook his head. "This entire situation is so skunky I don't know who to believe."

"And I feel the same. With a minor difference."

"Which is?" he asked.

"I'm holding the gun."

Cloud cover edged across the moon. The river dulled into

invisibility. I stepped a half pace back of Moses Muldoon.

"Yes, indeed," he said. "You are holding the gun. And edgier than a mouse in a fox den anyway. It's enough to convince me you ain't part of all this."

"So tell me what you know." I wasn't going to let my guard down.

"First of all," he said, "I have traveled two days by train just to be able to speak with you. That should tell you plenty."

"It does. Tell me plenty more."

The moon broke loose of the clouds. He turned to stare down at the river again.

"We've been on McCabe's trail for almost a year now," Muldoon said. "He was in on the Guadalupe Pass robbery."

It was my turn to whistle. Meant it too. A gang had blown up the Texas & Pacific railway tracks, just west of the Guadalupe Pass, stopping the train on its way to El Paso, some 80 miles down the line. Every paper in the country had carried the story, gleefully including the lurid news that not a single man on the train had been left alive to testify to the events of one of the biggest robberies in the history of Texas.

Muldoon nodded. "Thought that might get your attention."

"News made it to the territories that twenty soldiers died," I said. "What were they guarding? Half a million in fresh treasury notes?"

"Sixteen soldiers. Three hundred thousand worth of notes. No surprise the story gets blown up some."

He rubbed his chin. "Still, it was something. First sign of trouble was the wires down. No messages getting through to El Paso. Then the train was late. Real late. So the Rangers were called in. Me and Stockton and French, we was with the riders sent down the tracks to see what had happened."

A picture came to mind. The arid desolation of west Texas and a long line of horses moving from telegraph post to telegraph post.

"The gang had chosen a curve through one of the canyons. Ripped all the track out. The train hit it a full speed during the night. Some kind of wreck, let me tell you. Freight cars piled one atop the other. And bodies flung in all directions."

The newspapers had found a dozen different ways to describe the scene, each more grisly than the description before.

"Thing was, when we rode up," Muldoon was saying, "we didn't think it was anything more than a wreck. Curve was at the bottom of a steep grade, we figured maybe the brakes had failed or the tracks had given way. We'd no idea the train carried treasury notes. Or the soldiers. Railroad and government folks had kept the shipment a good secret. Fact is, they even used an ordinary freight car to hold the soldiers and the notes."

Muldoon shook his head at his recollections. "We got our first idea something was wrong when we seen the first body. One of the engineers. Laying rag doll on the ground the way dead folks look, and Leroy sees the man didn't die from getting thrown from the wreck. Nope. He'd been shot in the back of the skull. Execution."

Back of the skull. I felt the prickle of cold blood again. Franky Leonard had been executed the same way.

"From what we could tell," Muldoon said, "anyone left alive after the gun fight was executed. We had some Apache trackers with us to read sign. The tracks showed a half dozen dead gang members had been dragged away. What it meant was we were left with no clues as to who'd done it. Dead ones gone. All witnesses dead. We had no idea where to start in tracking down the treasury notes."

"Except on figuring it was an inside job," I said.

Muldoon jerked his head in surprise.

"Find out who knew about the shipment," I explained. "A railroad person, maybe. Or someone from the treasury. Anybody who could pass on the schedule early enough to let a gang plan this out in plenty of time."

"Not bad," Muldoon allowed. "We did start there."

"My guess would be railroad."

"Why's that?"

"How many hundreds of miles of track?" I asked, not expecting an answer. "Seems to me there wouldn't be a lot of places in west Texas with a downgrade leading to a curve. Chances are, of anybody, a railroad person might know best where to stop a train in the dead of night."

"Smart man. Maybe we should pin a Ranger star to your vest."

Despite his friendly tones, I kept the Colt steady.

"Marshal, you hit the nail on the head. Pinkerton Detective Agency was hired to look into this. Turns out it was a railroad man."

"Tom McCabe."

"Yup. Vice-president of The Texas & Pacific Railway. He quit the company a week before the robbery, said he had to tend to his ailing mother back in New York. It took Pinkerton some time, as they had dozens of other directions to follow, and they finally got to checking his story. Discovered McCabe didn't have a mother. Nor father. By the time they unraveled things, they discovered he'd been orphaned at a young age. Lying about his mother was enough to get us looking real close into his life. To save me from getting long winded, why don't you take my word for it that they know McCabe's the one who set it up."

I nodded. "Seems to me someone that bright wouldn't be stupid enough to keep his name if he was on the run. He drifts into Laramie, a dusty, small town a thousand miles north. Hides out as a aimless drunk named Franky Leonard."

It seemed, however, the more answers I got, the more questions I had.

"Pardon my curiosity," I said. "How'd you or Pinkerton find out he'd moved on to Laramie?"

"Well," Moses Muldoon said, "Pinkerton's good at learning things. Crack the door for them, soon enough they've levered it wide open. All it took was finding one gang member. From there, asking questions to folks who knew him, they found another. Then another."

Out came a wolfish grin. "What the Texas Rangers is good at is hunting men. Quiet-like. Which we did, one by one. We didn't want bounty men chasing them."

"Or newspapers learning about it," I said. "There hasn't been a single paragraph about the robbery since last fall."

"Exactly. And there's good reason the railroad folks want all this kept quiet."

I waited.

"See, Marshal, the treasury notes ain't been recovered."

THIRTY-ONE

AS A WORKING MAN earned a dollar a day, three hundred thousand in missing treasury notes was a considerable prize. I could see why railroad folks wanted this on the hush. If bounty hunters ever got word of that kind of money. . . . Maybe they *had* gotten word.

"You sent some men north to bring in McCabe, right?" I asked, almost before I had completed the thought. Muldoon nodded. "Though we weren't certain they would. See, sometime late April, a letter reached us in San Antone. Denver postmark. It said if we were looking for Tom McCabe, we'd find him living in Laramie, calling hisself Franky Leonard."

"Spelled out clear, I'd say. Interesting letter, as all of it was true."

"Granted, but we had no way of knowing at the time. Still, McCabe, he was the one behind this all. He was big enough game it seemed best to chance it and send someone there. Again, quiet-like. Which was why we didn't telegram the local law to get involved."

"I'm with you to here," I said. "Except—"

"Except the two men who rode into Laramie weren't the two men I sent out. They were Texas Rangers all right, but not Leroy Stockton and William French."

Muldoon spit. "I had two other men in the outfit. Was never quite sure about them. They'd run an outlaw down. More often than not, bring him back dead and claim they'd not found the stolen money or stolen cattle. But they were crafty, those two. I could never prove what I figured."

He spit again. With vehemence. "Outfit like ours, word leaks. That letter was no secret among the Rangers. A day after Stockton and French rode north, these two said they were going into Mexico after renegade Apaches. Took two weeks, I finally realized they weren't coming back from Mexico."

Muldoon ignored my Colt and paced tight circles in his rage. He only stopped once—a horse and carriage crossing the bridge interrupted him and forced me to hide my Colt beneath my vest—as he told me what he'd been able to gather about Stockton and French.

North of Amarillo, a cowpoke had tracked maverick long-horns into a remote gully. Along with the cattle, he'd found two men, dead on their backs, tied down to stakes as if they'd been tortured by Apaches. Apache squaws have a reputation for disfiguring their victims—and taking pleasure in it. These two men were unrecognizable. What the Apaches had missed removing from their faces, vultures and a couple weeks of hot weather had finished.

The two men might never have been identified, but one of their horses had escaped, still bridled and saddled, and had wandered to a nearby ranch. The ranchers saw the Texas Ranger brand, and the description of the horse matched the one Stockton had been riding.

Muldoon had traveled the 500 miles from San Antonio to Amarillo. It triggered his suspicions that the two bodies were so entirely clean of any way to be identified. Their clothing had been stripped and stolen. He'd looked for a pucker scar he knew existed on French's right shoulder—an old arrow wound—and it had either been cut away or been lost to vultures. Muldoon did know that a couple of years earlier Stockton had lost the tips of two of his fingers to a shotgun that misfired. But all their fingers and toes had been removed, and Muldoon was unable to identify them that way.

Gut feeling told him, however, these were two of his men. He'd not heard from Stockton and French since their departure. Unusual in itself. The other two had disappeared completely.

By the time all of this came to light, seven or eight weeks had passed. Muldoon, in fact, was on the verge of sending more men to Laramie when he received my telegram with its inquiry about two Texas Rangers riding into town.

When Muldoon finished telling me all of this, I understood why he had taken a train journey lasting two full days to arrive in Johnstown. My second telegram would have told him little, save that Stockton and French were almost certainly dead, and that his two renegades were onto a trail to the missing treasury notes, a trail taking them east from Laramie. Muldoon wanted the renegades, and Muldoon wanted the treasury notes. Distance was not going to stop him from pursuing them.

Immediately upon arriving in Johnstown, Muldoon had identified the bodies—they were the renegades—and then he'd set about finding me, an easy enough task as he knew I was at the Washington Hotel.

I understood Muldoon's reason for deciding to follow me before approaching me. He was as frustrated and confused as I was, more so when I told him Franky Leonard was as dead as a man could be, that three men, including a physician, had clearly identified his body, and that no magician could fake the death of a body chopped into frozen parts. Because he knew so little, he wanted to get the lay of the land before trusting me.

We were both wondering, then, how all of this was tied together.

For now, I was prepared to believe Muldoon was telling

the truth. Tomorrow, however, I would send another telegram to San Antonio and easily be able to verify his story.
For that matter, I'd even request a return telegram with
Muldoon's description. I was getting to the point where I
could not trust anything anyone told me.

Muldoon's story rang with truth, however, and it explained much of the renegade Rangers' involvement to this
point. Only they were dead. And Franky Leonard was dead.
Aurelia had been possibly murdered—to all appearances an
unrelated death—with the enigma of an improbable connection to an industrialist so wealthy and powerful he was considering a run for state governor. And there were the attempts on my life. On Leigh's. What was behind all of this
that had gotten the Rangers killed?

As the cloud cover flitted patterns of silver light and darkness across the bridge and river, I pointed out all these puzzling aspects to Muldoon.

"I'd be pleased to work with you on this," he said. "Trouble is, it's difficult to be partners when one's holding a gun on
t'other."

I grinned. "Trouble is, you could just as easy be one of
them renegades who crossed into Mexico. And Stockton and
French truly could be Stockton and French, with you hoping
to find the missing treasury notes."

"That sir, is an odious accusation." His voice chilled with
restrained rage, so low I hardly heard. "Those two men were
friends. We fought Apaches shoulder to shoulder. I gathered
the pieces of their bodies and buried them myself, had to tell
their wives and children."

He began to walk toward me. "Shoot me now. And you'd
best shoot to kill. Because unless you retract what you said,
I'm wading in to fight."

The clatter of hooves at the end of the bridge told me
another carriage was approaching.

"You may have my apologies," I said. If I couldn't trust
my instincts on this, I was a useless man and better off dead

anyway. "You may also have your revolver."

He stopped, lowering his clenched fists. I tucked my Colt into my waistband. Reached for his. The clattering hooves became the staccato of a horse whipped into a trot.

"Sam!" A voice reached us from the end of the bridge. Louis?

He was running from behind a building.

"Sam!" He shouted something I couldn't understand above the clattering of hooves on stone.

Louis?

The carriage was maybe twenty yards away, moving briskly. Louis stopped. The moonlight only gave enough illumination for me to see movement of his arm.

A flash. A single clap of thunder. The whine of a bullet careening off stone.

Louis was shooting at us?

I spun, threw Moses his revolver, grabbed mine.

The carriage was almost upon us.

Then a man swung the door open and leaned out, hand extended. Unmistakable his intentions, for outlined against the pale gray of the stoneworks was an extension of his hand. In it—a huge pistol.

The carriage swept toward us.

I fired. Maybe before the explosion of his first shot, maybe after. Heat seared the outside of my gun arm. My Colt fell to the stone.

Then the carriage rushed past in a swoosh of spokes and iron wheel rims.

Louis was sprinting toward us again. "Muldoon!" I yelled. Louis was big, deadly. And armed when I wasn't. "Muldoon! Shoot!"

No reply. No reply of gunfire. And Louis was closing in.

I whirled. Muldoon! On the ground, writhing.

Louis had the revolver. I didn't. Muldoon's was too far away. Mine kicked away by the passing horse.

Fists lose to bullets.

I didn't see a choice.

I stooped, grabbed Muldoon by the shoulders. Heaved.

Brought him to the edge of the stone wall overlooking the river. Clutched his knees. Lifted him high and toppled him over into air. Didn't wait for a splash. Dove after him.

The water welcomed me like the darkness of sorrow.

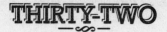

THIRTY-TWO

LEIGH HELD AN ENVELOPE in her hand when I met her downstairs for breakfast the next morning at a table near the window.

"Good morning," I said.

"It is not." Her voice had a ragged edge to it. I noticed the tender flesh around her eyes was swollen and red. Had she been crying hard? "Those two Texans, the ones you were chasing here. They're dead."

"I'd heard." I had no urge to tell her how I'd discovered their deaths. Nor did I have the urge to tell her about what I'd learned the night before about those very same Texas Rangers. I was not going to trust this woman.

"You'd heard? And you didn't tell me?"

Until I understood her role in all of this, I was going to tell her little. I wasn't going to tell her about diving into the river and surfacing to help Muldoon. Nor that Muldoon was safely mending in the residence of a private doctor, his lung nicked by the same bullet which had grazed my arm and left an ugly red burn. I wasn't going to tell her how Louis helped us out of the water. Nor why. For unknown to me, Louis had taken it upon himself to play the role of my guardian angel, staying nearby and out of sight as I traveled through Johns-town. Louis had seen the carriage, seen a man inside loading and priming his pistol. As the carriage gained speed toward Moses and me on the bridge, and with me unable to hear his shouted warnings, Louis had decided the fastest way to get me to draw my gun was by firing at the carriage wheels. He'd been running toward us to check our condition when I mis-judged his intentions by going over the bridge.

Leigh Tafton was hiding secrets from me. She was hot one moment, seductive and charming. Cold the next. I'd keep looking for answers all right, but had no intention of revealing anything to her.

"Don't you care about those dead Texans?" Her voice nearly broke. *Skilled actress?*

"It is not an ending I would have wished upon any men, regardless of what they attempted back in Laramie."

"Death is everywhere!" She too caught the hysteria verging in her voice. She gulped a breath. "It is not supposed to be this way."

"No?" I was asking mildly, but an inner excitement surged. How did she know which way it *should* happen? She must have realized the implications of her words, for she held up the envelope. "This is for you. From Cornelius Harper. I didn't realize your friends had the address of the Washington Hotel." Not much of a smile on her alluring face.

"I sent them a telegram letting them know where to find me. Just in case they needed to telegram any news."

"Such as?"

I shrugged. "You may recall I marshal in Laramie. I don't expect anything, but nothing would surprise me."

The table was set with fine china and a linen tablecloth. A waiter reached past my shoulder to pour coffee. I'd been here long enough that mail had already managed to cross the dis-tance between Laramie and Johnstown. It struck me I was weary of being pampered. Yet with the considerable amount which I did not know about Franky Leonard's death, I did not feel able to leave.

I reached for the envelope. Leigh withdrew it and tucked it under her plate.

"Samuel," she said, "would you ever be able to love me?"

Why is it that women seem to have little difficulty with any discussion on how a person feels? A man would have had to work up to a similar question, and even then stood an even chance of choking on it instead.

"Love you? For your money?" I asked, hoping to grab the reins of what I feared was already a runaway horse. "Or for your looks?"

"I am in no mood for banter. The events of the last few days have shaken me greatly. I see life differently. I almost—fear it."

I saw it as a stretch to make the connection between the issue of love and her fear of life. But then my gender put me at a disadvantage here.

"You have a strength," she said. "How? Why?"

I gave up on trying to make sense of her conversation. Especially before I'd first tasted coffee for the day. "People around us have died," she continued. "You nearly died in jail. Nearly died to poison. Yet I don't sense fear in you."

I sipped on coffee. Breakfast arrived, covered by the silver tops which the waiter dramatically pulled away to present ordinary eggs and ordinary ham. She remained silent as he dished the food onto our plates.

"Well . . ." she prompted me as he departed.

"If you make peace with death," I said, lifting my fork and choosing my words carefully, "much of the fear goes."

"And how have you made peace with death?"

"I know there is a reason for it."

She fixed intent eyes upon me. I would have preferred the eggs hot, and aside from a delay in eating, I did not feel comfortable sharing my thoughts. Not with someone I could not trust.

"Reason?" she asked.

Fork poised, I left my eggs untouched. "Death is the end of a long journey. Home. To God. If death has a reason, life has a reason. There's strength in knowing both. And when you think of passing through the curtain into eternity beyond, it puts this life into perspective."

"That's why money interests you so little?"

"That's why money interests me so little."

"Would you be able to love me?"

I set my fork down. Why is it a locomotive is easier to derail than a determined woman?

"Love you. Why should that matter? I doubt you love me."

"But I *could*," she said. "And it's not because of your looks or what I've come to think of you during our time together."

"Thank you for a special moment. I shall remember this breakfast forever."

"No," she said, "I mean I could love you because I decided to. Could you decide to love me?"

"Are we headed into territory with any landmarks to help me recognize my whereabouts?"

"Be patient with me, Samuel. I want a husband. I do not want to be alone. I think you would be an excellent husband. You could become accustomed to money."

I believe what she really meant was I could learn manners suitable to wealthy circles.

"I don't think love is that easy," I said.

"It's her, isn't it, Samuel." She spat the name out like an accusation. "Rebecca."

I took my first bite of eggs. No, it isn't Rebecca, I wanted to shout. But I smiled and swallowed instead of shouting. The eggs could have been lumps of candle wax.

And it wasn't Rebecca holding me back. No, she was gone from me forever. Hope for her, then, did not keep me from anyone else.

Yet, of course, it was Rebecca.

I'd heard an old-timer named Lefty Macgregor tell about the day he was out riding his horse, hunting for deer. He said close to half a day passes without spotting any game so he decides he might have better luck afoot. He comes upon a meadow, grass as deep as his cayuse's knees, with a dead cottonwood in the center as if it had been put there to stake his horse.

He dismounts. Instead of reining the horse to the cottonwood, he uses a long rope, expecting to be gone awhile and wishing to let the horse graze good and proper. He ties one end to a branch, the other to the horn of the saddle.

Mac said that he's less than quarter mile away from the meadow, and he sees a chokecherry bush moving a little farther down. There was no wind that day, so he figures right when he figures it might a bear busy berrying. A big silvertip, plenty of meat and bear grease. Mac moves within a couple hundred yards and fires his Sharps carbine, but only manages to comb the bear's hair. It spins and charges.

The Sharp was only a single-shooter, and Mac decides it'd be wise to turn the bear hunt into a foot race. He's real close to coming second, he said, when he reaches the meadow, grateful his horse had grazed to the near end of the meadow, not the far end. Old Mac said he didn't stop to bridle, but leaps directly onto the saddle.

About this time, Mac said, the cayuse sees what's hurrying the rider. The cayuse needs no spurs to get a good jump and for the first hundred yards Mac thinks he's out of trouble. Then whomp, next he knows he's flat on his back, horse almost squashing him flat as it drops out of the sky. Mac's trying to decide if it was a hurricane or cyclone, then remembers the rope tied to the cottonwood. Only good news is that it's enough confusion and horse squealing to turn the silvertip the other way, as it's tired itself plenty by then anyway. Mac waits a couple hours for his head to stop ringing, especially as the horse wobbles pretty good too for a while. Then they continue on their way.

Mac paused at that point in the story, scratching himself thoroughly before delivering what he'd worked his way toward.

Seemed that for months he had to walk that cayuse for a hundred yards before he could spur him into anything more than a lope, and even then the horse would be looking back to see if it was tied to anything. Moreover, Mac swore, he could stake the horse to a hairpin and it would stay.

After Rebecca and last summer, that was me, staked to a hairpin.

"Samuel, you haven't answered me. It's Rebecca, isn't it?"

"To tell the truth, it's a long rope and a horse dropping from the sky."

"I told you I am in no mood for your humor." She grabbed her napkin from her lap and flung it on the table as she rose. "You are the most troublesome man I have ever met."

I reached across the table for the envelope tucked beneath her plate.

THIRTY-THREE

THE ENVELOPE held two letters. I read the one from Jake first, sipping on my coffee as I strained to make out the splotchy ink scratches in ragged lines across the page.

Sam, you'll forgive my handwriting as I was never good at ciphering with my other hand before the stallion got me and this one's had even less practice. Not much to tell, except for what you'll be reading for yourself anyway, and that's plenty I reckon, don't you?

I can inform you that I've had a real bad run in poker lately and barely made over a hundred dollars since you departed. Don't get the wrong idea because it's a real certainty I don't miss you none, but that hound of yours is carrying on something dreadful without your ugly carcass to comfort him, so you best get back soon's you can. Your friend, Jake.

I grinned, so wide a white-haired old lady across the restaurant caught it and commenced to waving her fingertips in my direction and winking in return. I never figured I was much of a prize to look at, so it gave me a healthy fear of her desperation for company. I pretended to wave at someone past her, and when she craned her head to see who I meant, I dropped my eyes quick and got to Doc's letter.

Samuel, I want you to know I haven't mentioned a word about your eastern travels with a rich, beautiful heiress. You are there to look into the death of Franky Leonard, and that is all which has been said about you. As for that heiress, well Leigh, as I recall, had a certain light in her eyes when she asked about you. Had I known then of the change of events, of course, I would not have encouraged her admiration of you.

As it is, I pray you have made no promises placing you in a difficult position. However, do not blame yourself if you have, for you could not have known. Godspeed, my friend, if you are able to return to Laramie upon receiving these letters. You are well missed here. Cornelius.

Postscript: Kam Yee Chung inquires fondly after you. He instructed me to inform you he would be honored to prepare a celebration upon your return.

I read and reread the letters, with my next cup of coffee untouched and cold before I gave up trying to make sense of the puzzling aspects of the letters.

What had Jake been referring to that I would be reading for myself and was plenty news?

Was it the same reason Doc had warned me about Leigh? And what had Doc learned about Leigh? How could he have learned something in Laramie which I was incapable of learning here? And why, if I was in danger from Leigh, hadn't he told me more?

Altogether, it was disturbing.

I worried it also meant Leigh had kept something else back from me, along with the implication of her rash words in regards to the Texans' deaths. Was it another letter which would shed light on this situation? A letter which had been sent along with Doc and Jakes' notes? The more I thought of it, the more I was convinced. After all, Leigh had removed pages from her sister's diary to keep certain information from me.

Yet asking Leigh would serve no purpose. She would deny it, of course, and at the same time learn that I had further suspicions. It would be better for her to underestimate me, although I wasn't confident she had any reason to fear my useless efforts thus far.

So I would keep my mouth shut and my eyes open. And my Colt .44-.40 in easy distance of my right hand.

THIRTY-FOUR

MORTY," *I SAID*, "I'm looking for information."

"No 'good morning'? 'No how are you?' "

Mortimer Shaw was sitting behind his desk, his spindly arms resting across the ball of his belly. I'd raised my voice to speak, because the presses outside his office churred and clanked. Not, however, with newspaper production. Today's issue of the *Daily Democrat* had long since hit the streets. I'd noticed instead the papers now coming off the press were a copy of the speeches from the latest senate proceedings; as this was probably a lucrative, on-going contract, I decided it paid to have well-defined political leanings.

"Good morning," I said. "How are you. By the way, I'm looking for information."

"It is a good morning. And I'm fine." He took his attention away from the papers on his wide desk. He removed his spectacles and rubbed his face with both hands before he spoke again, a wry grin to match his voice. "Might this be information on trade?"

"Same trade as before. Before I leave town, you'll hear plenty." Which couldn't be soon enough.

"Sure, cowboy." His grin became sly. "Or maybe I should

ask instead for a chance to write your story. Folks here love legends."

"Somehow your train jumped a track."

"Samuel, Samuel. I'm a newsman. Did some of my own asking around. All the way back to Laramie. Seems you've got a couple of stories of your own. Gunfighting reputation. A governor's pardon after years on the run. Last summer's involvement in the Sioux uprising."

He wagged his index finger at me. "I believe you kept quiet because you knew I'd hound you. Sioux uprising indeed! Folks can't hardly believe Custer lost his stand at the Little Bighorn. We ran it front page every day for two weeks. I could run me a dozen more stories on it now, just by asking you what it was like a year earlier. I'd sell thousands more papers and—"

"Hear about the two men found shot dead in the lower part of town?"

"Inside front page," he said without pause, untroubled by my curt interruption. "This morning's edition. Couldn't learn enough about it for the front page. Not sure many readers might care anyway, that part of town."

"Both men were Texas lawmen," I said. "You knew that?"

He leaned forward. *"Texas lawmen?"*

I nodded yes.

He grabbed a fountain pen, dabbed it in a bottle of ink and poised it above a sheet of paper.

I shook my head no. "Before I leave town, remember?"

"I can make it worth your while," he said. "Unless you already know."

"Know what?"

"If I tell you, it doesn't leave me much to trade."

"If you think I'm budging an inch, you're mistaken." Leigh Tafton wasn't going to get anything from me. Last thing I wanted was for her to get it from a newspaper instead.

He sighed. "What kind of information?"

"I heard Blackburn rid his mansion of all the servants who worked there before Aurelia died. Maybe you can help me find some of those servants."

"Are you hiring?"

"Very humorous," I said. "Ever consider giving Mark Twain a run for his money?"

"As I believe you meant to mock me, I'll ignore that."

"The servants?" I asked.

"It should be easy enough. If the rumors are true, he's gone through his staff twice since in the last six months. Once in January. Once after Aurelia's drowning. I'll ask around for you. I can leave word at the hotel."

"I appreciate that," I said. "But don't bother with the hotel." Leigh had taken my letters from the front desk. The disturbing implication was she could take my messages and my telegrams. It had crossed my mind that Hawkthorne could very well have already replied to my request for information on Blackburn. Did Leigh already have his return telegram?

"If not the hotel, then where can I find you?"

"You can't," I said. "I've already booked a train passage."

"You said you would tell me the whole story before you left town!"

"Jump right down from that cactus," I said. "I'm headed east. To Harrisburg."

"The capital? Why?"

"That's the other information I wanted. What's the name of the orphanage you heard Blackburn supports?"

He studied my face. "What are you on to?"

"Nice try. Deal hasn't changed."

"An orphanage set up by some dowager. Husband set up one of the first banks. Old money, you know." He snapped his fingers. "Clark. Gladys Clark. The orphanage should carry her name."

"Thank you." I went to tip my hat, remembered this time halfway up that Louis had it, and saluted to spare myself the embarrassment of grabbing for a tip that didn't exist.

"Keaton," he said.

It stopped me halfway out of his office.

"I told you I had something in trade. If you hadn't already heard."

"Yes?"

"Another man was found dead. It reached me too late to make this morning's paper."

"I take it he didn't die in his sleep."

Mortimer Shaw was studying my face again. I decided it was the kind of look other men give when they are trying to decide if you filled your flush.

"They found him just off the Franklin Street bridge."

If Shaw hadn't prepared me to keep my face blank, I would have twitched. The Franklin Street bridge. That's where Moses Muldoon and I had been standing during our conversation last night.

"He'd been shot, Samuel. In the belly. Died slow, they say. The blood had pooled on the carriage floor."

"Carriage?"

"Did I forget to mention the carriage? With a bullet hole in the door?"

"You did forget."

"My apologies. It was a horse and carriage down past the bridge. The horse was eating roses out of someone's front garden. Still attached to the carriage. Naturally, someone thought to look inside. And there he was. You wouldn't know anything about this, would you?"

Shaw was sharp. He'd sat on this the entire time we'd talked, patiently waiting to hear if I would say anything to link myself to the carriage.

"That's a peculiar question," I said. "Why would you ask me such a thing?"

"I'll note you didn't answer the question directly."

"I assume there must be a reason behind your question. And I also assume the reason will be of particular interest."

"It should," he said. "This man came into town on the same train you did."

"Really?" It was difficult to keep a poker face. Somewhat because I did not want Shaw to know I'd been involved. And more so, much more so, because I had little doubt I'd pulled the trigger to punch a bullet hole in the carriage door. Carrying the burden of another man's death is a slow, sad horror which never leaves.

"Really. In fact, he traveled with you all the way here from Laramie."

I refused to give Shaw the satisfaction of knowing how much my curiosity burned. So I waited.

"While he was alive," Shaw said, "he worked as a manservant for Leigh Tafton."

THIRTY-FIVE

DOES A TOWN take on the personality of its river? I'd been in mining towns, high in the mountains, where the water tumbled and bounced from boulder to boulder; the men there lived the same way: fast, hard, relentless in pursuit of their dreams. I'd seen towns like Pueblo in Colorado, where the Arkansas was a muddy brown trickle; its residents gave life the same effort, rousing themselves only to wave away flies. In Johnstown, the Connemaugh curved efficiently through the narrow valley, a practical tool well used by the industries on its banks.

The Susquehanna River at my feet was giving me cause to think such wandering thoughts. It was a broad river, at first glance almost sedate. Yet as I looked down from my bench upon its eastern bank, I saw the power of the massive dark current as it tugged against a fallen tree. This river would hold its secrets.

Harrisburg too had the same feel. Behind me on cobblestone streets, the pedestrians and carriages moved with restrained elegance among the town squares shadowed by tall brick buildings. Yet there was the sense of power in this town, the feel of old money, frowning bankers and unsmiling judges. As capitol of one of the most powerful states in the union, Harrisburg, I was sure, held its share of intrigue, mystery, and old secrets.

I hoped to unearth one of its secrets. Not an earth-shaking secret, and insignificant, perhaps, to anyone but myself, but a secret nonetheless.

Mortimer Shaw had mentioned Frederick Blackburn's contribution to an orphanage in Harrisburg. That had not been significant at the time, but upon reflection, it was odd for a man with his reputation for stinginess.

Although I still had no understanding of the connection —and I imagined arguing through this with Jake or Doc— Frederick Blackburn was connected to Tom McCabe, the man who had lived in Laramie as Franky Leonard. After all, Blackburn had traveled west in the dead of winter to visit the man just before he was killed and cut into frozen parts.

At this point, were I back in Laramie, Doc would nod, Jake would shrug, both indications I should continue until I arrived at where I was headed.

I also knew the entire matter was important enough that Moses Muldoon had ridden a train all the way up from Texas. The Rangers were somehow part of this. And one of the things Muldoon had mentioned about Tom McCabe was his past as an orphan.

All of this was a ball of yarn, with the answers to Aurelia's death, McCabe's death, and the murders of the others hidden in the center. Until now, there had been precious few loose ends to grab and pull. But it could not be a coincidence, two references to an orphanage in Harrisburg from two widely different sources. Even if it happened that this loose string was nothing, it was much better to be here, hardly more than a hundred miles down the track from Johnstown, than to be uselessly pacing my room in the Washington Hotel.

Would Doc or Jake have agreed? I hoped so, and hoped even more I would find enough answers to return soon to

Laramie. I was tiring of heavy, sweltering air, of a low-hanging, white, hazy sky and of thickly foliaged hills which blocked my view in all directions. My body and soul belonged back in the freedom of the wide open territories and the pure air of higher skies. I wanted home.

****

The Gladys Clark Memorial Home for Orphaned Children was a brick mansion set halfway up a gently sloping hill. It had been a fifteen-minute walk to reach it from the river. The humid heat had one benefit; my muscles remained loose, and the walk had been nearly painless. Most of my bruises had disappeared, and Currie's blackjack beating had finally faded into a shivering memory.

A brick sidewalk led up to the home. No weeds grew between the cracks, the bushes on each side were neatly trimmed, and the large lawn of the grounds manicured. It spoke much for the caretakers of these children.

A small, engraved, brass plaque, set into a rounded boulder, also spoke for the orphanage. Gladys Clark, I read, in the later years of her life at the turn of the century had begun to take in homeless children, donating the mansion and grounds upon her death, along with an annual stipend from interest earned by money held in a separate trust fund. I thought of Leigh, and wondered if she would understand the world was not about money, but about how one used or misused it.

I walked up the brick path, grateful for shade provided by large oaks lining both sides. On the veranda—as wide as most streets—I paused. This was too peaceful. I had expected the laughter and screaming of children, not the settled air of a country estate.

I lifted the knocker and let it drop. Twice. It was loud enough that it stilled the chirping of birds in the bushes around the veranda.

Long minutes later, the door creaked open. I looked down

on a shriveled woman with unnaturally dark hair. It took only seconds to understand she wore a wig, skewed sloppily atop a face collapsed with age.

She, in turn, had craned her head upward to stare at me. "Afternoon, ma'am. I—"

"Peddlers must make appointments here." Her voice was surprisingly strong. No warble. No croak. "There were no appointments on the book today. Good-bye."

She shut the door in my face.

I blinked. Grinned. Lifted the knocker and let it drop. Four times.

She opened it. Craned her head upward again. "The children are in class at present. Please desist."

That, at least, explained the quiet.

"Ma'am, I—"

"What are you peddling?"

"Do you see peddler's wares, ma'am?"

"With my cataracts, I can barely see enough to know whether I'm awake or asleep."

I caught the sweet thickness of sherry on her breath. That, of course, was her business, not mine.

"Ma'am, I'd like to see the administrator."

"You're not one of those fools from the school board are you?"

"No ma'am. I am a duly sworn marshal from the territory of Wyoming." I said it on impulse, hoping curiosity might sway her into inviting me inside.

"A marshal! Ever been in a gunfight? Ever fought off redskins? Ever met Bill Cody?" Her wrinkles danced with her enthusiasm.

"Yes. Yes. And yes."

She beckoned me inside. "Iced tea, marshal? I'll bring you some while you're sitting in her office. It's a hot spell."

"Iced tea would be fine," I said. A long hallway, richly finished with burnished walnut, stretched ahead of us.

"Care for a little nip in it? The color of the tea stays the same. The old battleax won't know."

I did care for a nip. The whiskey urge, like my love for Rebecca, would always be with me. Especially with my new heaviness at the regret of shooting a man on the Franklin bridge.

"I'll pass on the offer," I said. "But I appreciate it nonetheless."

She tottered on ahead of me, informing me in great detail about many of Buffalo Bill Cody's greatest exploits, all learned from Ned Buntline dime novels, all highly improbable. Bill was a fine man—I'd been on the hunting crews with him as the Union Pacific laid track through the territories a decade earlier—but he would be the first to admit the dime novel tales were highly exaggerated to please an eastern audience like the old lady in front of me. I was beginning to understand that easterners had a falsely romantic vision of the land west of the Mississippi, and aside from the distorted pictures given them by dime novels, I could understand why. A man here was hemmed in by buildings and crowds morning 'till night. It never hurt to dream of freedom, and, many as were the drawbacks of the territories, it did offer freedom.

"What is it a Wyoming marshal wants in an orphanage?" she asked. This woman shuffled. An ambitious snail could outrace her. I fervently hoped the administrator's office was less than a day's journey down the long hallway.

"I'm not quite sure," I said. "I'm hoping to learn about a man named Frederick Blackburn."

"Frederick Blackburn!" She stopped. It took her some time and complicated shuffling, but she eventually got her body around to facing me.

"No sense in trying out those questions, Marshal. She's got a firm policy never to discuss an orphan's background unless it's folks looking to adopt a child. And Frederick Blackburn, why she'd say even less about him. Especially as he hasn't donated a penny since the February when his wife brought a cashier's note herself. And we've come to rely on it."

I was struggling to absorb that when another implication hit me. "Frederick Blackburn was an orphan here?"

"Hush. I'd best get you outside, Marshal. It takes little enough to set her off. She'd be nattering at me all day if she knew I'd even said that."

She peered ahead. Once she'd established she'd picked the right direction, she began the painfully slow shuffling toward the door.

I followed. After all, what choice did I have? It would be a simple matter to outpace this old woman and physically get my body in the administrator's office, but what would I accomplish from there if the administrator would not reply to my questions?

I followed slowly.

My entire tour of the orphanage had consisted of the main entrance and the first quarter of a hallway. Not much progress.

I decided however, I could make a safe conclusion about the elfish old woman in front of me. The administrator was efficient and orderly. The grounds told me that. The uncluttered hallway told me that. Yet the administrator still employed a slow, nearly blind, sherry-tipping old woman. There could be only one reason for it. Loyalty, perhaps ensured by a foundation stipulation.

"Was Gladys Clark a fine woman?" I asked.

The old woman stopped again. She lifted her head, perhaps staring into distant memories, but did not turn to face me. "Yes, she was, young man. I was in my teens when she took me in. I miss her dearly, and it's been fifty years since her death."

"You've been here all that time?"

She tucked her head down and began her determined shuffling toward the door. That was her goal, and sure as shooting, she was going to get there.

"I was here when the first orphans came in to the mansion. Haven't missed a single day since."

I thought of my marshal's badge, pinned inside my vest. I removed it and warmed it in my palm.

When we reached the door, I lifted one of her frail wrists and pressed it in her hand, closing her fingers over it.

"This is a marshal's badge, ma'am. The real thing. It's been pinned to my vest through gunfights, injun fights, flash floods, and cattle stampedes. It would be an honor, ma'am, if you accepted it as a gift from me."

"Gift?" Suspicion tinged her strong voice.

"A gift. As a token of appreciation for any time we might spend outside in conversation."

"You want me to tell you about Frederick Blackburn." An accusation.

"Yes, ma'am."

"You have anything else to offer along with your marshal's badge?"

Louis had my Stetson. I needed the Colt .44-40 tucked in the back of my waistband. "I could mail you some wanted posters of the toughest desperadoes in the territories."

Her shuffling did not abate. After all, we did need to reach the door. "Make sure you send an even dozen," she said. "Because what I know will make it worth your while."

THIRTY-SIX

I *WAS ON THE AFTERNOON TRAIN* within the hour, headed back to Johnstown. This was another marvel about the East. Train traffic. And train punctuality. In Laramie, one eastbound train a day passed through, one westbound train. A conductor never knew what might delay his schedule. Perhaps a herd of buffalo crossing the tracks, although that was getting rarer these days. Or tracks washed out. Mud slides in the passes. The occasional bandit attack. Not here. Trains crisscrossed between Philadelphia and Pittsburgh so frequently that boarding a train to get to Johnstown was as easy as hiring a carriage.

I took a seat by the window and let the trees become a green, unfocused blur as I stared at the passing countryside and dwelt upon the implications of what I had learned.

A story came to mind. I hadn't been there on the stagecoach from Sante Fe to Durango, but had heard about it from an old cowpoke who swore every word was true.

Ben Holladay, who ran the Overland Stage, was infamous for his orders to drivers: "Pack 'em in! Pack 'em in like sardines!" This added greatly to the discomfort, for coaches were often little more than crude wagons with canvas sides.

The Overland wagons were considered the worst. Holladay hated spending a nickel more than necessary and had a habit of establishing a rival service along a given route and carrying passengers for one-tenth the going fare. After his competitor folded, he'd raise his fares higher than before, cut back on the run schedule, and remove his best coaches from the route. Without suspension, the coach rides were bone-jarring nightmares on wooden bench seats. As the coaches moved through hills and over mountains on roads barely more than rutted trails, passengers endured bad weather, choking dust, breakdowns, runaway horses, and occasional drunk drivers. And, of course, stick-up men.

The Sante Fe to Durango run was notorious for road bandits. While the first part of the run out of Sante Fe followed the relatively flat valley of the Rio Grande, as the road climbed to reach Abiquiu, the treacherously steep and narrow trail curved through rugged hill country ideal for ambushes.

As the old cowpoke explained in his story, the passengers on this particular run had good reason to be nervous. They'd heard of three stick-ups on this stretch in the previous ten days. All seven passengers discussed with great animation and nervousness, their chances of getting through unscathed.

One of the passengers, a plump, middle-aged woman in a gray dress, could barely sit, she was so scared. She informed the other passengers she carried the last of her money, fifty dollars that her widowed daughter in Durango desperately needed.

A gentleman in a bowler hat across from the plump woman gave her sound advice. As he practiced shuffling a deck— one of many signs he was a professional gambler—he told her to divide her roll into two, and stick one half in each of in her shoes, but to save a couple of dollars for her pocket, because once the robbers found those few dollars there, they wouldn't think of looking elsewhere for the remainder.

Sure enough, they hadn't gone five miles into the hills when the coach stopped suddenly and they heard a rough voice bark, "Step out folks, and keep your hands up while you're doin' it."

The cowboy told me they all knew what they were up against, and weren't slow getting out. All the bandits wore bandannas to keep their faces hidden. One had the driver covered, another had the reins of the horses. Two more kept shotguns trained on the passengers.

The gambler calmly dusted his fine suit with both hands before stepping forward and motioning the leader of the bandits to the side where they spent a few minutes in whispered conversation.

None of the other passengers heard what the gambler said, but when the holdup men finished taking money and jewelry from all the passengers, one turned back and pointed the shotgun at the plump woman's belly. "Ma'am," he said, "why don't you step out of your shoes."

She did, and he grabbed them and shook the money into his hands. With a tip of the hat he returned her shoes, and all the bandits rode away, disappearing into a nearby canyon.

The coach ride continued. Inside the carriage, the plump lady sobbed and sobbed and all the rest of the passengers stared at the gambler in the bowler hat. He stared back calmly, but the tension was building, as coaches don't have much interior room and everyone was thinking the same thought.

Finally, the cowboy blurted out the question all shared. "Hey, mister," he said, "what was the low talk between you and that there stick-up man?"

Without even blinking, the gambler said, "I told him the twenty dollars I had was my entire bankroll, but if he'd pass it up, I'd let him know where to find fifty. He agreed, and I took him at his word. I'm not ashamed. If you don't take care of yourself, nobody else will. And as you might have noticed, those skunks took my twenty dollars anyway."

The rest of the passengers—all men except the sobbing woman—became wolfy at that point. No more than a couple miles passed before they began to discuss stopping the coach again and looking for a rope.

"Who needs a rope," one of the passengers said loudly. "If this feller is as light in pounds as he is in principle, we can hang him with thread and we'll probably still have to put a boulder in his pants to give him weight."

The man on the other side of the cowboy drew a short-barreled revolver and trained it on the gambler's chest, and they shouted for the driver to rein in the horses.

Still, the gambler just smiled peacefully.

They rousted him out of the coach. The middle-aged lady sobbed louder, saying she didn't want him strung up, but that time in jail would be enough. It didn't help. The other passengers—mad at being trimmed and with no way to track down the bandits—were looking for any blood to satisfy themselves.

As they searched for a high branch to let the gambler swing, he finally spoke again.

"If you folks will let me play out my hand," he said, "you'd find out who wins, but if you're bound to, go through with this hanging."

They were bound.

They had the noose knotted and the rope dangling from a strong branch. The traditional method for a necktie party like this was to set the man in a horse, drop the noose over his head, and slap the horse's haunches or fire a pistol into the air. When the spooked horse jumped into a gallop, the man would drop.

As the stagecoach driver worked a horse loose from the stagecoach team, the gambler spoke again.

"If you're this determined to hang me," he said. "I'll be taking off my boots. It's part of the promise I made to my dearly beloved and departed mother, not to die with my boots on."

He set his bowler aside—all the while under the watchful eye and ready revolver of one the passengers. The gambler slipped off his boots and set them beside the bowler.

He didn't appear scared or nervous at all. He turned to the middle-aged woman, who was wide-eyed at the seriousness of the situation. "Ma'am, I've been a gambler all my life, whereas none of these men ever played anything but solitaire. They don't understand much about bluff. And they don't know it's honor among gamblers to split their winnings in the middle if someone stakes them."

The middle-aged woman in the grey dress could make no sense of his statement. She simply nodded hesitantly.

"And ma'am," the gambler continued, "by staking me your fifty dollars, I feel I owe you half the winnings."

He leaned over to reach into his socks, but the man with the pistol ordered him off it, as a sock was an ideal place to hide a derringer.

The gambler asked the middle-aged lady if she would unroll his socks. It was such a strange request, he had to ask her three times. When she finally did reach down and dig into his socks, she discovered five one-hundred dollar bills in his left sock, and five others in the right one.

"First five hundred is yours," he said to her. "And I hope everyone here agrees it's fair I keep the other five hundred for myself."

It didn't take but a moment for all the passengers to realize the sly trick the gambler had played on the road bandits. The plump middle-aged woman commenced to sobbing again, this time with gratitude, and the others rushed around to congratulate the gambler. And when the stage coach resumed its journey, the passenger who had first suggested the lynching bee dug out a flask of whiskey and began to pass it around to show there were no hard feelings.

Whether the story was true didn't make any difference to me. I'd enjoyed hearing it, and told it occasionally myself when it seemed like folks had time for a story.

It meant much more to me now, however. The gambler's deception had been skillful because the stick-up men had been convinced they'd found what they were looking for, and

more importantly, were also convinced they'd found everything there was to find. Once convinced, they'd departed,
with no clue the real treasure remained safely behind.

That's the phrase which stuck in my mind as the train
steamed upward in the wooded highlands of the Allegheny
Mountains. *The stickup men had been convinced they'd found
what they were looking for, and more importantly, were also
convinced they'd found everything there was to find.*

I now believed that Franky Leonard—I had difficulty
thinking of him as Tom McCabe—had played a version of the
gambler's trick.

In fact, because of what I'd learned from the old lady at
the The Gladys Clark Memorial Home for Orphaned Children, I also believed I knew what had happened in Franky
Leonard's shack the previous January. Thanks to the old
woman, much of the other information I'd learned recently
made sense. There was a reason Aurelia noted in her diary
Blackburn's visit to the territories and the gleam in his eye
and his awakened hunger for her upon his return. I understood why Blackburn had fired his servants in January, and
why he'd stopped taking Aurelia to high-profile social functions. I believed I knew too why he'd withdrawn from pursuit
of the governorship. And why Aurelia had been murdered.

When I added it all up, it also gave me reason to understand many of Leigh's actions, including her inordinate anger
at Blackburn's canceled appointment.

All of this would be simple to prove too.

If I could find a way to reach Blackburn.

THIRTY-SEVEN

IT TOOK TWO DAYS to decide how to break through the barrier of wealth which protected Frederick Blackburn. Even then I had help in the form of the letter which finally reached me from Boston.

It was two days in which I had learned from Mortimer Shaw that the former servants of the Blackburn estate had scattered from Johnstown; none could be found still living within the valley. This information confirmed further my suspicions.

It was two days in which Leigh Tafton avoided my company. Just as well, I might have confronted her with some of my guesses.

It was also two days in which Louis and I spent time visiting Moses Muldoon. The three of us traded stories for hours, Louis matching each one of our western tales with an equally exaggerated yarn about circus life. The Texas Ranger was a tough bird. When he heard how I finally intended to deal with Blackburn, he insisted on joining, even as he was coughing spots of blood.

I told Muldoon no, and because of that, was alone as I dropped the knocker on the door of the Blackburn mansion, punctual for my two o'clock appointment on a drizzly afternoon, protected from the rain by the alcove.

"I am expected," I said when the butler opened the door. I extended him a calling card. Mortimer Shaw had agreed to print some for me at the *Daily Democrat*, chafing at my refusal to tell him why.

"Ah, yes," the butler said after he scanned my card. "Mr. Elliot Hawkthorne. Mr. Blackburn expects you indeed. Please step inside."

I did, removing my overcoat and top hat. It had cost Leigh several hundred dollars to dress me as a high financier. She, unlike Shaw, had neither grumbled nor asked questions. She'd simply agreed with tired resignation.

The butler craned his head upward, briefly staring at me from behind his thick spectacles. It gave his eyes the appearance of pickled eggs inside a jar.

The tight lines of his prissy mouth opened in a small, startled "o."

"You were with—"

I was hoping the butler would not recognize me, dressed as I was and here in an entirely different situation. It had been a futile hope. Fortunately, the recognition had been delayed until I was inside the mansion.

He began backing away from me. I grabbed his collar with my left hand. "Yes?"

"You were with . . . with . . . Baily Pense. And that miserable woman. . . ." His voice trailed off because he noticed my Colt .44-.40. Difficult not to notice, as I'd pulled it from my waistband and thumbed the hammer back.

He dropped my overcoat and top hat, wilting like a flower in a furnace.

"Pretend like it's the first time I've held a revolver," I said, tightening my grip on his collar. "We'll both be afraid one of these nasty, big bullets might accidentally put a hole in your lovely black suit."

"Mr. Blackburn does not carry gold or jewels in the mansion. You would be wisest to turn and leave now while you have the opportunity."

I admired his renewed efforts at bravery. But could not afford it.

"This is not a robbery." I turned him and placed the barrel of the pistol between his shoulder blades. "This is an arrest."

I'd wrestled long and hard trying to decide the best way to approach this. I'd finally realized what so often is true about any difficult situation. The most direct manner is the best.

"You will lead me to Mr. Blackburn because you have no choice," I continued. "You will not try to warn him as we approach, because if you do you will bleed through the holes these nasty, big bullets put in your lovely black suit."

He seemed to understand. "Mr. Blackburn is in the library. I shall lead you there straightaway."

Straightaway meant an awkward tandem shuffle, as I maintained my grip on his collar with my left hand, kept the revolver against his back with my right hand. He walked gingerly, the walk of a man who did not know that for safety reasons I only carry five bullets in the Colt, with the hammer always down on the empty sixth cylinder.

He took us down a long, wide hallway. Dark walnut panels to finish the walls. Ponderous oil paintings. Persian rugs. Delicate crystal sculptures.

No other servants crossed from any of the corridors we passed. The silence was almost uncanny, broken only by the distant clanging of a grandfather clock.

"Please do not misinterpret my next move," the butler squeaked. "Very soon I will stop and turn left to lead you to the library."

"Your caution is exemplary," I said. "I commend you for it. I also advise you to retain it for the remainder of the afternoon."

The library's paneled doors were opened outward for us.

In the manner he'd warned, the butler spun sharply to his left, taking us into the library.

It was a room larger than my entire hotel suite, lined on three walls with books on shelving at least 20 feet high.

The fourth wall of the library was not wall, but windows, cathedral-like in their immensity. Oiled with the water of rain, these windows gave me a blurry view of the Little Conemaugh and the green valley hills stretching up the other side into a gray mist.

Frederick Blackburn faced away from us, looking out his windows, hands behind his back, left hand clenching the right wrist. A suitably nonchalant, yet business-like pose of the lord of the manor, pretending not to know his visitor was studying him. I might have been impressed, had I been here under the pretext which had gotten my appointment. And had I not known what I did about the man.

The butler coughed to get Blackburn's attention.

Blackburn turned toward us, his face lighting up with a jovial grimace of greeting. He took a step in our direction, extending his hand. "Thank you, Randolph," he said to the butler, "you may return to your duties."

I suppose to Frederick Blackburn there was nothing yet unusual about the situation. He saw Randolph his butler. He saw me standing behind Randolph, perhaps too close behind, but not so close to draw attention. And my Colt, of course, was hidden from his view.

Then Blackburn saw my face. And froze. Only momentarily, but he froze.

He reinstated the jovial grimace and hailed me. "Elliot Hawkthorne. So very glad we could meet. I've heard much about you, of course. And now I can see the legend for myself."

So his first reaction was going to be a bluff. Which didn't matter to me.

"Sit," I told the butler. I pushed him into a nearby chair which dwarfed him. "Stay."

I raised the Colt toward Frederick Blackburn, stopping him a half dozen steps away.

"Hello Franky," I said. "Quite the improvement, isn't it, compared to the last place you lived."

THIRTY-EIGHT

"**T**HIS IS OUTRAGEOUS," he sputtered. "Waving a pistol at me in my own residence."

"Get in the chair next to Randolph. And keep your hands in your lap."

"No one orders Frederick Blackburn in his own library."

I pulled the trigger. It clicked dry on the empty cylinder. Blackburn flinched.

I cocked the Colt again. "Notice how the cylinder turned?" I asked. "That means I now have a bullet in place. Next time I pull the trigger, you'll hear a big bang. That's how these things work."

Slowly, trying to maintain dignity, the man moved into the chair beside the butler.

"Thank you," I said.

Without removing my eyes from Blackburn, I reached behind me for the unlocked handcuffs hanging from my belt. I tossed them to Randolph.

"Lock his wrists," I told the butler.

"Touch me and you will be dismissed forthwith," Blackburn said to the butler.

Randolph hesitated.

I had explained how a Colt revolver worked. I could continue my helpful manner. "Randolph, by nightfall you will be looking for new employment anyway, as your employer will be on a train, headed for the noose in Texas. May I suggest it is much easier finding new hire when all of your body parts are intact."

He handcuffed Frederick Blackburn.

Only then did I begin to relax. I swung a chair from the opposite wall of the library and slid it closer to Blackburn and his trembling butler.

I sat and took a close look at what Franky Leonard had become.

The Franky Leonard I remembered had worn clothes crusted with filth. His hair had been wild, unkempt, like a buffalo hunter three months on the plains. He'd been stubble-whiskered in gray, greasy patches, his high cheekbones and forehead smeared with accumulated grease.

The Franky Leonard in front of me now resembled much more closely the photograph of Tom McCabe I had first seen in the hands of Stockton and French during their visit to my marshal's office in Laramie. He wore a suit and bowtie, with a laundered and starched white shirt. His hair was clipped short again, with the difference that it was now parted on the left side, not down the middle. Unlike the photograph of Tom McCabe, the man now staring at me had no goatee, but had a full beard, neatly trimmed. He was not tall or large, but blocky, and power did radiate from the way he sat.

For a moment, my confidence faltered. What if this truly was Frederick Blackburn, noted industrialist and touted as possible governor? I had thrown all my chips into the pot, however. This was no time to fold without playing out the hand.

"Randolph," I said. "You can relax now. I'm a lawman." I reached into my inside suit pocket and pulled out a folded sheet of paper. "I've got an official writ, giving me warrant to arrest a man named Tom McCabe."

"Tom McCabe? I . . . I . . . I don't understand."

"You'll understand plenty soon enough," I said. "I can't send you out of this library in case you get a silly notion to search for a rifle, or call others in for help. So you'll just have to sit and listen."

"I can't call others for help," he said. "Mr. Blackburn has been running a skeleton staff. It's only me here." He was still trembling. Behind his spectacles, the pickle-egg eyes had grown to the size of watermelons.

"Randolph, stop shaking. I have no intention of using my revolver. The man I've come to arrest is in handcuffs. He too would be a fool to do anything but sit and listen."

"*You* are the fool," snapped Blackburn. "I've got enough influence that you'll hang for this outrage. Kidnapping a man under false pretense is—"

"Murdering your own brother is a hanging offense," I said.

We locked eyes. At that moment, he knew that I knew. The savage hatred in his stare was almost enough to rock me.

"Whatever your story is," he said in a soft voice, "it would be filled with so much conjecture that no jury would find it believable."

"You mean lack of proof? You mean his body parts have been in the ground for months now and are totally beyond recognition?"

No answer, because to answer would be to acknowledge understanding. In front of a witness who could testify against him later.

"Randolph," I said, "my name is Samuel Keaton. I marshal in Laramie, Wyoming. Out in the territories."

He still clutched the calling card I had handed him. "But this. . . . "

"Randolph, your employer has been away from Johnstown for what, a week?"

He looked to Blackburn for guidance.

"You've already handcuffed him," I said. "I doubt answering a simple question will make it worse."

Randolph frowned. "He has been away for the last week."

"Philadelphia," I said. "Business."

"That's not unusual," Randolph said quickly. "He's often away."

"He would have been away until long after I left Johnstown. He didn't want to meet me. I knew him from Laramie."

Which explained the canceled appointment. Blackburn could have avoided me almost indefinitely.

"Your employer has returned today for only one reason," I said. "He believed Elliot Hawkthorne had an urgent reason to discuss the sale of his steel mills. Hawkthorne's opinion carries great weight in financial circles. I, of course, came as Hawkthorne."

I didn't know the exact logistics of how Hawkthorne had done the favor I had requested of him. My world is not one of secretaries and documents. I guessed the way of that world was telegrams and messengers. The end result, however, I did know. Blackburn believed Hawkthorne was traveling through Johnstown and wanted to speak about possible bank arrangements to purchase the steel works through a cash settlement. It had been enough bait to ensure Blackburn would return for me to be able to arrest him.

"Sale of the steel mills!" It came out as a yelp from the tiny butler.

I nodded. That in itself should have told Randolph there was much more to this than what met his darting eyes. Frederick Blackburn's entire life had been in building his empire. Why dismantle it?

It had been the same question in Hawkthorne's letter to me. His inquiries had brought him whispered confidences from the financial elite. Frederick Blackburn, in a highly secretive manner, was seeking buyers for the Washington Iron Works.

"Sale of the steel mills," I repeated. I settled back in my chair. Were this a normal arrest, I would already be hustling the handcuffed man back out to the carriage in front of the mansion.

Instead, I intended to spin this conversation as long as I could. I didn't want to believe it was a matter of vanity, showing off what I had learned. Yet a man's most unsolvable mystery is often himself, and I wasn't going to discount that possibility. After all, I'd been beaten, shot at, and nearly poisoned; this man was responsible, and perhaps I was taking satisfaction where I could, justifying it with another reason. I was waiting to see if Leigh would arrive, armed with the revolver I'd given her from Moses Muldoon. If she didn't arrive, it would tell me one thing. If she did, it would tell me another. And what she did with the revolver, of course, would tell me that much more.

THIRTY-NINE

YESTERDAY," I said, directing my words to the man in handcuffs, "I spoke with an old woman in Harrisburg. You should be able to recall her. She's the one who gave you the switch for breaking into the money box at the orphanage. That was what, forty-odd years ago?"

I saw a muscle bulge at the back of his jaw. Other than that, nothing. If the old woman's conversation weren't so fresh in my mind, I would have been far less assured.

"You weren't difficult to remember, the old woman told me. And I understand why. Twins are rare enough. Twins like the two of you. . . ."

I rambled, taking sweet time, watching his handcuffed hands carefully for any sudden movement. Randolph was mesmerized by the story, sighing incredulously every so often, squinting disbelief at his manacled employer.

At the orphanage, they'd been called the Blackburn Boys. Father dead in a coal mine accident. Mother dying during delivery of the two boys a few months later. Frederick and Harvey Blackburn. They were so closely identical on a physical basis that until Frederick had fallen from a tree at age six and ripped skin on the inside of his lower thigh against a branch stub, no one could tell them apart, not even during the weekly communal baths.

In personality, however, no one could ever mistake Frederick for Harvey. Frederick was serious, scholarly, diligent. Harvey was cruel, rebellious, dishonest; the money box incident was only one of many for which he'd received a switching. Other matters—like the time Frederick fell from the tree—were suspected, but unproved. The old woman said she always felt Harvey, up there in the tree, had pushed his brother. Once, another boy had awakened in screaming terror because of a small timber rattlesnake which had crawled into his bed and bitten his arm; only that morning this boy had won a fistfight with Harvey Blackburn, who vowed to take revenge.

Because of the incidents over the years, no one was surprised when Harvey robbed a jewel shop in the marketplace center of Harrisburg, knocking the elderly owner over the head and fleeing with uncut rubies and diamonds. Two witnesses recalled him near the shop at the time, and final condemning proof was the small bag of uncut gems hidden in a hole in his mattress, less than a third of the missing jewels. Harvey Blackburn was thirteen at the time. The orphanage released him to a reform prison. Within a year, he had escaped and disappeared. No one had seen him since, and all guessed he had retrieved the remainder of the uncut gems and squandered them elsewhere.

Frederick, however, had continued his serious, hardworking, scholarly existence. At seventeen, he'd apprenticed with local attorneys. He had risen through the ranks, and eventually begun to handle legal matters for a steel firm in Pittsburgh. At age twenty-five, he'd put together a consortium of investors for the Washington Iron Works. Ten years later, he had purchased all the shares of the company for himself. And every year, he had faithfully contributed to the Gladys Clark Memorial Home for Orphaned Children.

None of this was conjecture on my part. I'd heard it all

from the old woman at the orphanage. She'd clucked dismay while telling me about Harvey, and nodded approval during her recital of Frederick's opposite climb in the world.

It took nearly half an hour for me to pass on what I'd heard from the old woman. I fully expected Leigh to walk into the library at any time during that half hour. She did not appear, however, so I pushed into the territory that was based on guesswork.

"Here's what I think, Harvey," I said to the man who called himself Frederick Blackburn. "You ran from Harrisburg as a teen-aged orphan. Took a different name. Tom McCabe. Eventually you hired on with the Texas & Pacific Railway. Maybe you enjoyed it, maybe you found it less tiresome than a dishonest life. Or maybe it was a way to bide your time."

"_This_ is tiresome," Blackburn said. "I'm sure my brother Harvey died long, long ago. A death he probably deserved for the ways he chose."

"You reached the rank of vice president, Harvey. And got wind of a treasury shipment of bank notes into Texas. Was it something you'd been waiting for all those years? Or once you heard of it, did it strike you that you had the perfect way to disappear?"

Blackburn shook his head. "Listen to yourself. You are speaking utter nonsense."

"What I'm thinking, Harvey, is that you could have been much, much less sloppy in planning out the robbery at Guadalupe Pass."

"Guadalupe Pass?" Randolph squeaked. "Guadalupe Pass?"

The Eastern press must have given it as much attention as the press in the territories.

"Yes, sir," I said. "Sixteen U.S. soldiers dead. Three hundred thousand in treasury notes. Stolen but not recovered."

Randolph's jaw dropped. He stared at Blackburn with awe. Why is it that a spectacular crime makes a man a hero?

"Harvey. You quit the Texas and Pacific after years of employment. That in itself would seem odd in light of the robbery, as you were one of the few who knew the date of the shipment. You gave the excuse about an ailing mother, knowing it would be an easy lie to discover. When all was said and done, it was as effective as sending a letter announcing you'd set up the train robbery."

"You are wasting breath, Marshal."

"I don't think so. You had good reason to get the law after Tom McCabe. Because you wanted the trail to end at his coffin."

Blackburn gazed at me, a half smile on his face. He'd masked the savage hatred and showed smug confidence. It rattled me more than I cared to admit.

"You hide out in Laramie," I said. "You don't do anything stupid like spend money and draw attention to yourself. You live in squalor, knowing soon enough you will have all the luxury a man could dream of. Had you been following Frederick's career, noting his fortune and waiting?"

"These handcuffs irritate me," Blackburn said. "Remove them now and I'll let you leave unpunished."

"And how, I wonder, did you convince Frederick Blackburn to travel as far as he did? It was winter. He was reaching for the golden ring, the governorship of Pennsylvania. What was in the letter you sent him?"

No answer. I doubted I'd ever find out. This man did not strike me as the confessing type.

I rambled on, keeping an open ear for Leigh's arrival. "Here's what I think happened last January. Frederick meets you in Laramie. You take him to your shack. Maybe he felt pity enough to follow you. Maybe you forced him at gunpoint. You execute him the same way you had the others shot in Texas. A single bullet in the back of the skull. You dress Frederick in your rags, and put on his suit and overcoat. You shave Frederick because Franky Leonard didn't have a beard. It leaves a man who the local marshal is convinced is Franky

Leonard. You saw him into parts—"

Randolph reacted by dramatically clasping his hand to his mouth.

"—because that will make it that much more difficult to identify the body if it is ever exhumed. Then you return to Johnstown, waiting until your beard has grown to finally enter the mansion your brother built."

"You tell an amusing tale," Blackburn said. "If it ever came to trial, which I assure you it wouldn't, the jury will be highly entertained at such a preposterous notion."

"Preposterous? Aurelia's diary more than hints at your strange behavior, the behavior of a man who is only posing as her husband. You fired all the servants, because after too many little oddities they might notice you were a different man from the one who first hired them. You drop out of the political race and social functions because there it would be too difficult to pose as Frederick Blackburn among men who have had many conversations with your dead brother. And, of course, when enough time has passed so the body in the coffin has disintegrated beyond recognition, you send a letter to the Rangers in Texas, letting them know where to find Tom McCabe. Because when they get to Laramie, they'll find him dead. And the search is over. All you need to do then is rid yourself of Aurelia and no one will ever know that Frederick Blackburn is really his blacksheep brother Harvey."

I leaned forward. "The trouble started when Leigh Tafton read Aurelia's diary. You forbade Aurelia to invite Leigh here, remember? What if the sisters shared confidences? And they did anyway. Aurelia's words remained for Leigh to begin to search for the reasons behind her drowning."

I knew there was more to be explained, but I could guess at the rest. Had I been Harvey Blackburn, I would have bribed one of Leigh's servants to keep me informed of her activities. It would have been simple at one of the train stops for the servant to wire ahead my impending arrival here in Johnstown, simple for Blackburn to arrange for my arrest and death in the jail cell. When that failed, the poison attempt. And later, the shooting on the bridge. Blackburn needed me dead so I would not see the physical resemblance between Blackburn and Franky Leonard. The Texas Rangers too had to die for the same reason.

"Marshal," Blackburn said. "I feel a degree of admiration for the effort you have put into all of this. You are sorely misguided however, and it is a pity you hadn't consulted even the greenest of attorneys before you visit here. You see, it will be impossible to prove any of this in a court of law."

No sign of Leigh. I was ready to give up on her arrival and take Blackburn into custody. Ready, finally, to believe I had been mistaken in some of my suspicions about Leigh.

"Yes, Marshal," Blackburn said, "I cannot deny my past at the orphanage. Nor can I deny the sad circumstances of my twin brother's life. Did he become Tom McCabe? Was he involved in the train robbery? It is neither here nor there and has nothing to do with me, Frederick Blackburn. If you did find witnesses to place me in Laramie last January, I might even admit I did visit him in the territories, that I received a plea from someone claiming to be the brother I had long thought dead."

He gave me a wry grin of sympathy. "But beyond that, Marshal, what can be proved? Harvey, if that was him in Laramie, is dead. We were identical twins. There is no way in this world to show I am not Frederick Blackburn."

"A trial lawyer would test you on events which occurred in Frederick's past."

Blackburn snorted. "I've kept a diary for years. If it's in the diary, I can answer. If not, a failing memory proves nothing."

His answer was one I could have anticipated. Yet I had not taken a carriage up here in the rain without reason. Blackburn's attitude of superior confidence irritated me, and I saw no harm in flipping over my ace in the hole.

"There is one other way," I said. "The single difference

between Frederick and Harvey Blackburn."

"Yes?" He was smiling. "Pray tell."

"Frederick fell out of a tree at six years of age. The old woman told me about it in great detail. He tore his leg on a branch stub so badly, they feared he might limp the rest of his life."

"Please continue," Blackburn said. "This amusement is almost worth forgiving you for the indignities and accusations you have inflicted upon me."

"Frederick had a scar on the inside of his left thigh, just above the knee," I said. "Harvey did not."

Blackburn's smile widened. "That of course is true. And that is why I instruct you to release me from these handcuffs."

He leaned forward. My Colt was ready and cocked almost instantly.

"Don't be tiresome," he said. "I'm merely going to roll up my pants leg. My left pants leg."

I allowed him to do so. He wore silk socks, held up by an elastic garter above the thick of his calf. He unrolled the pants leg higher, and there, just above the knee, was a long jagged scar.

FORTY

I *WAS TOTALLY ABSORBED* in what I could not believe. *This could not be Frederick Blackburn.* Because of my disbelief, I was hardly aware of Leigh as she made her entrance into the library.

Only she was not alone.

Bailey Pense stood directly behind her, a revolver barrel pressed into her ear.

"Keaton," he said, "set your pistol on the floor. Then move away from it."

I hesitated. *Bailey Pense?*

"Sam," Leigh was nearly in tears. "I'm sorry. He took the pistol from me. I didn't expect. . . ."

Bailey cocked the revolver. "It won't bother me to pull the trigger." He might have been commenting on the possibility of more rain.

Moses Muldoon's Colt .45. The one I had given Leigh. That knowledge was enough for me to obey Pense's command. I gently set my own pistol down on the hardwood floor of the library and pushed it away from me.

I hoped the action would give Pense enough boldness to talk. I'd never figured him into any of this. Of course, I'd never figured Blackburn to have the scar on the inside of his thigh either. My only consolation was that I had done one thing right.

"You, Bailey?" I asked.

"Me, you hick-town marshal. I was the one trying to kill you off before you could spoil my little game. What a fool you are, bungling your way through all of this. How you've managed to live this far is testament to your incredible luck."

He pointed Muldoon's Colt at my forehead. "But your luck has ended."

If he pulled the trigger now, I'd never learn what I wanted.

"Wait!" I said, hands up as if they could really ward off a piece of lead traveling faster than sound. "At least tell me why."

He smirked. "Money. Ever since Aurelia approached me in April, I've known he wasn't Frederick Blackburn."

Pense redirected his smirk to the two men in the chairs opposite me. "Right, Harvey?"

Blackburn's nostrils flared in anger, but he contained any reply.

"It was enjoyable, actually, listening to you from the hallway," Pense said. "Despite your stupidity, cowboy, you figured out most of it. Yes, Harvey Blackburn killed his brother and returned here to take his place."

Pense waved the Muldoon's Colt casually, emphasizing his words. "I killed Aurelia. That made it a secret only Harvey and I shared. And as a secret, it was worth a great deal of blackmail money."

Pense spoke to Blackburn. "You've been a naughty boy, Harvey. Imagine, trying to sell Washington Iron Works. Did you hope to escape me by running to Europe with the money?"

Blackburn turned his gaze out the window.

"I suppose I owe you a favor, cowboy," Pense said. "You warned me in time. I would have been extremely disappointed if my cow escaped before I managed to milk it completely. Fortunately, you trusted Leigh with the details of this appointment. I have all of you together. The ending will be tidy, I assure you."

Pense smiled. "Very tidy, actually. Blackburn here will be signing over power of attorney privileges. He'll disappear, of course. I have already picked out a coal mine shaft for his body. And in his absence, I'll plunder the estate the safest way possible. Through documents and legal work."

He lifted Muldoon's Colt again and pointed the barrel at my forehead. "As for you, Marshal, it's going to appear that you and Leigh had a lover's quarrel here. The butler interrupted and you shot him. Then you shot Leigh. And in remorse, you shot yourself. Very, very tidy. However, I will shoot you first as that removes the greatest danger."

"You should aim lower," I said.

"Really?" His smirk stretched across his face.

"Really," I said. "I assume you aren't familiar with revolvers. Not if you hired out to have me killed. The recoil on a .45 is surprisingly powerful. It tends to kick the barrel upward if you're not ready for it. My head's a small target. You'll shoot high and miss me completely. Aim for my chest. It's a much safer shot."

He lowered the pistol and centered it on my chest. "Is this bravado intended to impress Leigh?"

"Nope. Wanted to find out what you knew about weaponry."

I stepped toward him. " You knew as little as I figured. I feel much safer now."

"Stop. I know enough to pull the trigger."

"Can you see I'm terrified?" I took another step. Blood rage filled my veins. I wanted to take Muldoon's Colt and pistol whip him with it.

He pulled the trigger.

Leigh yelped.

I took another step. The only thing I'd done right today

was to give Leigh a pistol loaded with brass shells. No powder. No bullets. Just empty brass shells on the off chance she opened the cylinder to see if it was loaded.

Bailey Pense dry-clicked another shot. And another. And another. He kept frantically pulling the trigger as I stepped within reach.

I grabbed the barrel of the pistol. Yanked it from his hand. I raised the barrel for the petty satisfaction of seeing him cringe. I had no intention of slamming the butt of the pistol against his face, for my rage had faded into weariness.

Leigh screamed. Her eyes were looking past my shoulder.

I remembered. Too late. My own Colt on the floor where I'd set it to lull Pense into a sense of security.

I was turning and ready to dive, but Blackburn, on his knees where he'd scrambled forward, had my revolver in a two-handed grip, unwaveringly solid. This revolver was loaded.

His knuckles whitened as he began to pull the trigger. I drew a breath. Waited to die.

And he turned in one swift move and fired the bullet into Randolph's chest. It blew stuffing out of the other side of the chair. Randolph's face crumpled. He opened his mouth noiselessly, looked down at his chest, blinked in surprise and sagged dead against the armrest.

Blackburn spun the revolver back toward us.

"Stand aside, Keaton," he said. "I shall enjoy greatly my next shot."

Pense must have understood Blackburn intentions, because he pushed off me and took a single frantic step toward the library door.

My Colt bucked and roared again. And again. Large as the library was, both shots were still echoing deafening sounds.

The bullets seemed to pick Pense off the floor. He careened into the door frame and fell into the hallway.

In the moments of forever which followed, the acrid

smoke of gunpowder drifted upward. Leigh was clutching my upper right arm so fiercely it felt like bear jaws. We stared at the revolver pointed in our direction.

Blackburn grinned at us. "That does put a damper on this tea party, doesn't it?"

FORTY-ONE

BLACKBURN WAS CAUTIOUS. At gunpoint, he forced me to give Leigh the handcuff key. He directed Leigh to move to the side so that he could keep the revolver trained on me as she unlocked his handcuffs. He also directed her to handcuff me and give him the key. Blackburn however, was more prudent than I had been; he handcuffed my hands behind my back, not in front.

His smile remained bright and cheerful during the process.

"I like Pense's idea," he said. "Only now it will look like the marshal from Wyoming killed a butler and an attorney, then ran away with the rich widow. An abandoned mine shaft is an excellent place to hide your bodies."

"You'll be caught," Leigh said at my side.

"Shut up, child. Whoever gave him the writ to arrest me knows he came here. Who else can they suspect? I, of course, will have witnesses to say I never left Philadelphia to meet him. There might be an investigation, but I won't be touched. And when everything is settled, I finish liquidating my brother's empire and disappear myself."

"With no regrets," I said dryly. "Like Cain and Abel, but

you won't have a mark on your forehead."

"Spare me the religion, Marshal. And my brother deserved what he got."

"Why is that?" I did have reason to try stalling for time. While the mansion was empty of servants who might appear to ask about the three gunshots, I could still hope I had done one other thing right this afternoon. *Louis.*

Blackburn's eyes blazed with the hatred I had seen earlier. "Why is that, Marshal? I am far too brilliant to rob a jewel shop in daylight, then hide the jewels in my mattress. Where do you think Frederick found the money to pay for his initial investment into the iron works? From those uncut jewels which he had saved for years. Yes, *he* robbed the store and played them for fools, knowing my reputation would condemn me. He coldly put me into the hell of prison. Every indescribable night I swore I'd get revenge on him. It was there I decided I'd wait until his life was the way he wanted it, and then I'd take it from him and give it to me."

"How did you get him to visit the territories?"

Blackburn laughed softly. "In the letter I threatened to publicly accuse him of that crime unless he bought my silence. He didn't want any rumors to damage his governor's campaign."

"The scar on your knee?" I asked.

"After all I endured in prison because of him, I felt little pain cutting my own flesh in the shape of his scar."

I remembered the peculiar remark in Aurelia's diary, about Frederick limping on his return from the territories. Now it made sense.

"And you removed the scar from your brother's body. . . ."

Again, he laughed. "How would you remove a scar from a dead man's body? Cut the skin away in a patch the same size as the scar? Then even the dumbest marshal would guess there had been something to hide. If I burned his body and the shack, you'd never have been certain it was Franky Leonard, and those Texas Rangers would have kept on searching. No, I decided to remove the entire piece of his leg. And to keep anyone from asking questions about his leg, I took apart the rest of his body."

"Convenient for you it was January," I said, trying to extend this conversation as long as possible. *How long was it going to take for Louis to appear?*

"Convenient? I'd been thinking this through for years. I *chose* January as the month to murder him. The one month of the year his body would freeze that quickly."

"You are a snake," Leigh said.

"Coming from you, that is laughable. I've had my own weapon ready for you for months."

She became rigid.

"Oh, yes, Marshal. You should be pleased that some justice will be done when this pretty woman joins you at the bottom of the coal shaft. Her story is much more interesting than mine."

Blackburn waved the Colt toward the library door. "Move ahead of me," he commanded. "I'll tell you as we go to the carriage."

Leigh and I stepped around Pense's body.

"Don't try anything hasty," Blackburn said to our backs. "You, I'm sure, want to cling to life as long as possible. As for me, I'd rather you walked instead of forcing me to carry your dead bodies."

His consideration was overwhelming.

"I anticipated the day that Leigh might prove difficult," Blackburn continued, "so I engaged a private investigation firm in Philadelphia to look into the circumstances of her husband's death. He was a frail old man. Did Leigh ever tell you that? Poor man simply died in his sleep one night in France. Or so it seems."

I kept my eyes open for any warning movement, listening with half attention, readying myself to dive into Leigh during any instant. *Where was Louis?*

"Strange thing is, Marshal—and it took a substantial amount of money to learn this—the physician attending the old man's death found two small goose feathers stuck to the roof of the old man's mouth. What would that tell you?"

He answered his own question, the tone in his voice showing his obvious enjoyment at the recital of his knowledge. "A frail old man. Unable to fight off a stronger, heavier young woman and the pillow she placed over his face one night."

We had progressed down most of the hallway. Where was Louis?

"Normally," Blackburn was saying, two steps behind us, "a physician might make note of such a strange thing, those goose feathers, and pass it on to the local police. But not when the beautiful young American woman has been his lover for the previous month."

I noticed Leigh had denied none of this.

"It is furthermore strange, is it not, that the physician was able to afford a villa by the seaside, only weeks after the rich young widow departed from France."

We were at the front entrance. Only the steady drizzle of rain greeted us.

"So Leigh, my dear, perhaps you and I could have become a pair. Your sister was too sweet for me, and well on her way to dying anyway when Pense killed her. You and I, however, could have shared the fortunes we stole from others."

I stopped at the front door.

"Push it open," Blackburn instructed me. "And remember, I have your revolver pointed at your back."

Slowly, to give as much notice as possible, I eased the door open with my shoe.

Nothing outside, except the drizzle and the horse waiting in the harness of the carriage I had driven here. Beside it stood the carriage used by Leigh and Bailey Pense. No sign of Louis. For the first time since leaving the library, I began to fear for our lives.

****

Blackburn shut the carriage door on us. The door had an open window cut into it, and under normal circumstances a passenger latched and unlatched the door by reaching through the window and pushing or pulling a pin through the eyehole of an elegant bolt.

He pounded on the pin with the butt of the revolver. "Bent beyond repair," he said. "You'll not be escaping."

He grinned inside at us, malevolent. "I doubt you'll have a chance to yell at passersby for help. Not on a day like this. Not on the road up into the hills that I'll be taking."

Blackburn wagged a finger at us. "And if you do yell, I'll simply stop the carriage and shoot the both of you."

With no further ceremony, he climbed onto the driver's seat and flicked the reins. The carriage moved forward and down the estate drive toward the road which would lead us to our deaths.

It was a luxurious interior. Velvet lined, padded seats. The door window, as with the rear window, was too narrow to crawl through. There was only the one door too. It was an effective prison.

"I feel so old," Leigh said. She sat opposite me. Her head was bowed, her face lost in her long hair. "Very, very old."

She lifted her head. "I did kill him, Sam, my husband. He was a monster. A cruel, demanding ogre of an old man who degraded me in private. I was chattel, purchased by the money he used to arrange our marriage. Does that justify it?"

"I cannot say," I said. "I'm not the One you need answer to."

"I was a child!" She moaned. "I thought I knew so much, but I was a child. The French physician, I loved him. He promised he'd leave his wife for me. I thought that's all it would take to be happy. One single act to free me. Then the physician forced payment from me and stayed with his wife."

The carriage picked up speed as we moved into a trot.

"It took my heart," she said. "Made me realize I should fend only for myself. And when word reached me that Aurelia had died, I decided to do whatever it took to destroy Pense and Blackburn."

"What?" I'd been slouching, trying to relax. At her words I sat upright so quickly I almost banged my head against the interior roof.

"Aurelia sent me a letter, Samuel. She told me she knew Blackburn was not her husband. She had suspected for some time, but said nothing, only looked for proof." Leigh's voice dropped. "In her letter she described finding a tiny scar on his ribs. An old scar she knew Frederick never had. Yet still she kept her doubts to herself, afraid even to record them in her diary. But the scar was enough for her. She knew of Frederick's previous contributions to the orphanage. The only explanation that made sense was the obvious one. A twin brother. So when Blackburn went on yet another trip, she visited the orphanage. Sometime in February. She discovered the same thing you did, and wrote me for advice."

Tears began to stream down Leigh's face. "I wrote back, telling her if she could prove Frederick Blackburn was dead, she would inherit his estate. Samuel, I sent her to Pense! I sent her to the man who would kill her!"

"Let's back up here. You—"

"Don't you understand? Pense thought she was the only one who knew. He killed her so he could blackmail Blackburn."

"Leigh," I said, gently. I needed to know something. Badly. I guessed we were halfway down the drive. Once we got on the road, I doubted we had much of a chance of survival. Not if what I feared was true. "Leigh. Pense told us he killed your sister. In the library. Remember? But you said you wanted to destroy Pense and Blackburn. How could you have known beforehand Pense killed Aurelia?"

Leigh wiped the tears from her cheekbones. "I didn't for certain. But I knew enough not to trust him."

"How?" I felt like shaking her.

"The same reason you knew something was wrong. Her diary. The missing pages. It was Pense who gave me her diary from her personal effects. He told me he had no idea who had taken the pages out. But I knew Pense had done it, removing anything she had written about the orphanage and her discussions with him, because that was the week she was going to meet him."

I spoke very slowly. "From the beginning, you did not trust Pense."

"No, Samuel. And from the beginning, I knew Frederick Blackburn was dead. I guessed it had something to do with his visit to Laramie. So I went out there."

I put my hand up to stop her. "And when you saw the photo that the Texas Rangers carried that night they took you from the hotel. . . ."

"I knew the rest. I told them enough to send them out this way." She bit her lower lip. "I thought it would spare our lives. But. . . ."

They'd decided to kill us in a spectacular way. It explained why they hadn't bothered to try to torture any more information out of Jake and me that night. They must have come to Johnstown and been waiting for a chance to confront Blackburn. Only his wealth was too much of a barricade, and they didn't have someone like Elliot Hawkthorne to arrange a meeting. And once Pense discovered they were in town, he had them killed.

"Leigh." I couldn't grab her shoulders because my hands were handcuffed behind my back. "If you didn't trust Pense, why did you let him know I was meeting Blackburn this afternoon at the estate?"

"I didn't," she said. "He knocked on my hotel room door and took me away. It wasn't until our carriage was halfway here that I realized where we were headed."

It felt like every one of my hairs rose to attention. "If you didn't tell him," I said, "how did he know?"

She squinted, puzzled by my heated concern. "I assumed you told him."

I slumped back. No, I had not told Bailey Pense. Only two other people had known of this afternoon's appointment. Moses Muldoon, who had no acquaintance with Bailey Pense. And Louis, who did know Pense. The same Louis who had traveled to the estate with me to remain hidden as final backup if anything went wrong during the appointed meeting. The same Louis who had not made any move to help me thus far.

I opened my mouth to tell Leigh this. And a shot rang loud and clear above the spattering of drizzle on the carriage roof.

FORTY-TWO

THE HORSE SCREAMED. The carriage lurched forward a few paces. Then swayed and stopped, all motion dying as the horse's screams faded.

"That's a warning, McCabe! Now you git your carcass down from that buckboard before I shoot more than your horse."

Moses Muldoon and his unmistakable Texas twang.

I grinned and shook my head in admiration and cussed his stubbornness. All in about the same heartbeat.

Blackburn should have listened. Busted up or not, a Texas Ranger is one of the most formidable enemies a man can have. And I doubted Muldoon was standing in the open road with a rifle. More like he was behind a tree, ready to make the next shot considerably more than a warning.

Blackburn, however, did not share my respect for Muldoon. Best as I could tell, hampered by my limited vision in the interior of the carriage and guided only by sounds, Blackburn snapped a shot in the direction of Muldoon's voice, and used the distraction to attempt to scramble off the buckboard.

Another rifle shot from Muldoon.

The dead horse and carriage must have shielded Blackburn from a third shot, for in the next instant, his face and shoulders blocked the open window of the carriage door. I saw, however, Muldoon's second shot had not missed Blackburn. Blood was already gushing from Blackburn's right shoulder.

He grunted with pain as he tried to lift the revolver with his right arm. Maybe his brain still refused to believe he'd been shot. It happens that way some times.

He grunted again, and brought the Colt up in his shaky left hand until the barrel pointed directly at my heart. I was helpless. Handcuffed, I couldn't even swing my hands to try knocking the revolver aside.

Two things saved my life. The extra heartbeats it had taken Blackburn to switch the Colt to his left hand and raise it to the open window. And Leigh's decision during those extra heartbeats.

"No!" she cried. And dove in front of me.

The Colt exploded again. I felt as if I'd been punched in the chest. Leigh tumbled across my lap. And I was staring in Blackburn's face again, his features distorted with pain and rage.

Slowly, with a trembling hand, he lifted the Colt. He pushed his hand inside the carriage. Pressed the hot barrel into my forehead directly above my nose.

Leigh's weight was across me. My hands behind my back. The moment hung like an eternal regret.

"Die, cowboy. Die." His voice was a croak. He pulled the trigger, a snap of metal against metal.

I blinked disbelief to be alive.

Snap. Snap.

It had been one bullet into the butler. Two into Pense's back. A shot at Muldoon. And the bullet Leigh had taken in her dive across the inside of the carriage. Five bullets. Because of my habit to leave the sixth cylinder empty, I was alive.

Snap. Snap.

Blackburn hissed rage and flung the revolver at my head. I ducked. It clattered against the wall behind me. When I lifted my head, I saw only his back and shoulders, dipping and rising as he ran a broken line into the woods.

Another shot exploded from Muldoon's rifle, the bullet thunking a tree.

I took my eyes away from the fog and drizzle and the man disappearing into the trees.

In my lap, a woman who had taken the bullet intended for me was losing her life's blood as it soaked through the material of the fine suit she had once purchased for me.

****

Leigh's body was twisted, her ribs and shoulders bent awkwardly and lolling down beyond the edge of my legs, her head almost against the carriage wall. I shuffled my body toward the side of the carriage until I was able to prop her head in my lap. I could do nothing else except watch; the handcuffs were a curse of futilely.

She groaned and stirred, shifting until the back of her head was solid against the top of my thighs. I was looking down at her exquisite face, now pale with shock, framed by blood-matted hair.

"Samuel. I want your hand. Hold my hand. Please."

I wiggled forward to make room behind my back. "Reach around my waist. It's the best I can do."

It caused her tremendous pain, but she managed to lift her arm and let it fall behind me. I moved my manacled hands until I found hers. It was cold. She gripped tight.

"I'm afraid," she said. "So afraid."

I could not brush the hair from her sweating forehead. I could not hold her to console her. I could not find any words to give comfort.

"I used you, Sam," she whispered. "I went to Laramie

looking for someone to come back here and expose him. I'm sorry."

I shushed her gently.

"No," she said, forcing energy back into her voice. "Listen. I wanted to prove Aurelia right, that Frederick had died in January. Because then his estate would fall to her."

She groaned. "Believe me Sam, I would have traded everything to see Aurelia alive again. But she was dead. And I knew I would inherit everything that had been rightfully hers after Frederick died."

Leigh blinked away a rush of agony. When it subsided, she continued. "I thought money would be a consolation. For what happened in France. For Aurelia. I thought money would put me beyond pain."

A wan smile. "I was wrong."

She closed her eyes and stilled herself for several moments, braced against spasms.

Above us, the bleak gray rain drummed onto the carriage roof.

She took a deep breath, opened her eyes. She smiled. "Remember breakfast, Samuel? When I said I could learn to love you, I believe I was already there. I couldn't let him shoot you, not when it was my fault you were here."

"Leigh, I. . . ."

"Shhh, Sam." She coughed, a rattle of weakness. A trickle of blood ran from the corner of her mouth. And I couldn't reach down to dab it from her porcelain skin. She swallowed hard. "Not much time," she said. "Let me talk."

I nodded, filled with rage against my helplessness in the face of death. Helplessness only a Man from Galilee had ever defeated.

"The letter, Sam, the telegram. Forgive me. I wanted you for myself and it was—"

Pain rocked her again, bringing her half upright before she fell back again.

"Oh Sam." She was weeping. "I'm so afraid."

How long had it taken me to accept, how many conversations with Doc, how much of my own uncertainty and fear before I was able to embrace the blood and guts story of a Man mutilated on the horrors of the cross, pierced, embalmed, and shut into the darkness of a tomb? How many days still did my heart and soul struggle to believe with the simple faith of a child that God gives us grace because of the resurrection of the torn body of His Son?

Leigh did not have the years and months I'd been given to finally understand. How, then, could I ease her terror as the black of eternal death came with her ragged, last gasps of life? In that moment, raging against the brutality of death, I knew the answer. I found myself speaking in a manner I had never expected of myself.

"Leigh," I said. "Three men—each nailed on a cross. The Easter stories you heard as a child. Calvary."

"I'm afraid, Sam."

"Three men—each on a cross, Leigh. One looked over and asked to be remembered. That's all it took."

"Sam, I'm not ready." Her voice barely a whisper. "It's dark, Sam. I want light."

"Ask, Leigh. Look over at the cross in the middle. Ask now for Him to remember you."

"Sweet Jesus," she said. "I'm afraid. Oh, Sweet Jesus, help me, I'm so afraid."

Her hand tightened on mine, almost crushing in her intensity.

Her eyes widened. In surprise. "Light, Sam! Oh . . . look. . . ."

There was nothing for me to see. Just a woman, frail and weightless across my legs, eyes now closed, a calm smile of peace on a face that would never cry bitter tears on this earth again.

I bit my lip and rested my head against the sill of the carriage window and watched the rain soak into the trees and earth.

FORTY-THREE

I WAS STANDING on the platform between passenger cars as the steam locomotive pulled out of the Union Pacific station in Cheyenne. The vast expanses of Nebraska were behind me; the immensity of the plains had filled me not with my usual delight of open skies, but with impatience, for I could not wait to finally see the mountains outlined against the western horizon. Even then, it had seemed like days until the mountains became more than a purple smudge, days to reach Cheyenne with the final leg of my journey just ahead.

I remained on the platform as the train rocked and picked up speed, leaving Cheyenne and its open plains behind, moving into the first of the pines which dotted the eastern slopes of the Laramie Mountains. I knew well the terrain ahead. The train would climb into the Sherman Pass, where it would stop at the summit for water. And then the western slopes would lead down into the Laramie Plains, with home only twenty miles ahead.

I ached for the moment I would step off the train and walk through Laramie's streets, nodding and smiling at familiar faces. I'd find Jake and Beau first, knowing Doc was probably out on a call. Jake and I would swap stories; he'd pass on local gossip and I'd answer his questions about the Texas Rangers and Franky Leonard. Tonight, I'd have the chance to reflect on the Johnstown happenings with Doc and we'd sift through, both trying to understand a little more about life and people from those events.

Much of what I'd pass on I knew for certain. Pense had shown up at the appointment because he had been trying since my arrival to ensure neither Leigh nor I unmasked Harvey Blackburn. Once that appeared imminent, Pense was prepared to kill Leigh and I to maintain his access to the money which had flowed with plentitude while he was able to blackmail Blackburn. Blackburn, of course, had been in the process of liquidating as much of the empire as possible to escape the blackmail, another reason for Pense to take the drastic action he did.

I had told Leigh of my appointment and taken her with me simply because I knew so little of her involvement in all of this. I had given her Muldoon's revolver and told her to wait in the carriage. If she was innocent, she would let the arrest happen without protest. If she was playing a different game, I would have found out by her actions with the unloaded revolver.

Unfortunately, Bailey Pense had arrived in a second carriage, warned by Louis. I doubted I'd ever be able to confirm Louis' motives, for example. Louis had not arrived on horseback because Louis had been shot dead the night before, something I didn't know until Muldoon informed me later.

All I could do was guess why Louis had made the final decision to betray me. From the beginning, as I'd known all along, Louis had been in Pense's hire. Even while working with me, as I'd also known, Louis had continued to work for Pense, for Louis and I had agreed it would serve our interests best if Bailey Pense was unaware of Louis' shift of allegiance. Louis had saved my life with his warning at the bridge, Louis had helped drag me and Moses Muldoon from the river; this even while Pense had hired Leigh's servant to make sure

Leigh and I were dead. Yet in the end Louis must have decided a bird in the hand was worth two in the bush. Yes, if Leigh paid a reward as promised, he would have gained more by finally siding with me. But it was still a risk; my plan had to succeed, and Leigh would have to keep her word. On the other hand, he could have been certain of a sustantial amount of money from Pense by going to him with my plans. After all, it would tip the odds in Pense's favor, and Louis knew Bailey Pense definitely would pay what he promised, for they had been together for years.

Although Pense had bribed Leigh's manservant to report on us, and to attempt to kill us to keep us from exposing Blackburn, I believed—but could not prove—it was Bailey Pense who had shot Stockton and French at point blank range, for this was the same method used to kill Louis. Pense would have known from Leigh about the Rangers' arrival in Johnstown and the reason for their arrival. As Pense did not want Blackburn exposed, he needed those Rangers dead. He could have set up the meeting, promising them help, but shooting them instead.

I'm guessing, then, Pense and Louis met during the evening before my appointment with Blackburn, hours after I had told Louis and Moses my plan to arrest Blackburn. Pense heard what he needed from Louis and shot him.

If this was true, it was a shot which saved my life from Blackburn. The morning of the appointment—while I was readying myself to travel up to the Blackburn estate—Moses Muldoon heard that Louis had been found dead in an alley near the steel mills.

Muldoon knew Louis had been my final backup. It was enough to get Muldoon out of bed and on a horse into the hills. If Louis couldn't be there, then Muldoon would take his place. When Muldoon saw Blackburn at the reins of the carriage, he knew something was wrong, and reacted with the instincts of a Texas Ranger, shooting the horse first to ensure Blackburn had no method of sweeping past and getting away.

Blackburn? Muldoon later described to me how he had followed Blackburn into the woods. Muldoon, still fragile from convalescence, had been forced to move slowly as he trailed Blackburn through the moss and underbrush of the thick woods. He was able to follow much as he had often followed wounded game, by watching for splotches of blood darkly contrasted against the gleaming wet foliage. Muldoon had no idea, however, that Blackburn had emptied the Colt of bullets, and proceeded even more cautiously. Because of that, he did not find Blackburn until an hour later. I can only imagine Blackburn's final minutes, running to exhaustion, becoming weaker each step to blood loss, and then, stumbling in fatigue, slipping in the wet moss at the edge of a ravine, and dropping face first twenty feet onto a broken branch of a fallen tree. Death would not have come quickly to Blackburn, for the branch had impaled him through the belly.

I wanted to pity him for such an ending, hunted like an animal and writhing in primal agony, fully understanding his impending death.

Yet this was the man I believed had been cold-bloodedly poisoning Aurelia over a period of months. When I recalled his single statement—*your sister was too sweet for me, and well on her way to dying anyway when Pense killed her*—and compared it to her diary entries and the mysterious malady, it fit together, something Doc Harper might be able to confirm for me as I described the symptoms.

Blackburn was the man who had engineered the execution of sixteen soldiers at Guadulupe Pass. I knew this because in the days following Blackburn's death, Mortimer Shaw was able to establish that close to three hundred thousand dollars had been deposited in his accounts in late January, within a week of arriving from Laramie.

I did repay Mortimer Shaw for his help. Because of the stature of the murdered man, investigators were called in by a special governor's commission, and I'd been forced to stay in Johnstown for an additional week, answering questions again and again as they confirmed all the different pieces. Had Moses Muldoon not been there in an official capacity, my story—and the story behind Franky Leonard might never have been believed. As it was now, for all my time in Johnstown, I had three souvenirs.

Two were in my chest pocket, a folded newspaper page with Shaw's front page story of the saga, and a folded cashier's check for five thousand dollars, which was my portion of the reward offered by Texas & Pacific for the capture of Tom McCabe. The third souvenir, less happy, was the fading bruise on the skin beneath that chest pocket. Leigh Tafton's body had absorbed most of the brutal killing power of the last bullet from my Colt revolver. It had punched through her body to strike me as a thrown rock, not enough force to break cloth and skin, but enough force to leave me with the reminder of the sacrifice she had made for me.

That was part of the sorrow upon me as the train began its descent of the western slopes. From the swaying platform, I saw the plains spread out before me and, as always, thought of how Rebecca and I would never ride those plains together, the other portion of sorrow which would never leave me, no matter how much the valley had become home to me.

****

I caught Jake napping in my chair, head down on my desk in the marshal's office.

"Hey, you knot-headed, mangy, old dog," I said, stepping lightly inside.

It felt great to be on the warped floorboards, looking around at the familiar potbellied stove and locked gunrack.

Jake sat up with a startled thump, banging his knee on the underside of the desktop.

"Sam?" He frowned. "Sam?"

"Relax, Jake," I said, "don't put yourself out jumping up and down with happiness to see me."

My turn to frown. "Where's Beauregard?"

"Sam?" Jake was on his feet now. "What are you doing here?"

Served me right, I guess for building up the homecoming in my mind. I'd figured Jake might do some whooping and hollering, maybe thump me on the back, drag me down to the saloon and make me tell him the happenings out East. All the weeks away, maybe I'd painted too rosy a picture about the home I missed.

"What am I doing here?" I said, turning my disappointment into anger. "I'm the marshal. Unless you—"

I caught the details on his badge. "You did, you lowdown polecat. You took the job for yourself."

His mouth was gaping.

"Where's Beau?" I said. "Him and me, we'll go visit Doc. Might be the air's a little less chilly there."

Jake walked around the side of the desk. "Sam. . . ."

"I suppose you sold old Beau?"

Now Jake's face was twisting into anger. "Don't get high and mighty on me, Sam. You's the one who said you wouldn't be back."

"What?" I squinted at him. Sniffed the air. "Little early in the afternoon to be painting your tonsils, ain't it?"

"As town marshal," he said, indignant, "I never step inside the saloon before three o'clock."

"And you can say 'town marshal' in good conscience?"

"In the same good conscience you could just leave us for some uppity rich widow."

"Jake, I ought to bust you one. I'd never do no such thing."

"She send you packin', Sam? Sent you back to Laramie with your tail draggin'?" He thought about that a second. His features softened into a grin. "Shoot, at least you came back. Forgive me for getting my back up so stiff. It's just it hurt some, thinking you'd leave us behind with hardly more than a good-bye. No invitation to the wedding or nothing else."

Jake unpinned the badge from his vest. Held it out to me. "Sam, you take the marshal job. It never felt right without you around anyhow."

I set the badge on the desk. "Jake Wilson, you explain to me right now what this is about."

"Me? I can't hardly explain when you're the one who waltzed in here out of the blue."

"No," I said, "Explain it to me like it ain't me you're talking to. Like you were telling it down at the Red Rose Saloon."

Jake lifted his hat and scratched his head. I grinned to see the familiar gesture, as a one-armed man has to grip the hat a certain way to make the action practical.

"Well, it's like this. A few weeks back we get a telegram from Sam Keaton, saying he was getting hitched to Leigh Tafton. Said he was taking a ship to Europe to do some traveling with her. Said maybe he'd get back in a few years to look up his acquaintances."

"Jake, you most surely are fabricating this."

"Does a snake walk on its hind legs?"

I shook my head no.

"That's your answer then. I'd show you the telegram plain as the paper it was writ on, 'cept one night I got pie-eyed and shot it up." He cast his eyes at the floor. "But don't go figuring it upset me any."

"Jake, I didn't marry no widow." I closed my eyes briefly at the memory. "Fact is, she passed on."

"Sorry to hear that Sam. Real sorry." His eyes shifted from the floor, to my face, then shifted away again, glancing at the wall to one side of me, then the wall to the other side. "I'm not sure, though, you'd be advised to take your hat in your hand and propose again."

"Dog gone it, Jake. I wish you'd make sense. I didn't propose to the widow."

"Then why'd you send the telegram saying you was about to get hitched?"

I grabbed his collar and shook him. "I didn't send the telegram. I didn't propose. Understand? And I sure ain't going to propose to anyone else in the near future."

"Maybe we should back up some," Jake said. "I can see you're a mite touchy about all this."

"Back up some," I instructed, releasing his collar and brushing off the shoulders of his shirt. "Back up as long as it takes."

"Well," he said. "We sent you the letters."

"Which I got," I said. "Some of what Doc said didn't make sense, but I figured I'd ask him tonight at Chung's Eatery."

"There's a man with a long face too, Sam."

"Doc?"

"Doc took the telegram news without saying much. I mean Kam Yee Chung. He was figuring on throwing a big celebration dinner. As a wedding gift."

I wanted to stamp my feet. "Will you get this widow off your mind Jake?"

"Which widow?" he asked. "Leigh Tafton? Or Rebecca?"

"Of course I meant Leigh Taf—" *What had Jake just said?*

"Sam, I got a bad feeling about this. You look like someone just whomped your head with an axe-handle."

I groped for the edge of the desk and leaned against it. "You said Rebecca."

"I did," he said, "and it's what's giving me this bad feeling. You knew Rebecca had been widowed. Tell me you knew, Sam."

I shook my head no. I could hardly think.

"She sent you a letter, Sam. Along with ours."

"I didn't get the letter, Jake." I believed I knew why. Leigh. Who had asked for forgiveness in the carriage. Forgiveness for a letter, for a telegram. "I didn't know Rebecca had been widowed."

"At the Little Bighorn. Up against Custer. Newspapers never spent much time talking about the Sioux women and children left behind. Plenty braves died, though. His name was Thunder Voice, Sam. Rebecca told us what little she knew. He took a bullet in the chest on the first charge."

Rebecca had told them? I took a breath. I was queasy with fear, my mouth like it was filled with sawdust. "She was here, Jake? Rebecca was here?"

Jake leaned against the desk beside me. "Sam." I'd never heard his voice so gentle. "Sam, she was here. Stayed at the Union Pacific Hotel. Went to the train station everyday, waited each time until the last passenger had stepped off. Went every day for a couple of weeks. You never wrote back. You never stepped off the train. Then the telegram arrived and—"

"What? Rebecca believes I got married?"

"It broke Doc's heart to show her the telegram. She didn't say a word, Sam. Got quiet-like. Asked if it was okay to take Beauregard, as you weren't coming back anyway and she didn't want to travel alone."

"Travel? Alone? Jake, where's she headed? When did she leave? Where's my horse? Saddle and gear? Come on, man, can't you move faster?"

Jake had difficulty answering, as he was trying to keep up to my half run in the direction of the livery.

EPILOGUE

I *DID NOT EXPECT* to be able to find trail signs of her travel. Some rain and too much wind had blown through the valley plains in the time which had passed since her departure from Laramie. Instead, I pushed hard with a remuda of three horses which allowed me to ride a fresh mount every few hours, traveling up to fifty miles a day, knowing my best chance of finding her among the thousands and thousands of square miles of uninhabited territory would be to aim squarely for her destination.

Jake had told me she was headed north, to return to the Sioux, who had fled north into Canada. She was convinced she could help them—with her excellent British education—during interpretation sessions, fight for vaccine supplies, and contribute in a more traditional sense as a woman in camp.

I'd expressed worry about her safety through the Wyoming Territories and up through the territory of Montana. Jake had pointed out she'd lived among the Sioux for nearly two years; she probably had more plains savvy than I did. Jake expected she'd move along the rivers. While a longer route, it was a simple way to navigate and the best way to guarantee a fresh water supply.

I didn't hesitate in deciding to do the same, on the off chance I might catch up to her, despite her considerable head start.

I followed the North Platte downstream to the mouth of the Sweetwater River, then moved west, upstream on the Sweetwater toward the South Pass of the old Oregon Trail which had been deserted for years now that the train had cut through this land. At the Seminole Cutoff just before South Pass, I turned north again, spending a day's travel across rugged, arid hills until meeting the Beaver River, going due north on an almost straight line until it entered the Wind River.

I'd then continue north along the Wind River until it became the Bighorn River, which would take me well into the Montana Territories.

I never made it to the Bighorn.

****

There is a point where the Wind River cuts through giant canyon walls hundreds of feet high. The gap between the canyon wall is too narrow to be a valley; it is as if a giant axe cleaved the earth in a series of twisting, deep gashes which quickly filled with a stream of water.

I was a half mile into the canyons, dwarfed by the high walls. Although it was midday, I was in shadow, such was the narrowness of the canyon. Wind sighed as it pushed against the steep rock. The river, almost stoppered by the walls, gurgled and frothed in its rush through.

I was down from my horse, dipping my hat into the river, when I lifted my head at a deep, throaty bark.

Beauregard. Trotting toward me from a draw which disappeared into the canyon walls.

I grinned.

"Hey, Beau," I said, squatting as he approached. "How you been keeping?"

He'd been well. No ribs showing, no burs in his fur. Wet nose. Glossy hair.

Beau nuzzled my neck. Placed a front paw on my thigh. Rumbled contentment as I scratched his head.

I was looking past him, not daring to hope, watching, praying for more movement to come from the gap folded in the canyon walls.

It was that simple. She walked out, leading a roan horse by its reins. Maybe fifty yards between us.

I straightened, tied my horse's reins to a nearby bush, and walked toward her, Beau at my side. If it hadn't been for the wind and the river, Rebecca would most certainly have heard the echoes of my beating heart.

We walked toward each other. Five steps away, she stopped, long hair tied back, she was gravely dignified in blue jeans and a checked cotton shirt. She'd changed in a subtle way. Tiny wrinkles of sadness creased her eyes. The laughter in the set of her mouth had disappeared.

I moved no closer. Nothing in her stance encouraged me to cross the distance between us.

"Rebecca," I said.

"Beau let me know a rider was approaching," she said. "I never expected it to be you."

I wanted to open my arms, pull her in close, but I was afraid. She'd been in my dreams every night, but now was holding herself back like a stranger.

"Doc showed you a telegram."

"He did. I understood. You couldn't know I'd be back. You have every right to begin another life."

"I never sent the telegram," I said. "I never married. Never even proposed."

She maintained her grave dignity.

"I did not receive your letter, Rebecca. Otherwise I would have been back on the first train." I grinned. "Even though she was spectacularly beautiful, rich beyond a man's dreams, and unsuccessfully threw herself at my feet every night."

She closed her eyes. Gave me the first hint of a smile. Opened her eyes again.

"Samuel, it nearly broke me to love you so much. Can I trust this is real?"

"Hold me," I said. "Find out for yourself."

She moved into my arms and rested her head against my chest. We said nothing, only listened to the wind and the river in the shadows of those canyon walls. Later, there would be time to let words break the peace of the end of a journey. A long journey.

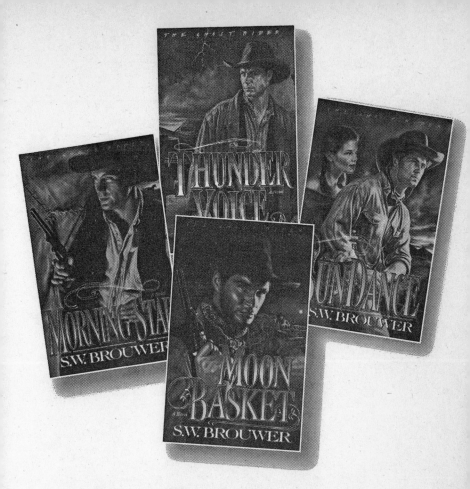

Don't miss a single story from the Ghost Rider Series!

In the rough-riding tradition of the great American Western, the Ghost Rider Series brings you all of the excitement, drama, and energy of life on the frontier. The vivid world of Samuel Keaton comes alive in *Morning Star, Moon Basket, Sun Dance,* and *Thunder Voice.*

Look for them at your local Christian bookstore.

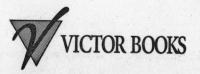

Enter a medieval world of ancient secrets, an evil conspiracy, and a mysterious castle called Magnus.

The year is 1312. The place, the remote North York Moors of England. Join young Thomas as he pursues his destiny—the conquest of an 800-year-old castle that harbors secrets dating back to the days of King Arthur and Merlin.

You'll find *Magnus* at your local
Christian bookstore.

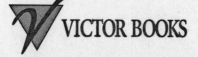